Madeleine Reiss was born in Athens. She worked for some years in an agency for street performers and comedians and then as a journalist and publicist. She has two sons and lives in Cambridge with her husband and her younger son. *Someone to Watch Over Me* is her first novel.

SOMEONE TO WATCH OVER ME

Carrie's life collapses when her five-year-old son, Charlie, disappears on a Norfolk beach. She turns her life inside-out to find out what happened, but nothing prepares her for the most shocking discovery . . . Molly is desperate to protect her young son, Max, from his estranged father — a violent and unstable man. She can't do it alone, however, and time is running out for help to reach them . . . Carrie's and Molly's lives are about to collide — but will their love for their children have the power to heal?

MADELEINE REISS

◆

SOMEONE TO WATCH OVER ME

Complete and Unabridged

CHARNWOOD
Leicester

First published in Great Britain in 2013 by
Harper
An imprint of
HarperCollins*Publishers*
London

First Charnwood Edition
published 2014
by arrangement with
HarperCollins*Publishers*
London

A catalogue record for this book is available from the British Library.

ISBN 978–1–4448–1988–5

Published by
F. A. Thorpe (Publishing)
Anstey, Leicestershire

Set by Words & Graphics Ltd.
Anstey, Leicestershire
Printed and bound in Great Britain by
T. J. International Ltd., Padstow, Cornwall

This book is printed on acid-free paper

To my dearest three — David, Felix and Jack
And in love and memory of my father,
Barry Unsworth 1930–2012

Acknowledgments

I would like to thank my agent Luigi Bonomi for his sound advice and support. Kate Bradley at HarperCollins for her enthusiasm and the clever way she remembers all the things I forget. Most of all I would like to thank my mother Valerie Unsworth who is full of dreams and who always thought I had it in me.

Prologue

He held her hand tightly. It was dark and it was hard to see the path. She had told him to watch where he put his feet and not to get too near the black channel of water. He knew for a fact there were bad things hidden right down deep at the bottom of it. There were supermarket trolleys and stolen cars and rotting cows, which had toppled out of their fields into the canal and not been able to get out. There were snakes that swam all twisty through the coldness. He thought that there were people in there too. He thought of bodies floating upright, anchored to the slimy bottom by curling fronds of weed. He had once seen an eyeball coming out of a drowned person's head on a TV programme. He had watched through the crack in the door and afterwards he had wished he hadn't. Once you saw things they stayed with you forever. Even though they were walking so fast it made him breathless and even though her nails were digging into his hand, he was glad to get out of the house. He just wished he knew where they were going.

'Will we be able to stop soon?' he asked.

'Just a bit further. We can't stop yet.'

Her face gleamed all white and her mouth was stretched out thin. He knew they would never be able to go fast enough or far enough, however hard they tried. He wished they could change

1

themselves into giant birds and fly as far as Africa. Big, yellow birds that could see in the dark and camouflage themselves against the sand in the daytime. In his brain he sang the song that made him feel better and tried with all his might to escape into clear open spaces and a sea without edges.

1

Carrie stood on the pavement outside the shop. It looked even better than she had imagined it would. The window, trimmed with lace stencils and silver stars, framed a display of what she hoped were the most irresistible Christmas gifts ever. There were creamy cashmere dressing gowns, strings of crystal beads, amber earrings with ancient insects trapped in their glowing depths, vintage cake stands laden with glittering brooches, elegant party shoes with buckles and curved heels, old silk scarves traced with faded Eiffel Towers and caped matadors. Tomorrow, *Trove* would open its doors to the paying public, and all the months of work would have been worthwhile.

Back inside the shop she checked that everything was perfect; the pan of mulled wine was ready to be heated up on the tiny stove in the back room, the cinnamon-scented candles were lined up along the counter alongside the piles of brown bags, each stamped with the name of the shop and fastened with red ribbon. She took one last look round, then set the alarm and clicked off the lights. Her bike was locked up at the back of the shop, the saddle already sheened with frost. Tucking her coat around her legs and sitting gingerly on the hastily wiped seat, she set off down the road hoping that her flickering front light would last until she got home. She had bought the bike from a shop just round the corner from where she lived and she had realised, even as she was buying it, that it wasn't the most practical of purchases. She should have looked more closely at the state of the tyres and at the chain clotted with rust rather than been seduced by its green and silver stripes and large wicker basket laced through with plastic daisies.

As she cycled down the largely empty streets, she looked into windows warmed with lights and decorations and clouded with cooking steam and the moisture from people talking and laughing in small rooms. Carrie felt the familiar sadness settle around her heart. She could distract herself for some of the time, but it always came back to this. This dogged pain that refused to let her go, but carried her mercilessly out to that wide-open sea and sky.

★ ★ ★

It had been Carrie's decision to go to the coast that day; Damian would have preferred to have stayed at home to read the papers and fix the fence that had blown loose sometime over the winter. She loved expeditions, particularly those that involved chill bags and flasks, and she got up early to fix a feast of cheese and tomato baguettes and crisps and some sinful sundae-type desserts in their own plastic glasses. Charlie, who had just turned five, hadn't yet mastered the sandwich. Cheese was fine, and bread, by itself, was more than acceptable, but put the two elements together and he acted as if she was

4

offering him something impossible to contemplate, a culinary monstrosity that made his small shoulders shudder. For Charlie she packed a hunk of bread, some Babybel cheeses and a cake with pink icing.

It was the sort of summer day that is called perfect because it is so very rare. They rolled down the windows as they drove, and the car seemed to be full of sun and the smell of warm plastic from the water bottles on the back seat. The Norfolk coast was only a couple of hours away from Cambridge, an easy drive on a chilly day, but likely to be slower today with the roads full of people making for the sea. Charlie had developed a taste for Ella Fitzgerald and sang along under his breath to the CD he insisted on having at full volume.

'*'I love to go out fishing, in a river or a creek, but I don't enjoy it half as much as dancing cheek to cheek . . .* ' What's a creek?'

'A stream, as in, 'I'm up shit creek without a paddle',' said Damian, who was better than Carrie at providing succinct explanations of the meaning of words.

'Umm . . . Dad said a rude word!' said Charlie with delight.

Carrie could see her son in the wing mirror. She loved looking at him. At his neat head, his serious dark brown eyes, the way his eyebrows rose and rounded every time he talked. Sometimes she went into his room and watched him sleeping, even climbed the first rung of the ladder of his bunk bed so that she could get close enough to smell that combination of salt and

5

sweetness that was unique to him. She wasn't a particularly patient mother. She wasn't fond of activities involving flour or tubs of poster paint and there were times when his chatter drove her to a kind of bored distraction, but most of the time he dazzled her. Her love felt overwhelming, liquid, like blood through veins or a sea, filled beaker-like to the very brim.

They arrived at the beach at about lunchtime and dragged food and rugs and buckets along the sand until they found a place that was far enough away from other people to satisfy Damian, who had a 'no radios, no dogs and no other people's children' rule which tended to narrow their options. Since having Charlie, Carrie also had a rule which she kept to herself that involved not setting up camp anywhere near young, firm girls who looked as if they might strip off at any moment and indulge in a vigorous game of volleyball. They settled at last for a hollow in the dunes, some distance away from a woman and a boy about the same age as Charlie, who were lying on their backs on striped beach towels. Carrie anchored the water bottle in the shade of the grass, which fringed the dip in the dune like eyelashes, and unpacked the swimming costumes. Then they took off their sand-laden shoes and walked to the sea. A day at the beach always began for them with this small act of homage.

The tide was coming in slowly and the sun glittered in patches where the water had gathered. The ridges of moist sand were so firm beneath their bare, car-softened feet that it was

6

almost painful to walk. Charlie squatted down to examine the intricate piles of wormed sand and to hook up fragments of mussel shell with pruned fingers. His yellow shorts were too large round his waist, despite Carrie having sewn up an inch on either side, and when he ran he gathered them up with one hand to prevent them falling down. The perfectly blue sky stretched away, until it imperceptibly merged with the sea at a point so distant that it was impossible to see where sea ended and sky began. It felt as if you were walking in a thin membrane stretched to infinity. Although the day was warm, after a couple of weeks of overcast weather, the warmth hadn't yet found its way into the sea.

'Can I go swimming?' asked Charlie, oblivious to the temperature. He threw himself forward in the shallows, kicking vigorously, churning up the sand, trying to tempt them in by pulling at their ankles. He was beginning to learn to swim, but still needed his inflatable wings. Carrie and Damian kept walking and Charlie splashed alongside them. It seemed as if the water would never get deeper and that the three of them would move forward forever. Hunger finally made them turn back to the beach. That, and the fact that Charlie's lips were turning blue. Damian lifted his son up and wrapped him in his shirt.

When they turned round and headed back for their spot in the dunes, they saw a flamingo standing in the water between them and the beach. Carrie thought at first it was a blow-up toy, too impossibly bright to be real. Its exotic shape and colour out of place in the pale, bleached landscape. But then it bent its neck and dipped its head repeatedly in the water.

'It must have escaped from a bird sanctuary,' said Damian.

The bird shook itself, as if, like them, it had expected a warmer ocean, took a clumsy run forward and then lifted off with a curious sideways movement, head and neck stretched out, its legs trailing behind like an after-thought. They watched it fly away until it was just a speck.

'Will it come back, Mum?'

Charlie asked her the question because he knew the beginning of a story when he saw one, and indeed, Carrie was already thinking about a possible bedtime tale which could feature a confused flamingo called Fabian and perhaps Florette, a lost flamingo wife.

'Why is it pink?'

Damian knew it was something to do with its diet, but was unable to say what it could find on a Norfolk beach that would be pink enough to maintain its plumage.

'Will it go grey after a while?' asked Charlie anxiously.

'I'm not sure, pal,' said Damian. 'Perhaps he will find his way home where his brothers and sisters and a bucket of fresh shrimps will be waiting for him.'

After he had been persuaded into a fleece, they had lunch. Charlie ate his bread and an apple and said he wanted to save his cake for later. He sat for a while, watching the boy whose encampment was nearest theirs. He was squatting on his heels and digging energetically. Carrie could tell that Charlie wanted to play with him by the way that he kept sliding his small feet through the sand.

'Why don't you go and make friends?'

'I think he's older than me,' said Charlie. She knew how much he hated to be at a disadvantage.

'He looks pretty much the same age to me.'

Charlie got to his feet and wandered in a self-consciously casual way over to where the boy was scooping up sand. For a while Charlie pretended to be looking for shells, but then he gave up dissembling and stood over the other boy, watching his endeavours with a critical eye.

After what he clearly considered to be the correct amount of time, Charlie finally spoke.

'My name's Charlie. I'm five. How old are you?'

The boy looked up at him and answered. Carrie didn't catch what he said, but it must have been encouraging because Charlie got down on his hands and knees and started burrowing too. They each began to excavate from a different point and dug along towards each other. Whenever their hands made contact under the cool sand and another tunnel was formed, they exclaimed in surprise. Carrie watched them for a while, but then the effects of lunch and the sun began to catch up with her and she lay back on the picnic rug.

9

She could hear Damian turning the pages of the newspaper, the occasional voice shouting, and once, what sounded like a helicopter, but the sounds were muffled. Black shapes swarmed behind her eyelids and she dozed. She woke when Damian tickled her bare feet.

'Sorry to disturb you, sleepy head,' he said, 'but I need to go to the toilet. I'll have to go back to the car park.'

Carrie shook herself awake and sat up to look at Charlie, who was still playing with his new friend. She got her magazine out of her bag, rolled over onto her stomach and tried to read but the words swam in front of her eyes and she laid her head down on the paper and slid back into sleep. Charlie's voice woke her the second time. She rolled over onto her side and squinted up at him, but the sun was too bright to see his face.

'Can I go down to the sea again?'

'Only if you go with your father.'

'Dad's still not come back.'

'Well you'll just have to wait until he does. Where's that other little boy gone?'

'He had to go for a walk with his mum.'

'Is he nice?'

'Yes.' Charlie made his case by ticking off his new friend's attributes on his fingers.

'One, he is five. Two, he has yellow hair. Three, he isn't mad on bats. Four, he likes *Scooby Doo*. *Please* can I go down to the sea?'

'Just wait a bit, I can't leave the bags. Wait till Dad gets back.'

Carrie sat up, and Charlie sat down next to

10

her, looking up every now and again to see if Damian was coming. Finally he spotted him in the distance making his way back down the beach.

'Can I go and meet him . . . *please* . . . and then we can swim . . . ?'

'Only if you give me a kiss first,' said Carrie, lying back down. He knelt next to her and planted his lips on her cheek, stroked one sandy hand across her face.

'I love you every single day,' said Charlie.

'And I love you every single day too,' said Carrie, and shut her eyes.

★　★　★

Afterwards, she wasn't able to say how long she had been asleep. She thought it could only have been a matter of minutes.

'Where's Charlie?' asked Damian, appearing suddenly above her.

Carrie, like every parent, was always only a moment away from panic. All it took was for her to lose sight of him when he lagged behind in a crowd, or when he was hidden by a slide in a park, and she felt a dip in her stomach. She felt that familiar lurch now.

'I thought he was with you.'

'No, I left him here when I went to the toilet. I've just been for a run.'

Carrie stood up and scanned the beach. There were a number of figures in the distance that could have been him. It wasn't easy to see that far away. She couldn't immediately spot anyone in the distinctive yellow shorts he was wearing.

'You stay here in case he comes back. I'll go and look for him.'

Carrie started running towards the sea.

2

Molly watched Max as he lay on the floor, lining up his plastic animals in strict formation. He was using the geometric design on the border of the carpet to ensure that all hooves and paws toed the line. The ark stood waiting with its gangplank down and its tiny bearded Noah standing to attention on the deck. Max's tendency to place things in lines was sometimes disconcerting — miniature soldiers faced certain death as if about to start a race; crayons lay in an orderly rainbow all the way along the hall. Cards trimmed the mantelpiece in royal flushes. He even rearranged the food on his plate in sequence, with the least desirable items bringing up the rear. Since this was a recent habit, Molly wondered if this behaviour was a sign of inward disturbance. Possibly she should be worried by his seemingly compulsive need to order the world. Maybe she was simply reading too much into it and he was disclosing a propensity that had always been there, waiting for the right set of animals or the new box of crayons. He had probably been born with the straight-line gene, and would grow up into an adult who was fond of graphs and trousers ironed sideways and pint glasses placed neatly in the centre of beer mats. She thought that what she was really looking for in his behaviour, were confirmations of her own sadness.

★　★　★

Although the Christmas tree bent slightly to the left, Molly thought it looked pretty, with its multi-coloured lights flicking out some sort of puzzling rhythm. They had gone and got the tree together and brought it back in the car with its tip sticking out through the window. She had resisted the temptation to take charge of its decoration, despite the fact that Max had adorned all the lower branches with the heaviest baubles so that they bent at the ends and almost touched the floor.

She started to put away the canvas she had been working on earlier in the day, a small watercolour of the view out of the window. It was the first thing she had painted for a long time and it felt good to be getting back into doing even a little of what she loved. She looked out of the window, across a wide, black field over which birds gathered and then dispersed. It was beginning to get dark although it was still only three o'clock. She felt oppressed and anxious, as if this small house was cast adrift on floodwaters, without a compass or proper provisions. Molly was keen on the acquisition and preservation of provisions. As a child the stories she had loved the most always involved families in extremis eking out bitter winters with a small box of onions and turnips and fashioning pathetic, yet admirable playthings out of twigs and balls of wool. She liked fictional characters who bottled and salted their way through their lives and nobly stacked their larders with the labours of their presumably very rough, red hands or who, when left on desert islands, conjured up ingenious accommodation and cunning ways of collecting rain water. She had always celebrated each season by preserving it. Jam from the warm strawberries she had heaped into smeared punnets. Blackberries brought home in jugs and Tupperware boxes and then stashed away in freezer bags. Each sloe carefully pierced and pickled with gin and put in the dark to marinate.

'When's tea?' asked Max, rolling onto his back, a rhino in each hand meeting horn to horn.

'Not for ages yet,' she said. 'Are you hungry?'

'Can I have just one chocolate bell from the tree?' he said. 'That should tide me over.' She recognised with pain that this was one of Rupert's expressions. She thought of him years ago, packing the boot of the car to go away somewhere with more food and drink than they could possibly need. 'That should tide us over,' he had said and smiled, and she remembered feeling the safety in the words.

Max untied a chocolate from the tree, careful to avoid touching the wire from the flashing lights. He had a morbid fascination with electrocution, and the slightest darkening of the skies would provoke dire warnings on the danger of standing under trees and wearing leather-soled shoes. It had been Rupert who had planted the horror in Max's mind by telling him some outlandish tale of putting his finger into a socket and being thrown through a window and biting all the way through his tongue until he almost choked on his own blood.

He always was a convincing teller of tall tales. Molly thought about the evening they had first met. He had seemed more vivid and distinct than anyone else in the room. Her eyes had been drawn to him straight away and she had found it hard to stop looking. Rupert had reminded her of a fox, or some other shiny-furred creature. She had always thought of herself, with her pale blue eyes and hair of an indeterminate brown, to be the very reverse of striking. She had often despaired at the soft, almost child-like contours of her face, wanting instead to have high cheekbones and dark, dramatic lashes, the sort of looks that made men catch their breath, and so she'd been astonished when he came straight over to her, as if he had been waiting for her to arrive, although they had never met before.

'You can sit by me,' he had said, steering her over to the table and the chair next to his. He had talked to her throughout the meal, his eyes never leaving hers, his hands solicitous with butter and wine. When her napkin slid off her lap and fell under the table, he insisted on ducking down and retrieving it. She felt, with shock and excitement, his hand brush her ankle and pause delicately, halfway up her leg.

They were married six months later. She had set her heart on a dress that she had seen in a shop window. The material was the palest pink and encrusted with crystal beads. It had a tight bosom-enhancing bodice and fitted sexily across the hips and made Molly feel like a decadent princess. Molly thought that being a bride was

16

your one chance to be voluptuous and get away with it. Rupert's mother, whom she had only met once and whose eyes, on that occasion had shifted over her swiftly as though assessing a metre of fabric, had insisted both on paying for the dress and coming with Molly to choose it. She dismissed the frock Molly had selected with a small sound of distaste and chose instead a severely simple sheath. Although its pale lines were exquisitely cut and it was four times the price of the dress she had wanted, Molly never felt like herself in it — but rather as if she was playing the part of the person that should have been standing by Rupert in the little church that was filled with the scent of lilac.

They honeymooned in Umbria in a villa that looked out over terraced olive groves and a night sky full of fireflies. They spent their days exploring the nearby towns where Rupert took hundreds of pictures of her by fountains or leaning against yellow walls threaded with caper flowers and quick lizards. Sometimes when he stopped her halfway up some steps and made her turn towards his lens or when he laid down his fork to frame her head exactly beneath an arch she felt as if the sequence of pictures were what made the story for him.

'Smile!' he said, and she had no trouble obeying, since everything was enchanting to her. She found it endearing that he wanted to record her happiness so minutely. In their muslin-draped four-poster bed Rupert gave her slender body the same earnest attention.

'You are so beautiful,' he said as his fingers

moved over her and into her as if his touch could read her secrets. He discovered the tiny, silvered scar on her breast caused by the removal of a cyst, the dent just above her ankle where she had been bitten by a dog as a child and the raised mole at the top of her inner thigh.

'It's a kind of inventory,' he said when she protested that she felt scrutinised. 'So I'll know you again if I was blind.'

He held her open with his fingers and stroked her with his tongue and she was glad and surprised that he wanted her so much. When they got back he carried her carefully over the doorstep of their new home. After advice from his mother, Molly had set about painting it cream, with the occasional wall in heritage grey or papered with large, muted flowers. The first year he took her to all the places he had been to as a child. There was a wood that smelt of wild garlic that was threaded through by a fast, brown river, and a garden with blue and pink hydrangeas the size of a child's head and a low wall against which they had nestled like lost lambs.

The phone rang and Molly came out of her reverie with a start.

'Hello?' There was silence at the other end of the line. 'Hello?' she said again, but no one answered and she replaced the receiver. She told herself it was a foreign call centre and that a young man with a made-up British name had been prevented from selling insurance by tangled lines or that a hand in a bag had unknowingly activated a cell phone, but she knew it was him.

He often phoned in the early evening, as if the fading light was his prompt to check on where she was.

'Are you alright, Mum?' asked Max. He sat down next to her on the sofa and put his arms around her neck. She could see her face reflected in the darkened window, as pale and as insubstantial as the ghosts that populated this area of the Fens. One such phantom Fenland farmer was said to regularly return to haunt his land. So precious was the rich black soil, that he ate great chunks of it. His invisible munching left clods disturbed where no tractor had been.

'I'm fine, darling,' she said to Max, and pulled him onto her lap. She stroked his head, feeling the shape of it under her hands. After a while he wriggled away from her and lay back on the floor and so she got up and drew the curtains against the dark fields.

3

Carrie woke early on the day the shop was due to open. She switched on the light in the still-darkened room, threw off the quilt that covered her bed and put on the Chinese silk dressing gown that hung on the hook on the bedroom door. In a pre-Christmas bid to lose a few pounds to accommodate the feasting to come, Carrie had decided to start each day with a bowl of porridge made with skimmed milk and a few raisins. She was half hearted in her attempts to lose weight and at thirty-seven, felt she was approaching the time when she would in any case have to choose between her bottom and her face. She had a theory that after forty, the skinnier the arse, the more prune-like the face, unless you overdid the surgery and then you just looked weird. Carrie was tall and long legged and had a face that was at its most beautiful when animated. Her brown eyes were spaced a little too far apart, but her mouth was soft and full and her black hair fell straight and smooth across a wide brow. When she talked she often rubbed her hand across her forehead, as if trying to shape her thoughts before they escaped from her.

Carrie sat on the sofa to eat her porridge and contemplated the day ahead. She found that for the first time in three years, she felt something that resembled anticipation — although it was such a long time since she had felt it that she barely recognised it at first, mistaking the small flutterings as her stomach rebelling against the dollops of oats she was sending its way. She had filled *Trove* with things that were beautiful and had real value, not in monetary terms necessarily, but objects that had been made with care. It was the perfect place to get a present for someone else or to buy yourself a treat when you were feeling down. Carrie hoped that it would become somewhere that people wanted to linger and touch things. She had worked hard to get the balance right between providing a good range of new, quirky objects and old reclaimed things that had a patina and a story. She had also spent weeks travelling around looking at the work of craftspeople and artists. She had found a woman in Northumberland who created the lightest, silkiest scarves out of wool that had been dyed the pinks and burnt oranges seen so often in north-eastern skies. She had also bought several watercolours from a Manchester artist who had barely managed a civil word to her but whose paintings had immense charm. They featured small figures bent absorbed over tasks or walking in old-fashioned formation through dappled woods. Carrie enjoyed the hunt for treasure, particularly if she found it in unexpected places.

She had thought in the first white, dazed months after it had happened, that she would have to move from Cambridge. The town was too small; there was no way to escape the memories. But after a while she welcomed what she had been left. She also understood that she couldn't move. She needed to stay where she could be found. There was, in any case, something in the gloominess of Cambridge, in the oppression of grey sky and buildings that soothed her. It was a town made for mourning. She was familiar with the open land and the dark earth of the surrounding countryside, where the beauties were subtle ones. They had explored it together as a family; Charlie, head bobbing over Damian's shoulder and later, running on ahead to blaze the trail through flat fields of corn or along chalky dykes. Now when she saw Charlie's first wobbling cycle ride across the common, or caught a memory of his face just on the edge of laughter at the top of a swing, she was comforted. She didn't want to go to a place that he hadn't marked, just as she couldn't throw away the tubs of play dough still pitted by his fingers.

After rifling through her wardrobe and leaving piles of discarded clothes on her bed, Carrie eventually decided to wear her favourite pair of just tight enough jeans, black boots with buckles on the ankle and wedge heels and a green vintage jacket with large buttons and a velvet collar. She pinned a diamanté bow-shaped brooch onto her lapel and wrapped three strings of dark green glass beads around her neck. As she left the house, protected from the early morning cold in a huge scarf and beret, she saw a small blonde figure, dressed in a flimsy frock and minuscule cardigan, coming out of the door of the house opposite. This was at least the sixth different woman she had seen emerging from the premises. It was a constant source of wonder to Carrie how her neighbour managed to keep up with his demanding schedule. The blonde figure scuttled off into the half-light, and Carrie got on her bike and headed for town. The build-up of traffic had not yet begun along Mill Road. In another hour or so there would be a line of car windscreens framing pale, Monday faces. A woman with neatly curled hair was unlocking the doors of the Co-op. In the newly refurbished church someone was shifting a font on castors across the laminated floor.

Trove was situated about fifteen minutes' walk from the centre of Cambridge and was tucked down a side street in a largely residential area of expensive Victorian terraces. It was in the middle of a small row of shops; a delicatessen whose clientele accepted the overpriced olives and mozzarella in exchange for the rakish charm of the owner who wrapped up their loaves of bread in tissue paper with exaggerated reverence, a greengrocer who had a tendency to use organic as his excuse for limp leaves and shrivelled carrots, a betting shop and small Chinese supermarket. Although the street was a little out of the way, it was on the main route into town and the shops benefited from the footfall of local customers.

Jen was there when she arrived, and had already turned on the feather-fringed lamps that were placed strategically around the shop. She had also sprinkled orange and clove oil on the radiators so that the place smelled delicious. She was engrossed in the task of dressing the old wire dummy that stood next to the racks of vintage clothes Carrie had sourced from charity shops, fairs, eBay and her own extensive hoarded wardrobe. With her head buried under the folds of silk, she struggled to pull the narrow-hipped dress down over the wire frame.

'I didn't know you were going to get here so early,' said Carrie, taking off her scarf and gloves.

'Gnnf . . . too excited to sleep,' Jen replied, the words muffled. She emerged from the fabric with her hair mussed and her eyes bright.

Carrie had met Jen at college on the very first day of term. She had been a young eighteen-year-old then with no experience of being away from home, let alone living in London, which seemed terrifyingly large and noisy to her and full of people who talked too fast or who looked at her strangely. She had seldom been to the capital and wasn't really prepared for the homesickness that engulfed her in the first months. Her mother had despatched her briskly at Coventry station with the words, 'Remember, the best way to avoid loons on the tube is to sit with a bit of string trailing out of the corner of your mouth. Works every time.'

Although economical in her farewell, Carrie's mother, Pam, was devastated by her daughter's departure and remained on the platform, hidden from sight behind the newspaper stand in WH Smith to watch the train pulling out of the station. Not usually given to public displays of emotion, she found to her surprise that tears were running down her face and gathering inside the collar of her pink cashmere coat. To cheer herself up she went to John Lewis and bought three skirts, four pairs of shoes and a hat for which she had no wedding.

Jen was older than Carrie and had spent the previous two years travelling and working. She had seemed very sophisticated to the other girl who had attended one school, dated one boy and had been drunk only once, after drinking half a bottle of peach schnapps taken from the back of her parents' kitchen cupboard. Unlike Carrie, condemned to live in smelly university accommodation, Jen had also been the proud possessor of a flat in Clapham, bought for her by her father just before he had absconded to France with a young lawyer who worked at his firm. After knocking down a few walls of their chateau and indulging in the purchase of some enamel jugs, the young lawyer (who it turned out was somewhat susceptible to rashes) decided that Jen's father wasn't, after all, quite what she had expected and she returned to home to Surrey and set up a sanctuary for maimed hedgehogs.

Jen had looked after Carrie during that first year at university, advising her on how to acquire and then ditch various hapless young men who were drawn to Carrie's legs, lustrous hair and air of vulnerability. Jen herself had to beat men off with a stick. Dark and curvaceous, she treated the smitten youths who had the misfortune to succumb to her charms with ill-concealed contempt. In her third year, much to her mortification, she fell hard for a high-profile, married politician, who treated her with just enough disinterest to keep her frantic. She finally gathered enough strength to call a halt to proceedings when, on her twenty-third birthday, she found herself having sex with him in a restaurant lavatory again. The thought came to her that perhaps she ought to want something more meaningful from a relationship than being rammed against a sanitary towel disposal unit.

Although Jen had a very warm heart and had a real aversion to hurting small creatures, when roused, she was scary. The twinkle in her politician's previously sparkly blue eyes dimmed somewhat when he discovered that a rumour (planted into the ear of his demoralised secretary) had been circulating, describing details only his wife (and the five other young women with whom he had enjoyed white tiles and the smell of bleach) could possibly have known. Information such as the fact he had a penis that curved sideways and that he had a tendency to shout out random French words at his moment of climax was used by his political enemies to such good effect that he was never again able to stand up in public without some wise ass muttering 'Brioches massive!' or 'Le fanny de ma tante!' *sotto voce*.

After her politician, Jen steered well clear of any serious or lasting entanglements, preferring to remain firmly in control. Every now and again she would meet a bloke on a Friday or a Saturday night with good teeth or an affable smile and invite him back to her dusty flat, with its battered sofas and heavy velvet curtains. In the morning however, she would always wake alone, ready for a solitary walk on the common followed by two butter-laden croissants and a bowl of milky coffee. Throughout college and beyond, Jen looked out for Carrie. She scrutinised prospective boyfriends ('Looks to me as if he might wear women's shoes on the sly'), doled out travel tips ('Never stand behind a donkey'), and advised on the best job interview techniques ('Look them in the eye and imagine them on the toilet'). In return, Carrie vainly tried to get her to have a decent haircut and dress in a way that showed off her ample breasts and tiny waist. Despite her best efforts Jen persisted in wearing droopy garments of the sort found on women who like to dress up as Anglo Saxons in their spare time and she stubbornly resisted any attempts at restyling her mop of curls. Over the years the two women stayed in touch, despite the fact they were often on other sides of the world and then other sides of the country.

Carrie smiled at the thought of what the two of them had been through. She was glad and grateful that Jen was still in her life. She looked at her watch. It was time to open the shop door for the very first time.

'Come on, girl,' she said. 'Let's open the doors to the hordes!'

4

Molly often woke with a sense of urgency; this morning it took her several minutes to realise that it was Saturday and there couldn't be anything that needed her immediate attention. Although she and Max had been living in the house for over a year she still wasn't used to its noises. The house was full of scratchings and creakings, as if the very bricks and wood it was made of were shifting uneasily. It was a house with a restless soul she'd decided, although the more prosaic side of her knew quite well that many of the late-night rustlings were due to rats. A couple of days after blocking a large hole in the edge of the kitchen floorboards with wood filler, the house had smelt unmistakably of rotting rat, a sweetish odour like overripe apples mingled with something more meaty and rancid. She thought that she had probably trapped a rat family beneath her floorboards. The smell didn't subside for almost two weeks, by which time she had almost become accustomed to it.

She stretched out underneath the pile of blankets she had heaped over herself. Some of the house noises were also due to a decrepit old boiler, which seemed to have a mind of its own. At the moment the temperamental creature was sulking and produced only enough heat to warm the very bottoms of the radiators. She hoped Max would sleep for a while longer. She knew that once he was up, she would have to marshal them both through another day. It was that exact time between night and morning when everything was holding its breath. When the new day seemed to hover in the distance, as if waiting for a sign.

Molly couldn't remember now exactly when she had stopped feeling happy. She sometimes wished that there was a way of recognising the end of things, so that you could properly acknowledge their passing. She always left rented holiday houses with a sense of ceremony. Thank you, she would say as she took a last look round. Thank you house, for giving us a good two weeks. I hope that I might see you again one day. She knew it was foolish and she would never say the words out loud, but it helped her to leave if she was able to mark both the happiness and its ending. She knew that being a mother set in motion a series of endings. Every child who was lucky enough to have a lap to sit in must surely also have a last time they indulged in this intimacy, but it was only when you looked back that you noticed that the last time had been and gone.

It seemed to her now that the first years of her marriage were part of another lifetime. It wasn't that Rupert changed suddenly, it was more as if the bits of his personality that she had previously only noticed out of the corner of her eye came into sharper focus. Living together had been wonderful at first. She loved her grown-up home with its matching china and scatter cushions. She loved her job as a teacher at a local primary school, but most of all she loved being Rupert's wife. Molly had felt like the most blessed of people, hardly deserving of the good fortune that had been heaped upon her. Rupert seemed to make it his mission to anticipate her needs and make her happy. There would be gifts hidden around the house, loving notes pinned up on the fridge. He would administer back rubs and hot water bottles at the first sign of period pain. He would remember passing comments she had made about books and films, and bring them home for her. He put batteries in her bicycle lights, paper in her printer and credit on her phone, and made sure her bottle of Chanel No. 19 never ran dry. He even once hunted down an unusual oval blue button that had dropped off the cuff of a favourite dress, finding a replacement on an obscure website. She laughed at the thought of him searching the whole of the internet for a button, but he looked at her as if he was surprised by her levity.

'You know I would do anything for you,' Rupert said, stroking her hair in that way he had; tugging slightly at the ends as if he was testing its strength.

They celebrated the first anniversary of their marriage by going back to their honeymoon hotel. Molly would have liked to have tried somewhere new but didn't want to raise churlish objections when Rupert had gone to the trouble of putting a copy of the menu from their very first meal, with flight details added, into the side pocket of her handbag. She found it at work when she was looking for her pen, and just for a moment, as she pulled it out and saw what it was, she felt breathless. She thought of him waiting for his opportunity. Waiting for her to go upstairs or out into the garden and then opening the bag, maybe looking through her things to see which would be the best place to leave it and then zipping the pocket up again quickly so that she would discover it later and think of him. If Molly was irked by the way it had all been decided without any consultation, she didn't show it, nor did she reveal her embarrassment when he caused a scene in the marbled hotel lobby on discovering that they had been put into a different room from the one they had stayed in before. Although the honeyed skin of the young receptionist flushed under the onslaught of Rupert's bad temper, she remained composed.

'I'm sorry Sir, we cannot ask our other guests to move,' she said, biting down with small white teeth on her bottom lip.

'I expressly asked for room number 8. I definitely put it in the email. Go and check. Go and check now.'

She checked and double checked and then a perfectly groomed young man tilted his head gravely at them and expressed the deepest of regret in impeccable English, but no amount of bluster from Rupert made the slightest bit of difference.

'I'm so sorry, Sir; we only have the one room free. Would you like me to arrange for your bags to be taken up?'

As Rupert snatched the key from the receptionist, Molly saw the little purse of her lips and the quick glance she gave Molly before lowering her head, and she knew that the other woman felt sorry for her. You don't understand, she felt like saying, you don't know what he is really like, how he loves me. She was angry, and then regretful, that this place that had been so full of wonderful memories had been soured by this second visit.

Rupert remained cold and irritated throughout their evening meal, barely speaking despite her attempts at gaiety. She ate slivers of duck that were pinker than she liked, and he moved his sea bream around his plate and drank quickly, ordering another bottle of wine before he had finished the first. Because he wouldn't talk to her, Molly spent the time looking at the other diners and wondering about their stories. At the table opposite there was an older man with a breathtakingly beautiful young woman who twisted her great fall of hair around her hand as he showed her how to eat langoustine. Next to them there was a woman with her head wrapped in a silk scarf patterned with butterflies. She was with a young man who was unmistakably her son. They had the same awkward thinness and sharp, pink-tipped elbows resting on the table. It looked to Molly as if the woman had been crying. 'What makes me sad,' Molly heard her say, 'is the fact that I will never see them.' Her son looked as if he wished he were anywhere else but sitting in this dining room with its sconces and tablecloths and extra cutlery.

'They'll probably be ugly sods,' he said,

shielding his face with one hand.

'Nonsense,' said the older woman, 'they'll be beautiful,' and she smiled at a point behind his head as if she could see them in her mind's eye, lined up, lovely and gleaming for her inspection.

★ ★ ★

Back in their room Rupert stroked himself, then held her wrists tightly and came quickly into her as if he didn't care if she was there or not. She waited until she could hear from his breathing that he had fallen asleep and got up, as quietly as possible. She put on the same white cotton dressing gown that she remembered wearing on their honeymoon and pushed open the wide doors that led out onto the balcony. At some point in the evening it had rained and the air was fresh and smelt of quenched dust. Two hot air balloons moved through the sky slowly like oil in water.

The next morning his moodiness of the day before was forgotten and Rupert was back to his loving, attentive self. He ordered breakfast for them both and insisted that she sat in bed while he fed her small spoonfuls of yogurt. Afterwards he pulled her off the bed and pushed her against the wall and she wrapped her legs around his waist while he thrust hard into her until she cried out so loudly he had to put his hand over her mouth to stop the people in the next room from hearing. Fiercely private, he hated the thought that anyone else might know what they were doing. She stood in the shower whilst he

33

knelt in front of her and washed slowly between her legs, his hands slippery with soap that smelt of honey, the warm water soothing against her back where the skin had been grazed by the uneven plaster on the wall. They went to Gubbio and took a swaying funicular up the mountain to the Abbey of Saint Ubaldo. She pretended that she was more scared than she really was of the sloping hillside beneath their caged feet so that he would hold her close and put his hand into her shirt to distract her, his clever fingers slipping through the cotton and plucking at her nipple. Above the Abbey, the evening landscape spread out, perfectly composed, just for them, and she wondered how she could ever think that she was anything other than completely happy.

★ ★ ★

Molly heard Max's feet padding across the landing floor and a quick glance at the clock showed that she had been lying in a stupor for some time. She felt a fizzing in her arms and hands that she recognised as a reaction to shock or fear; the unexpected lurch against her shoulder by a stranger on the edge of a train station platform, the sudden sound of beating wings rising up from a still hedgerow. The door creaked open and Max's head poked cautiously around the frame.

'Are you awake yet?' he said hopefully, his teeth chattering, his arms clutching his chest. In reply, Molly pulled back the blankets and he ran and jumped into the warm patch by her side.

5

He wasn't in the sea. It was the first place Carrie looked, scanning the water for his head, looking out to the very edge of the horizon that suddenly seemed even further away than it had earlier in the day. She ran along the beach, occasionally stopping and asking people if they had seen a small boy in yellow shorts. They shook their heads and got up and looked around too. Most of them parents themselves, they knew from her face what she was feeling. They said things like; 'He'll turn up,' and, 'Where shall I say you are if I see him?' but she barely listened. She stumbled on the sand, breathless, desperate already. She saw the boy who had played with Charlie earlier walking back across the beach and she ran up to him. 'Have you seen my boy?' she asked him. He shook his head and walked on, hands in the pockets of his shorts.

The tide had come in and the sun gleamed on the sea. The dazzling light and panic filled Carrie's head like static. She ran backwards and forwards, into the shallows and then up the beach again, searching the dunes for small hollows in which Charlie might be hiding. The desire to see the familiar shape of him was so intense it made her whimper. Maybe he was playing a game. She remembered how the year before he had crawled into a cupboard in a holiday caravan and fallen asleep. When they had found him he had a crescent-shaped mark across his cheek where his face had rested on the edge of a plate. He liked small spaces. Perhaps he had found his way into the old lookout post further along from where they had been sitting. Carrie ran to the concrete bunker and looked through the slotted aperture. At first she couldn't see anything but a small shape in the corner. Then her eyes grew accustomed to the dark and she saw it was nothing but a heap of abandoned clothes. She ran to where Damian was standing, still scanning the beach.

'I can't find him,' said Carrie, grabbing Damian's arm and holding on to it.

'Where did you last see him? How long ago?' asked Damian.

'Where we were sitting. I'm not sure. Not long. I'm sure it hasn't been long.' She could barely talk.

'I'd better go and tell the lifeguard. You stay here. You have to be here in case he comes back. It's alright. We'll find him. We'll find him, Carrie.'

Carrie stood and waited. She looked around her, turning from side to side. The empty world stretched out in front of her and she heard herself panting. Breath in, breath out. Where was he? Where was he? She picked up the fleece that Charlie had left half buried in the sand and held it to her face.

★ ★ ★

They sent two helicopters and little crowds gathered, thrilled by the glamour of impending disaster. 'He's how old?' they asked, so that they could be part of the drama. They watched the boat go out with a kind of awe. Afterwards, when they got home, still sticky with salt and sand, they would talk about it in hushed tones with half an eye on their own, safe children and turn on the news, hoping for the end of the story. Some people stayed and organised themselves into lines and walked methodically across the dunes as far as the car park and then back again. Some of them had sticks, and Carrie thought suddenly of similar lines of people going across a moor, turning over the heather for clues. The boat moved slowly across the water as if it had all the time in the world.

It started to get dark, but Carrie still stood waiting on the beach. Damian wanted her to go into the lifeguard's hut and have a hot drink but she had to stay where Charlie could find her.

'Come on, Carrie, there's nothing you can do . . .'

Someone had given her a coat to wear, but she was still shaking. She couldn't feel her body but it was moving strangely, as if she no longer had any control. He would come, if she waited long enough. He would surely come. It was inconceivable that he wouldn't. How could she leave this place without him? He would put his arms around her neck and she would lift him off the ground and hold him close and smell the salt on his warm skin.

6

The first day in the shop was a huge success. The story that Carrie had managed to muscle into the local paper and the fliers she and Jen had stuffed through countless letterboxes had done the trick and there had been a steady stream of customers, most of whom hadn't left without purchasing at least something. They had opened *Trove* at just the right time to catch the pre-Christmas buying frenzy. Carrie liked to think that it catered for all tastes; a necklace strung with silver filigree butterflies and seed pearls for the girl who had everything, or an old leather-bound volume of sea birds for the father who claimed not to want anything at all.

To Carrie's amazement, it turned out that Jen was an incredible salesperson. She might look as if she got herself dressed in the dark, but when it came to other people she knew exactly when to suggest a colourful accessory or to wait outside the changing room and turn disaster into triumph with the perfect garment for diminishing hips or emphasising lovely legs. 'Everyone has something beautiful about them,' she announced grandly, the effect of her words in no way diminished by the mince pie crumbs that had attached themselves to her frontage. Carrie watched, amazed as she sold a vibrant red cloche hat to a timid-looking young girl in beige who left the shop grinning from ear to ear, 'You look like a forties heroine, darling'; a cerise and black lace basque to a man who had come in looking for a bath set for his wife's birthday, 'Lingerie, so much more adventurous don't you think?'; and a set of vintage cushions covered in blowsy cabbage roses to a woman who had described her house as minimalist. 'There's only so much white a body can live with, after all.'

At around four o'clock, a group of carol singers from the local school gathered outside the shop, and Carrie and Jen propped open the door and stood on the step to hear a somewhat chaotic rendition of 'Away in a Manger'. The soft light cast by their lanterns gave their faces a radiance and a solemnity that was timeless. Except for the odd headphone wire that hung down from under their hats, they could have been children from any century. After they had finished, all fifteen of them shuffled in for mince pies and little star-shaped chocolates and then shuffled out again, being very careful not to knock into the glass baubles and candles that lined the shelves in the shop. Carrie put a ten-pound note in their bucket and they moved on up the road, lanterns swinging, pushing each other and giggling. Jen watched Carrie's face as she looked at the departing children.

'How you doing?' she asked, shutting the door after them and linking her arm through Carrie's arm.

'I'm fine,' said Carrie. 'Really. I always look for his face when I see a group of children. I probably always will. It's a kind of reflex now. I look at children two or three years older than he was when he went and it gives me an idea of how he might look now, how tall and stuff.'

'It's hard to imagine someone getting older when you can't see them. Those age progression images that you see on the TV news always look really strange,' said Jen.

'I imagine the parents looking at the picture a computer has generated of their child, and thinking, 'I would never have done her hair like that' or, 'I wouldn't have put her in that blouse'. It must be terrible to see an approximate child and know that's all you are ever going to see,' said Carrie, and Jen saw her clench herself against the words. The pain was always there, waiting to launch itself at her.

'Anyway, it makes me happier, not sadder to see children having fun and doing all the things they should be doing,' Carrie said, moving around the shop, straightening the clothes on the rails and re-stacking items that had fallen out of place.

At six they shut up shop and Jen went home to 'soak my feet and have a bloody big glass of red wine'. Carrie placed more orders, looked through some catalogues she had been sent and totted up the day's impressive takings. It was eight before she finally left the shop. When she unlocked her bike, she discovered that the back wheel had developed a puncture. Cursing the rip-off merchant who had had the audacity to sell her a bike with such worn rubber tyres, she started to push it home along the narrow streets. The air smelt of coal fires, once the fuel of the railway workers who used to live in these small terraces. Now of course, most of the houses had underfloor heating and shiny, wall-mounted radiators — real coal fires were simply a fashionable accessory, not a method for keeping warm. A couple walked past, sharing a bag of chips with two wooden forks. They looked so happy, so carefree in their matching hats, like another species thought Carrie bitterly, and the chain fell off her bike.

'Fucking. Fucking. Hell,' she said and gave it a good kick.

'What's that bike ever done to you?' asked an amused voice behind her and Carrie turned round to see the man from across the road walking towards her. She made the kind of small coughing noise that was shorthand for, 'Yes, ha, ha, very funny, now leave me alone,' but he stopped and surveyed the offending machine.

'Ah, the chain's off,' he announced. She bit back her impulse to congratulate him on his keen powers of observation and started wheeling her bike along the pavement. He fell into step beside her.

'I don't think I have ever properly introduced myself,' he said. 'I'm Oliver Gladhill. Carrie, isn't it? Mrs Evans at number eight told me your name. I was going to come round, so I'm glad I've bumped into you now. I'm having a party for Christmas. I've been in the house for almost a year, and I still don't know most of my neighbours.'

'What a lovely idea,' said Carrie. If he thought that getting the Roses and the Foxtons in the same room was a good way to spread festive spirit she didn't want to be the one to burst his bubble. Let him find out for himself that the two families were fighting a bitter, bloody battle that went back so long that nobody, least of all the participants, knew what had provoked it. If you asked Greta Rose, with her pinched mouth and singular lack of bloom, she would say that the fault lay with the Foxtons and a garden wall that had moved five inches to the right in the middle of the night. Ask Lydia Foxton — who had a competitive streak that made Paula Radcliffe look easy going — about the origins of the enmity and she would claim that the Roses deliberately blocked up their drain with balls of kitchen foil. Last year matters had reached a peak because it was discovered that Ben Rose who at fifteen was the eldest child of the family, had been shagging sixteen-year-old Emily Foxton, with much enthusiasm in the Roses' granny annexe, built to accommodate the worst Rose of all who had fallen down dead the year before whilst surveying the Foxton abode through a powerful telescope. Lydia said that Ben had seduced her innocent daughter and Greta replied that anyone in their right mind could see that Emily in her crotch grazing skirts and tendency to hang around outside the Guildhall was a complete slapper.

'Next Friday night? Eightish?' said Oliver.

'Thanks. I'll be there,' said Carrie, irritated by his confidence and the way he seemed to take up so much of the pavement. She resolved to develop an acute headache on Friday afternoon.

They parted company outside her house and

Carrie made her way down the dark side alleyway that led into her small garden.

★ ★ ★

That night she dreamt about Charlie again. This time he was sitting at the end of her bed, his shoulders rounded in his pale blue striped pyjamas worn soft by countless washings. He was reading her a favourite book, about a dog called Crispian who invited a boy to come and live with him in his very tidy two-storey doghouse where everything had its own place.

Charlie couldn't read very well yet, but he knew this story by heart. Carrie sat up in bed but she couldn't see his face in the dim light of her bedroom. For a moment she was overcome by a paralysing fear that she wouldn't be able to recognise him. She called out his name in panic and he turned towards her and smiled and she was comforted by the clarity of her memory. Of course she would never forget even the smallest detail of his face. It was engraved on her heart. She woke and lay flat on her back looking up at the ceiling, tracing the cracks from one end of the room to the other. Her face was tight with tears, the pillow wet under her head. It was at these quietest moments that she felt the most pain. It came in slyly with the thin grey light of morning and curled itself around her. It forced her to remember the way his hands held a spoon, his lurching run, the way he tilted his head and looked at her with such immaculate joy.

7

Damian and Carrie had not made it through. Loss has a way of multiplying like mould spores up a wall, and neither of them had found a way to stop the rot. In the first days and weeks after it had happened, she had clung to him, feeling as if letting go would cast her adrift, but in the end it was he who let go of her.

★ ★ ★

They had stayed on the beach until the early hours of the morning, despite everyone's efforts to get her to go home. She had watched the sun come up, hoping that its warming rays would touch the beach and restore her child. She thought that he would be there, waiting for her in the curve of a dune, his hair the same colour as the grass, his face alight.

'I want to stay,' she had said to the policewoman who had held her hand and rubbed her fingers as if against frostbite.

'There's no point. Come on home now. Come on,' said Damian, his face grey in the thin light.

'But how? *How*?' she said and she had fallen down then, her body feeling weak and boneless. Someone lifted her up, even dusted the sand from her coat and in the end she let herself be led away, back to their car which was littered with empty packets of stickers and smelt of the

44

banana skin he had left on the back seat. Afterwards, she couldn't believe she had been persuaded to abandon him. She thought with incredulity of her feet walking across the beach away from him. How had she done that? Why had she not just lain down and waited for the wind to cover her with sand? Why did she not run into the sea and let the waves take her? They had left him behind and driven back down the same roads that they had travelled earlier, in another lifetime. It seemed preposterous, obscene, that all was as before. As smooth as water that has closed up after a thrown stone.

Back at the house, Carrie lay on her bed thinking of him alone and cold somewhere, wondering where she was, unable to find her. Perhaps he would be calling for her and feeling puzzled by the fact she didn't come. The pain of it made her twist and bend, as if she was being consumed by fire. She writhed on the bed wrapping the sheets around her hands and arms, unable to stop pulling against them. She didn't sleep or eat for three days and nights. Instead she sat by the phone, willing it to ring, and then trembling in dread when it did. On the fourth day, she drove back to the beach and sat, fully dressed, in the sea. Damian, who had been at the police station, returned to find her gone and drove to the spot he knew he would surely find her. When he approached her she looked at him as if she had never seen him before. He led her past families eating their lunch unheedingly through another perfect summer's day.

At night she sat in Charlie's room holding on

to his pillow and the smell of him. Every day a policeman trained to keep his voice solicitous found new ways of telling them there was nothing to tell. Two weeks after Charlie disappeared, some yellow shorts were found on a beach further round the coast. The careful policeman brought them round in a plastic bag and placed them on the edge of the kitchen table. Carrie saw her own stitching in the waistband. She felt as if she was looking at something from another age. A kind of relic.

Then there was nothing else. He didn't turn up buried in the dunes or washed up on the shore. He had vanished. A woman rang the police and claimed she had seen a boy that looked like Charlie with a man on a bus, but it turned out that that she was well known for seeing the missing and murdered. She had once claimed to have seen a whole family on a fairground carousel, eating ice cream. It transpired that their father had killed them all the week before.

At first Carrie didn't want any news. No news meant that he might still be somewhere. Her mind threw up the pictures that had been imprinted from television footage and the retrospective chill of CCTV. She thought with horror of flickering computer screens and men with a taste for the pale, thin bodies of children. She imagined her boy in the back of a lorry on a mattress, perhaps with other children, being taken a long way away where he would never be found. She could see him dressed in unfamiliar clothes, sitting on the edge of beds in strange rooms. Sometimes she saw him in the clearings of woods, in shallow graves with soil only just covering his pale, purplish eyelids. As the days passed into weeks, not knowing where he was began to be the chief source of her pain. And all the time what wore away at her was the knowledge that his going had been her fault. She had fallen asleep on her watch and he had suffered for her negligence. She had not done her job and this was her terrible, cruel punishment. When she finally slept she dreamt of him, arms stretched out, floating on the crest of waves.

★   ★   ★

Putting her head to one side as if she had a crick in her neck, their counsellor stressed the importance of talking to each other about their feelings. 'Grieve together,' she told them in the tone of someone recommending a course of healthy exercise. The trouble was that Carrie's way of grieving was nothing like Damian's. Whereas she wanted to go over what had happened again and again, as if by repetition some sense would be made of the completely incomprehensible, he preferred to keep moving. He fixed the loose fence. He emptied out the shed. He sorted his CDs into alphabetical order. Then he decided he should go back to work.

'It's not doing either of us any good, sitting in the house,' Damian said, as she lay watching him getting dressed. He paused over his selection of ties, choosing one with a thin navy stripe. It was this slight hesitation while his hand hovered over the tie rack that so astonished Carrie and made her realise how alone they both were. On the days she had bothered to get dressed at all, Carrie had simply pulled on the same black sweater, the same jeans. Part of her knew that he selected one tie over another not because he cared about which tie he wore but simply because this little morning ritual was comfortingly familiar to him — but at the same time she felt excluded by his apparent control which seemed to her so much like coldness.

Damian took to saying that he had stayed on at the office to finish work, but when he came home his clothes were impregnated with the metallic smell of the city at night, a taint that you seemed to absorb when you walked for any length of time by the edges of roads. He avoided coming to bed at the same time as her, choosing instead to sit watching TV late into the night, while she lay silently in Charlie's bunk bed. When she was brought home from a store in town, because she had been found in the children's department, her arms full of small shorts and gaily coloured T-shirts, crying square-mouthed at the enormity of her loss, he was impatient with her.

'You have to move on,' he said but she didn't know where there was to go.

'Talk to me,' she begged. 'Tell me how he was. Tell me some of the things he did.'

'I can't,' he replied, but she couldn't stop herself.

'Do you remember how when he was a baby

his whole naked body used to shake when we trailed a muslin over his stomach?' she said. 'Do you remember the way he would hook raisins out of those tiny boxes with a bent finger and make a strange growling noise as he did it?'

Even worse than the way she wanted to talk about Charlie all the time, was the way Carrie picked away at the sequence of events that led to their son's disappearance. She reminded him of a bear he had seen years ago in a Spanish zoo walking forwards and backwards endlessly in its concrete canyon. She couldn't let it rest, but carried on down the same groove that gave them both nothing but pain.

'I slept. Damian. I slept. How could I sleep? Everyone knows that when you are looking after children on a beach, you can't take your eyes off them, even for a minute. Tell me, how could I sleep?' Each time she asked him she would look at him with the same wide-eyed incredulity. At first he felt pity for her and felt his own astonishment mirrored in her face, but when she asked him again and again he was maddened by her and no longer had the strength to spare her. It seemed that there was no way for them to help each other. It seemed that in suffering so differently they made each other's pain worse.

★ ★ ★

One night he found her standing in Charlie's room. He came up and touched her on the shoulder and she spun round at him.

'WHERE IS HE?' she shouted, her fingers

49

pulling viciously at the soft undersides of her arms.

'Come back to bed,' he said, scared of her and the way she had become.

'I can't sleep. I don't know where he is.' She tried to explain.

'Don't you wonder where he is?'

He didn't answer.

'Why won't you talk to me?'.

Damian saw his son's pyjamas folded on his pillow and he knew he was going to start the ending for them.

'You were supposed to be watching him. Why did you let him go?' said Damian, and Carrie knew that this was what he had been trying not to say since Charlie had gone. Despite the pain his words brought her, she also felt a kind of relief. She had been waiting for him to blame her because she believed it was what she deserved.

'I left him with you. I left him with you . . . '

Damian didn't hide his face, but looked directly at her as the tears poured from his eyes. He made a sound that was more like rage than sorrow.

8

Shortly after Molly and Rupert returned from Italy, a news story captured the headlines for several weeks. A young woman who had been jogging in their local park never made it home. She was found behind some shrubbery, her throat cut, her skirt pulled over her head to cover her face, then gathered up and tied with a ribbon.

'If that happened to you,' said Rupert, 'I would kill myself. I don't want you going out alone at night for a while, at least not until they get the bastard who did it.'

Months later, Molly saw a picture in a newspaper of the so-called Ribbon Murderer. He was looking straight at the camera as he got out of the police van. He had an ordinary, quite pleasant face. The sort of face you would trust. However much you scrutinised it, the signs of what he had done weren't there.

★　★　★

What had started as a short-term solution to the potential threat posed by the murderer became a way of life for Molly. Without really noticing it, she stopped going out by herself. She became so accustomed to her life being managed by Rupert that she forgot that other people didn't have to account for every minute of their day, the way she did. He had been so solicitous in the trammelling of her life that she had not noticed her imprisonment. First he started to ring her at work, and then more and more frequently he was outside the school gates at the end of the day, waiting for her to come out. One day he decided that the skirt she was wearing was too short, so he replaced it with two Diane Von Furstenberg wrap dresses. They were beautiful and they suited her, so she forgot that she had been angry that he had thrown something of hers away without asking her. He told her that she was getting too old to have un-styled hair that hung down her back like a girl and took her to an expensive salon, where a young man with sharp scissors and sharp hip bones transformed her curls into an elegant bob. The reflection of her face, with its newly framed eyes, looked strange to her. When the hairdresser moved smoothly round her with the mirror, she could see the exposed white length of her neck that had been hidden since she was a child and was reminded of the bleached bones of a prehistoric find.

★ ★ ★

Without really noticing it, her friendships started to fade away. People got fed up of being turned down all the time or discovering that where Molly went, Rupert would inevitably be. Many of them felt envious of what they saw as the romance of her relationship. Only one or two of her closest friends questioned this all-encompassing intimacy, but when this questioning became too strident, Rupert was adept at putting doubts in her mind about their motivations.

'I think they are just jealous of our happiness, darling,' he would say. 'They'd give anything to have what we have.'

They had been married for about a year and a half when Rupert suggested that she should stop taking the pill. Although in theory Molly was keen to have children, she found herself curiously reluctant to start the process.

'Couldn't we just have a couple more years enjoying being together?' she asked. 'Besides which, it wouldn't be a good time to get pregnant at the moment, with the school getting ready for an Ofsted inspection.'

Rupert's answer was to take the pills from the sponge bag that she kept by the bed and to pop them down the sink, pushing through the foil and firing each one down the plug hole as if they were tiny missiles, then pulling her down on the bed to perform his own 'Ofsted inspection' on her. He was so charmingly eager, so attentive to her every need from the first moment that the subject came up, that Molly quickly came to see her reluctance as simply a lack of confidence in her own readiness, in her ability to be a good mother. He set himself assiduously to the task of making a baby, reading about optimum times and recommended diets, researching a theory that if the man ate a high proportion of smoked foods he was more likely to produce a son.

'I'd like a son,' he said, as if the matter was decided. 'Girls are too complicated. Just look at the convoluted way *your* mind works . . . In any case you are the Queen of the House. You don't want any rivals for Daddy's affection now, do you?' and he set about preparing salads with smoked bacon and smoked salmon and looking into the benefits of water births.

She knew exactly when she conceived Max. Always a light sleeper, she had been woken that morning by the sound of clamorous birds and lay for a moment watching the muslin curtain at a half-opened window swaying in the breeze. Rupert had his back to her and she smoothed her hands along his spine and then moved over him, touching him gently so that he was still half asleep as she straddled him and guided him into her. Afterwards, she lay very still, feeling the air on her body, careful with herself as the very beginnings of her baby attached himself firmly inside her. Three weeks later the test confirmed what she already knew. She held the knowledge to herself for a couple of days, wanting, just for a while, for it to be something for only the two of them. Rupert, when he was told the news with candlelight and due ceremony, was delighted, and set about big plans for a nursery with an underwater theme, complete with circling sharks and lampshades shaped like jellyfish.

Three months after Molly fell pregnant, her mother developed terminal breast cancer. For once Molly ignored the fact that Rupert didn't like her going out without him and went to her parents' house as much as she could. Molly and her mother had never been demonstrative with each other and her mother's illness didn't change the reserve between them, but it did provoke in Molly memories of her own childhood she thought she had forgotten. She remembered how her mother used to leave secret messages around the house for Molly to find when she returned from school; a tiny scarf knitted for her toy monkey, a jigsaw puzzle stealthily completed, her pyjamas spread over the warm radiator. There was a doll called Beth, her favourite, who always went missing and which she would find eventually somewhere in the house or garden, mid adventure. Once she had been discovered halfway up a tree; another time, Beth had been in the fridge, her plastic fingers dipped into a pot of strawberry yogurt. The postman even delivered the doll one day with a stamp attached to its chest. Moving the doll around and giving it its own secret narrative was her mother's way of telling her the stories that she seldom spoke out loud.

* * *

Max was born in the last weeks of Molly's mother's life and on one strength-sapping summer afternoon, after Molly had brushed her mother's hair and pinned it up on her head in an attempt to keep her cool, she had placed Max in her mother's arms. He lay there, looking just like Molly's old doll embarked on another adventure.

'Thank you,' her mother said, looking down at Max, one of her pale fingers clutched in his firm red fist.

'What for?' asked Molly.

'For this. For him. And for you.' Her mother

55

answered and turned a peaceful face to her daughter. The lines around her mouth and her eyes had smoothed out as if she had begun some process of reversal. Molly could see that Max's birth had loosened her mother's hold on life; had provided the slipway that would launch her beyond them all.

★ ★ ★

Molly's father found he couldn't settle after his wife's death. After wandering round and round the empty family home, opening and closing doors, looking in cupboards, pacing through the night over the pale blue carpet they had chosen together only a year ago, he thought vaguely about the waste of both carpet and of life and bought himself a one-way ticket to Australia. For the first month or so he stayed with Molly's sister who had moved there ten years before, but then he moved on. Never settling in any one place for long, he rang Molly from time to time from towns she had never heard of. It was clear to her he would keep moving for the rest of his life.

★ ★ ★

'We are all the family we need,' Rupert said when he caught her weeping for her mother or worrying about where her father was. 'It's us three against the world.' Instead of being stifled by these words, she took comfort from his strength and certainty. And if sometimes, he retreated into dark, unreachable moods, or occasionally seemed to become suddenly and inexplicably angry about imagined slights or conversations that took a turn that displeased him, these times were more than made up for by the other things that he did during the first few years of Max's life. He had boundless energy and enthusiasm; waking them when it was still dark one morning and insisting that they put their coats on over their pyjamas and walk to a nearby hill to watch the sun come up. He once jumped over a fence that had been put up to keep the viewing public at bay during lambing season and put his hands out at just the right moment to catch a mucus-covered lamb as it shot into the world. He scrambled up trees showering conkers and apples and blossom depending on the season. He crowed at all of Max's milestones, as if no child in the world had ever before grown a tooth or hauled himself along a hallway and he still kept his attentive watch over Molly's body, stroking her soft curves, noting the old, familiar marks and watching for new ones.

9

When she woke up on the morning of Oliver's party, Carrie was sure she wasn't going to go. There was something about her neighbour that irritated her. He seemed far too sure of himself and she didn't want to give him the impression that she was in the least bit interested in his well-used charms.

It was raining on her way to work and her bike went through the puddles that had gathered in the uneven surface of the road, splashing her legs and sending muddy sprays up the back of her camel coat. Even quite light showers of rain seemed to saturate Cambridge quickly, streaking the fronts of buildings with ugly damp marks and causing the ancient, inefficient drains to overflow along the sides of the roads. On days like this and in this part of town it seemed like the sweet stretches of green that edged the parchment-coloured colleges were a long way away.

By the time she arrived at *Trove*, both her coat and the shirt underneath were soaked through. In the little toilet off the kitchen she tried to dry her hair with a hand towel and surveyed the wreck of her make-up in the mottled mirror. She rubbed at her face with some cucumber and lemon cleansing cream, which was from a range she stocked in the shop. Made from natural ingredients, the moisturiser, cleanser and body lotion in their beautiful green glass bottles were produced on a farm in Yorkshire.

Carrie wriggled out of her wet shirt and dried herself as best she could with the minuscule towel. She found a powder-blue cardigan with mother of pearl buttons at the back of a rack of clothes and put it on, grateful for the warmth of the soft cashmere. She wasn't sure where it had come from, but she would wear it and then wash it and sell it. There had to be some perks to having her own shop. Her jeans would just have to drip dry as the day went on. She clipped on some earrings the same colour as her sweater, shook her still-damp hair around her face and felt that she was at last ready for the day. She had a lot of work to do to make the most of the last couple of shopping days before Christmas, and she had to do it alone because Jen had taken the day off to do her own shopping.

★ ★ ★

She had just taken delivery of a batch of felt brooches, which were ideal as last-minute Christmas gifts. In beautiful dark reds and greens they were shaped like cherries and apples and embroidered round the edges in gold blanket stitch. She decided to use them as the inspiration for a whole display based on food and after putting on a CD of carols she set about covering the table in the centre of the shop with some red gingham material she had bought at an end of line sale. She was so absorbed in her task and so caught up in the purity of the singing, she didn't hear the doorbell go and jumped when Oliver Gladhill materialised in front of her.

'Morning!' he said cheerily, eyeing her still-wet jeans. 'I see you got caught in the rain.'

Carrie was conscious that her jeans were clinging rather closer to her curves than she liked.

'Party. Tonight. I need napkins and thought you might do me a discount?' said Oliver. He had no need of napkins, and in fact, they were something of an alien concept to Oliver, but he had spotted his neighbour's well-clad bottom through the shop window when he was passing and thought he would use this excuse to check that she was coming to his party. Although clearly grumpy, the woman had something about her, mainly legs that went on forever. Carrie showed him the paper napkins, thinking that perhaps lilac pansies wouldn't really be his thing, but he took two packets and placed them on the counter.

'Are you still coming tonight?'

Carrie, who was never good at lying, thought that developing a sudden migraine was unlikely to be convincing. Tempted though she was to say that watching ancient episodes of *A Place in the Sun* and eating piles of sardines on toast felt like a whole lot more fun, decorum took over.

'Yes' she said, 'I'm looking forward to it.'

He gave a kind of crinkly smile that Carrie thought sourly had probably launched a thousand girls into his bed, but to which she was totally impervious. Despite his nice shoulders and long fingers the man was a phoney, from his ever-so-slightly crumpled shirt, to his trustworthy brogues.

★　★　★

Carrie spent all morning serving customers and she was pleased by the positive comments they made about the shop. She was helping a small boy who was buying his mum a present and couldn't decide between a lace-trimmed umbrella or a photo frame studded around the edge with sequins, when Jen walked in, laden with bags.

'Finished!' she shouted with her usual exuberance. 'I've done every last bit. Even my pesky brother!'

Jen's brother Paul, who was coming back for Christmas between spells abroad, was probably the hardest person to buy presents for in the whole world, not because he had everything, but because he had nothing. Carrie had been to his house years ago and Jen had laughingly showed her the inside of his kitchen cupboard, which contained one small milk pan and a battered tin plate. He was very clever in the astronomical field and had his eyes firmly fixed on the stars rather than material possessions. It was hard to tell the difference between the academics who roamed the town muttering under their breath, and the fully certified loons. Carrie thought that often they were one and the same. She was in any case very grateful to Jen's brother who had gone off to an observatory in Chile for months of painstaking work on the spaces between galaxies,

61

and lent Jen his house. Needless to say, the kitchen cupboards were now full to bursting, mostly with spoils from *Trove*.

★ ★ ★

After Damian had moved out, Carrie had sealed herself in her house and refused to either go out or let anyone in. Once a week, she would go and get basic provisions, but the rest of the time she lay in bed staring up at the ceiling, or she sat in Charlie's room that was exactly as it had been the morning he had left it. Her boss at the small publishing company where she had worked for five years kept her job open for three months, but then was forced to fill her post because it was clear that she wasn't coming back.

Carrie's mother finally penetrated the barricade and insisted that she attend a bereavement support group. Carrie went just to shut her mother up, and although it helped a bit, she found that hearing about other people's sadness didn't lessen her own; it simply made her feel as if there was no escape from misery. It saturated every area of life. It lurked behind the ordinary curtains of ordinary houses. It was etched into the lines around people's mouths. She made a few friends from the group and she remained in touch with them, particularly a man called Peter Fletcher whose son and wife had been killed in a road accident. She still met up with Peter from time to time, whenever the need to go over familiar ground became necessary for either of them. She found that sometimes she still needed to talk to someone who understood the specific pain of losing a child. Who knew the incredulity a parent feels when a child dies before they do. Bereaved people have a high tolerance for listening to other bereaved people's stories again and again because they know that by listening they would earn their turn to examine and re-examine. They talked about small things; how long it had been between each breath, the way his head had turned at the end, last conversations about shopping or bins or the cat, the exact time of death. They talked about the details so that their loss could be absorbed slowly. They let it in, little by little, in an attempt to control the pain and stop it from engulfing them.

The only thing that really kept her going during this period was her search for Charlie. It seemed that despite continual pressure from her, the police had stopped doing anything useful. The nice police person who had rubbed her hands on the beach that morning was sent round to tell her that they were almost certain that Charlie must have drowned. When she said the words, she looked carefully over the top of Carrie's head as if looking at something in the distance and her mouth went very small, as if recalling an unpleasant taste. Carrie refused to give up. She returned again and again to the Norfolk villages and towns near the beach. She walked the streets, showing people Charlie's photograph and asking them if they had seen him. She put up posters on hundreds of lampposts. She started a website and a campaign to raise money to find him. She persuaded the local police to do a reconstruction of his disappearance, which went out on *Crimewatch* on the first anniversary of his death. During the filming, she stood in the same weather and with the same sea in front of her and watched another little boy in yellow shorts run away from her towards the horizon and her heart broke all over again. There were the usual crackpots who rang in to say that Charlie was with Jesus or with their ex-husband or even that he had gone swimming with dolphins, but there were no proper leads. It seemed impossible to Carrie that someone who had been as loved and cherished as Charlie could have disappeared without a trace, like a shaken Etch A Sketch.

* * *

Jen was the only person brave enough to suggest an event of remembrance. A funeral was out of the question of course, but she said tentatively that perhaps Carrie would find it helpful to have a memorial or celebration of her son's life. The first time Jen suggested it to her, Carrie reacted with fury and insisted that Jen leave her house straight away.

'He's not dead,' she sobbed. 'I'm his mother, I'd know if he was dead, wouldn't I?' She didn't talk to Jen for a fortnight and then rang her up and apologised.

'I'm sorry. I know you just want to make me feel better, but I can't give up on him.' It was only when she was persuaded by some other members of her bereavement group that perhaps she might view the event as a kind of vigil, that she changed her mind.

'I think it would be nice for people to be able to just think about him and tell stories about what he's like,' Carrie said and Jen's heart hurt at the firm use of the present tense.

Thirty close friends and family members met up at the beach one chilly April morning. No one else was there except for a few bird watchers, their chests bristling with binoculars, and they had the whole expanse of sand and sky to mourn him. Carrie stood frozen and dry-eyed, watching the waves furl and unfurl and remembering the feel of him inside her, rocked in her water.

The memorial on the beach marked some sort of turning point for Carrie. She understood for the first time that she had a choice. She could die without him or she could live without him and she needed to work out which she was going to do. She had kept some sleeping pills that had been given to her by her doctor in the weeks after Charlie went. She got the bottle out of her bathroom cabinet when the night seemed particularly long or when memory hit her like a wave, knocking her off her feet and sucking her under. There were times, when if she had believed that dying would enable her to see him again, she would have done it in a heartbeat.

Jen didn't pretend to understand; in fact she often said the wrong thing because there wasn't a combination of words anywhere that would do justice to what had happened. But she was there when Carrie raged against the poem by Henry

Scott Holland called 'Death Is Nothing at All', which had been sent to her by a well-intentioned relative.

'Of course he's not slipped away to the next fucking room. If he was in the next fucking room there wouldn't be a fucking problem would there?'

When Carrie finally decided the time had come to go through Charlie's things, it was Jen who helped her to sort everything into boxes to save or give away. She held her friend when the discovery of a Mother's Day card tucked between recipe books on the shelf made her scratch her own face. On the second anniversary of his disappearance she remained sober whilst Carrie drank vodka after vodka whilst clutching Charlie's jacket.

★　★　★

The two of them had thought about the possibility of opening a shop together years ago, but the suggestion in those days was only one of many. There was also the fantasy Bed and Breakfast project, which was to cater exclusively to broken-hearted women. Perched in a harbour in a Cornish village and painted the hue of clotted cream, this establishment was to be staffed by a team of young men with surfboard stomachs, dressed in cut-off denims. Each room was going to contain a mini fridge stocked with jumbo-sized tubs of ice cream and the price of the room would include complimentary beauty treatments and salsa dancing lessons. Another of their great ideas was the fantasy School of Chocolate project. This unlikely academy was a cerise-coloured chalet in the Swiss Alps. The students, footsore from the slopes, but chic in their Chanel ski wear, would learn how to transform the rich dark stuff into elaborate confections. Carrie and Jen would, of course, be in charge of mixing and tasting and if there was anything left, wrapping the end product in the finest tissue paper and placing it in heart-shaped boxes lined with purple velvet.

When Jen resurrected the idea of the shop, Carrie saw it as a chance for a new focus in her life. Since Charlie had gone, she had simply existed from day to day, with nothing to concentrate on except her pain. Carrie re-mortgaged her house and Jen sold the flat in Clapham that her father had bought her all those years ago and which was now worth a lot of money, despite the long line of students that had rented and trashed the place. She was between jobs and dumped boyfriends and had been spending so much time with Carrie anyway that the move into her brother's vacant house was the obvious thing to do.

It took them only two weeks to find and secure the little shop. The rent on the place was headache inducing, but they knew that with a bit of luck and a lot of graft, they could make it work. For a town the size of Cambridge, there weren't very many shops in which people could find things they hadn't seen elsewhere. In its previous life, the shop had been an opticians and had been painted a depressing shade of grey as if the owner had made the decision that vibrant colour would have been wasted on the visually challenged. They gutted the place, clearing out the shelves and mirrored glass and replacing them with pale wallpaper decorated with lavender-coloured birds perched on branches. They found a huge old mirror in a charity shop and painted the battered frame silver and a glass-topped counter that used to live in an underwear shop came from the same source. They discovered sturdy wooden floorboards under the carpet and painted them white.

On the day *Trove* opened Carrie received her divorce papers and a card from Damian wishing her luck with the new shop. 'It will be a new beginning for you,' he had written. 'A chance to move forward. I wish you happiness and no more pain.'

Carrie wished it was as easy as he made it sound to begin again. Beginning again implied there had been an ending — but for Carrie there would never be an ending until she knew for certain what had happened to her child.

10

At lunchtime, Molly got a message from the school secretary that the head teacher from Max's school had rung up requesting to speak to her.

'It's not an emergency,' the secretary told Molly, 'but she says could you try and phone her back before the end of the day if you get the chance.'

Molly hastily laid out the tables for the afternoon art session with pots of paint and glitter. She remembered the year before and the scramble to help decorate thirty cardboard picture frames with silver-painted pasta in the half an hour before term ended, and vowed that this time she would have the going-home presents ready well in advance. She stood outside the staff room and phoned Max's school on her mobile. She was put through to Mrs Plumstead, a woman who believed in getting straight to the point and who probably had never left anything to the last minute in her entire career. Max called her the Dalek because of the way she talked in little bursts of instruction. 'Wash your hands,' he would say in a Dalek voice. 'Get your lunch. Stop running. Stand behind your desk. Sing louder. Talk more quietly. We wiiiiill exterminate! Exterminate!'

'I'm rather worried about Max,' Mrs Plumstead said now. 'I am afraid he had another little episode this morning.' Molly's heart sank. She knew the use of 'episode' meant that Max had wet himself again.

'It's just that it's happening more and more frequently. I really think perhaps he should see a doctor. He seems a little stressed. I'm also rather concerned about his inability to write anything that bears the remotest resemblance to his real life. I've had to talk to him a couple of times about telling lies. We encourage imaginative writing, but in their day books the children are supposed to write about what they have done. It's like a diary.

'Sometimes it is just plain outlandish stuff,' she said, 'other times he writes things that seem quite credible, but I know they can't be true. Yesterday for instance, he wrote that his father was back in the country. I understood his father has been abroad for an extended period of time . . . '

'Yes, he's been in America for the last six months,' said Molly. 'I'll talk to Max. Maybe his father not being . . . with us is upsetting him more than I thought. I don't know.' Molly trailed off. The head teacher's silence felt damning. She clearly thought that here was yet another case of adults screwing up their children's behaviour by putting themselves and their own dreary affairs ahead of those of their offspring. After some more talk about the advisability of despatching Max to school with a change of clothes, Mrs Plumstead rang off, and Molly had to put her anxieties to one side for the next hour and focus on ensuring that most of the glitter ended up glued to paper rather than to the children's hair.

★ ★ ★

When she went to pick Max up he had already made his way out of the after school club and was waiting for her at the gate. He was standing apart from the others, wearing trousers from the school lost property box that were a little too short for him. He got into the front seat of the car, clutching a plastic bag that Molly knew contained the evidence of his humiliation.

'I'm sorry it happened again, darling,' she said, knowing that he would hate to have to tell her about it himself. He probably didn't know that Mrs Plumstead had already spread the glad tidings. Max shrugged his shoulders and looked away from her out of the car window. She could feel the tension in his body.

'Was it just that you didn't quite make it to the toilet on time?' she said, putting a hand on his tight little thigh. He flinched away from her slightly.

'Is something upsetting you, Max?' Molly asked. 'Or is someone being mean to you? Tell me darling.' Max turned towards her and she could see that he was trying not to cry.

'It's what little kids do. Wetting themselves. Ryan said I got wee on his shoes, but it's not true, it just went in my trousers and on the chair.'

'I'll go and wee on Ryan myself if he's not careful,' said Molly in the threatening deep voice that always made Max laugh. 'You can tell me anything,' she said. 'You know that, don't you? You can tell me anything and . . . ' Max interrupted, 'And you will still love me. I know.'

He looked out of the window for a while, but Molly could feel that some of the misery had left him.

'What if I stole all your money? Would you love me then?'

'Yes,' said Molly.

'What if I chopped a bear up into little bits?'

'Yes, I'd still love you.'

'What if I cut the ears off a baby?'

'Yup.'

'What about if I hit someone over the head with a hammer?'

'No problem.'

'What if you made chocolate cake and I got up in the night and ate all of it?'

'Now, steady on there. There are limits you know!' said Molly, and she was relieved to hear her son laugh.

When Max had had a bath and changed for bed and the offending clothes had been washed and draped on one of the reluctant radiators and were giving off a fug of synthetic jasmine, the two of them settled down to watch *Elf*. This was a pre-Christmas ritual that could not be missed. Max loved the absurdity of a man dressed in an elf costume doing all the things that grown-ups had forgotten they liked to do.

'Max?' said Molly, while Max squirmed with delight at the sight of Will Ferrell pouring sweets and maple syrup over his plate of spaghetti.

'What do you write in your day book at school?'

'Just what we've been doing,' said Max absently, his attention focused on the screen.

'Do you always write what has really happened?' asked Molly.

'Sometimes, when I can't think of what to write, Charlie tells me,' said Max, cracking up at the sight of the giant elf eating balls of cotton wool as if they were candyfloss.

11

Oliver's house was full and noisy when Carrie finally made it across the road. The front door was slightly ajar, so she went in without knocking. Although it had taken an effort of will to resist the comfortable sofa and the Friday night pyjamas that had become her habit, she had chosen her clothes with care. She wore a black lace dress with a high neck and tight sleeves, some large gold hoop earrings and the pair of burgundy velvet Max Mara heels that she had bought for six pounds at the Red Cross shop. Her hair was in a loose knot held together with a long gold pin. Oliver had clearly gone to town on the decorations — the halls were not so much decked in holly, but submerged under it — and there was a smell of warm wax and slightly overcooked mince pies.

With a quick glance, Carrie ascertained that both the Roses and the Foxtons had showed up, and were sitting glowering at each other from the opposite sides of the room. Mrs Evans, who was in a permanent state of anxiety about everything from the workings of the council to the workings of her innards, was examining the food very closely. Carrie saw her sniff her crostini before putting it cautiously to her mouth. Emily Foxton, wearing a sequinned dress so small it would have fitted a Chihuahua, was sitting on the arm of the sofa staring at Oliver — or at least she looked as if she was staring at him; it was hard to tell since her eyes were obscured under enormous false eyelashes. The family at number fourteen had brought ALL their children, even the one that still crawled, and she saw with dread that a few of them were clutching instruments. Carrie was very grateful that she only heard the strains of the harp, the tinkle of the piano and the crash of cymbals on her way past the house. She thought they must be a grave aggravation to the people who lived in numbers 12 and 16. Mrs Musical Family spent her time trying to either park or extricate her Musical Prodigy Carrier from Almond Street. She had the flushed, unmade-up face and the wide hips of a low maintenance woman. One that could be heard saying with a mixture of pride and defiance:

'I *never* go shopping. I have had this same handbag for thirty-two years.'

Mr Musical Family had the hunted look of a man who yearned for a glimpse of a black stocking and who suffered from extreme tinnitus. The children were pale and pinched after too many hours spent bent over music stands in airless rooms.

Oliver caught sight of Carrie and immediately came over.

'You're here. I thought maybe you had changed your mind. Have you got a drink?'

He steered her over to the table and ladled out a generous slug of mulled wine. He was wearing a white shirt tucked into dark trousers and his hair was more groomed than it usually was, combed back from his face and ending in a slight curl over the collar of his shirt. His fingers touched Carrie's as he passed her the glass of wine, and Carrie suspected that the contact was not accidental.

To her surprise, Carrie found she quite enjoyed meeting and talking to people that she had previously only seen walking past her house or getting in and out of their cars. From time to time as she chatted with her neighbours, she found herself looking at Oliver as he moved round the room and was surprised by the effort he was putting into making everyone feel welcome. At one point Mrs Evans, who had been hitting the mulled wine hard, came over all hot and had to be propped up against some sofa cushions. Oliver went to get her a glass of iced water and sat with her until she felt herself again. Carrie heard her telling Oliver that he had the most wonderfully strong arms.

Every now and again Carrie found Oliver by her side filling her glass from a jug of mulled wine, doing it in such a way that made her feel as if he had picked her out for particular attention. It was something about the way he looked at her; intent and admiring, but also as if she had just said something funny or was about to. She suspected it was one of the tools of his trade, this way he had of making women feel special.

Beginning to feel the effects of the mulled wine, Carrie went over to sit on an upholstered seat that had been constructed into the bay window. The bottom half of the sash was open and the cold air was welcome on her hot cheeks and neck. Outside, a group of girls with tinsel in their hair walked past singing ostentatiously, as girls in groups often do when they are in public, as if they are trying themselves out when it is safe to do so. She remembered suddenly what it felt like to be that age and to be caught up with the sensation of life. The fear in the very centre of you at the thought of being touched, and yet the yearning for it making your skin feel tender in readiness.

Oliver came and sat down next to her. There wasn't much room on the seat and she could feel the press of his leg against hers.

'Are you OK?' he asked. 'Can I get you something else to drink?'

'No thanks. I think I've probably had enough,' said Carrie.

'I don't know anything about you,' he said, and the genuine curiosity in his voice made her want suddenly and absurdly to tell him what she was thinking. Then she remembered that he was probably a master at the game of asking women the right questions, in just the right way. The man couldn't help himself. He'd even left Mrs Evans ('You really *must* call me Jean') in a state of heightened excitement about his forearms.

'I know quite a lot about *you*, however,' Carrie said acidly, thinking about the early morning departures of a series of slender and dishevelled blondes.

'Oh, yes?' said Oliver in an amused tone, looking at her in a way that made her think he might have seen her peering shamefully out of her window, spying on his love life. She found to her annoyance that she couldn't stop looking at his mouth, the smoothness of his lips, the way one lip just curled down slightly at the corner. She was aware again of his body pressed against hers, and of her own body responding with an equal pressure, an equal heat.

Just then there was an almighty bellow from the other side of the room, and the crowds parted to reveal Mr Foxton and Mr Rose entangled on the floor. Mr Foxton was sitting astride the other man and with one hand caught up in his wispy grey hair, was banging his head up and down vigorously. Roger Rose had blood pouring from both nostrils. Lydia Foxton, standing next to her husband, her face flushed and triumphant, was inciting him to greater excesses of violence. Greta Rose was talking urgently to the police on her mobile.

Oliver threw himself on the two men and after some undignified scuffling, managed to separate them. He had to partially sit on Gerald Foxton to prevent him from launching himself upon his enemy once more.

'What's this all about?' asked Oliver.

With a trembling hand, Roger Rose tried to wipe the blood off his face.

'He says I tripped him up,' he said.

'He definitely tripped him up. I saw the fucker,' screeched Lydia Foxton, flexing her hands as if contemplating joining in the fray.

Mrs Musical Prodigy put her hands over the ears of her nearest child. 'How about some musical entertainment?' she suggested in her brightest, most encouraging voice. 'Ophelia, go and get your harp, darling. We'll pour some oil upon troubled waters.'

The threat was enough to get most guests reaching for their coats and handbags, particularly since the sound of a police siren could be heard only a few streets away.

★   ★   ★

Long after the last of the guests had departed, Carrie went to draw the curtains across the window in her front room. As she glanced out, she saw Oliver on his doorstep, kissing a dark-haired woman. This was no casual good-night kiss. He was definitely taking his time about it. Anxious not to be caught staring again, Carrie made a show of closing the curtains with much swishing of fabric, and was almost certain she saw Oliver looking over the shoulder of his latest conquest and straight at her, but of course it was dark outside and she couldn't be sure. Anyway, she told herself firmly, she wasn't really all that interested.

12

After Max had watched *SpongeBob* for three hours straight, Molly made him go cold turkey and insisted, despite his reluctance, on a brisk walk as far as the village, past the duck pond edged with ice and through the small copse that led to the back of their house. When they got back Molly was struck by how dusty and unloved the place looked and she realised it had been a while since she had given it a proper clean. She set Max up in his room with some toys and started on the living room, clearing out the fireplace and laying it with new kindling and logs, sweeping the slightly sloping wooden floors and shaking the rugs out of the back door. The garden was small and square and almost entirely paved over with flagstones. If it had been her own garden Molly would have taken up the patio, cut down the looming hedge that smelt rotten in wet weather and instead made curving flowerbeds and a patch of lawn. As she stood there on the chilly step she imagined a different garden with a flowering cherry tree and bluebells, and perhaps a white lilac in the corner. This house, situated in the middle of the Fens about five miles from Ely, was not where she would have chosen to live — it was too exposed to the weather and too isolated — but since she had no choice it would have to do for the time being.

Molly went back inside, dragged the hoover from the cupboard, and began to vacuum the stair carpet. After about five minutes she turned the protesting machine off. Like everything in the house it was past its prime and had a tendency to overheat and needed regular rests. She went to the top of the stairs and, not wanting to disturb Max while he was so happily and quietly employed, stood by the half-opened bedroom door and watched him. He was sitting on the floor, with several sheets of paper spread around him. He had a habit of starting to draw something and then deciding it had gone wrong and abandoning it and starting afresh on another piece of paper. He got through masses of the stuff. It didn't matter how often she told him that he should persist with a particular drawing he would always refuse to continue once doubt had crept into his mind. Now he seemed to be drawing what looked like a castle surrounded by squiggly lines. She was surprised when he spoke and thought at first that he must be addressing her.

'I'm not exactly sure what you mean,' Max said. 'You'll have to be clearer or I'll get it wrong again.'

Molly watched as he stopped what he was doing and looked up and across his room in the direction of his bed. It seemed to Molly that he was waiting for a response, because he tilted his head the way he did when she was explaining something to him that he didn't really understand.

'Oh, OK. I get you,' said Max and he bent

down over his paper again and started drawing lines with a surer hand. 'We just have to make sure they are all connected.'

Molly went all the way into the room.

'Who are you talking to, Max?' she asked. She was unnerved by the way his eyes were not focused on her but were looking instead at a point just beyond where she was standing. So intent was her son's gaze that she found herself turning round to see what he was staring at, but there was nothing there. Just his rumpled bed with his pyjamas thrown aside and the usual collection of stuffed animals he insisted on sleeping with.

'Charlie, of course,' said Max in his 'doh, don't you know' voice.

Molly sat down next her son and pulled him close to her. She knew that children often had imaginary friends, particularly only children like Max, but she thought it was odd the way her son had fixated on a child he had only met once. She couldn't help worrying that what had happened with Rupert had damaged him in some way, made him odd and unreachable. Maybe she should try working fewer hours and spend more time with him.

'Why do you talk to Charlie?' she asked. 'You can always come and talk to Mummy if you get lonely.'

'Charlie knows what I mean,' said Max, and then, seeing something in his mother's face, said hastily, 'You know what I mean too, it's just that Charlie is the same as me.'

★ ★ ★

Molly thought back to that day on the beach that had started so happily and ended so terribly. Max had been around five years old. It was during a period with Rupert when, although things were going relatively well, he often needed time away from Max's chatter, so she had taken him off to the beach. It had been a perfect day until the boy had gone missing. Although Max had played with him, she couldn't really remember what he had looked like, but his mother's face was still vivid in her mind. Molly didn't think she would ever forget the other woman's expression when she had run up to her on the beach, panting with the effort and with fear. Her eyes had been dark in her white face and her body tight and set, as if readying itself for what was to come. At the time Molly had felt bad that she had not stayed on the beach and helped to look for the boy, but she had had a desperate, uncontrollable desire to get away from there and to take Max somewhere safe. Max himself had seemed to be unaware of what was happening, but a couple of months after the incident she had been astonished when he asked her about it.

'The mum on the beach didn't find her boy, did she?' he asked one night as she was putting him to bed.

'I don't know, darling,' she had said tucking him in tightly, the way he liked. Although she did know. It had been in the paper and on the news for a while and she had followed the story without really wanting to.

Max got up from the floor and stretched. Molly looked up at him.

'Would you like to talk about what happened with your dad, Max?' she asked.

'No,' said Max, and his face had that blank, shutdown look he always got when his father was mentioned. She had tried several times to initiate conversations about Rupert but Max always changed the subject. She didn't blame him, since she didn't really want to talk about it either. Just the thought of her husband filled her with a terrible sense of shame.

* * *

The first time that Rupert hit Molly she was so astonished that she didn't feel the pain of the blow. Rupert had been working hard and the little time they had together was dominated by rows and tension. It seemed to Molly that the slightest thing she did would make her husband angry. Everything from leaving a fork in the sink to Molly spending ten minutes longer than the allotted hour at the supermarket provoked raging outbursts, followed by prolonged, punishing periods when he would say nothing to her at all. Max, who had turned four and had just started reception class, was old enough to be puzzled by his father's erratic behaviour; sometimes smothering him in kisses and bringing home outlandishly expensive toys, then becoming impatient at the slightest noise his son made. Some days, just the sight of Max bouncing on a sofa or running down the hall would be enough to send Rupert into a black, terrifying rage. Once, Molly found Max under the bed in his room. He was hiding because he had knocked the wastepaper basket over in his father's study and he was scared about what Rupert would say.

★　★　★

Molly thought that some Cretan sun and a fortnight together might help Rupert to relax; they hadn't had a holiday abroad since Max had been born. She attributed a lot of Rupert's moods to the fact that he had mentioned potential redundancies at work. He was clearly stressed by the idea that even if he kept his job he was going to have to do more work to cover the gaps.

'Where did you get the money?' he asked, looking away from the picture of the villa she was trying to show him and continuing to cut his toast into four neat squares.

'I sold a couple of paintings and I have been putting a little money aside every month,' she explained. 'It will be lovely, it's a bit inland, but has a pool and we can hire a car.'

'We can't go,' he said. 'Get the money back. I can't get the time off work.'

But by the evening he had changed his mind and came back from work with a guidebook of Crete. He sat showing the pictures to Max and marking certain pages by bending the corners.

'Look, Knossos,' Rupert said. 'That's where King Minos imprisoned the Minotaur. It was his child but it was born half cow and half human.'

'Is it still alive?' asked Max. Molly laughed more loudly than his question warranted because she was so relieved that Rupert had agreed that they could go after all.

*   *   *

The villa was beautiful and overlooked the White Mountains and a sliver of sea. During the day the three of them explored hot hillsides thick with ancient stones and thyme and then swam in a warm, wavy sea. Each evening they ate bread and salad on their veranda, watching the headlights flickering on and off as the cars rounded the bends in the narrow road that snaked below them. They went out on a snorkelling boat to a place where the sea was such a deep blue you felt you could cut a slice of it. Max was scared to jump out of the boat at first, but Rupert managed to persuade him into his arms. He held him in the water and pulled the mask over his eyes and nose. Father and son swam holding hands, their flippered feet moving in unison. Later Max wouldn't stop talking about the new place he had discovered.

'It's just like our world,' he said, eyes shining. 'It's got hills and valleys and trees and everything, but it's underwater and it's secret. It slides away downwards under you and makes you feel dizzy.'

Molly bought him his own snorkelling mask and he spent the rest of the holiday with it clamped to his face, only peeling it off to eat and drink, his skin water drenched and his face marked around the eyes with the ridges left by the rubber. On the last whole day of their holiday they went into Hania and wandered around the shops in the narrow lanes close to the harbour. Rupert bought Molly some earrings in the shape of tiny mermaids. They sat at a café with cane chairs and a raffia awning and watched the silver fish moving quickly in thick clumps through the water.

In the evening they finished the last of their bottle of supermarket ouzo. Max had gone to sleep, hot and open mouthed, his snorkelling mask packed away in his red suitcase along with a sea urchin shell wrapped in layers of toilet paper. Molly had found Rupert standing looking at his sleeping son. 'He's great, isn't he?' he said turning to her, and she saw he had tears on his face. He spread the mosquito net carefully so that it covered Max's feet.

'I'm so lucky to have you both,' he said, and Molly felt that maybe it would be alright between them after all. Maybe their little family had a chance. Maybe they could even think again about having another child. She stroked her husband's face and led him out to the pool. He pulled the cushions off the sun loungers and they lay down together. He began at her feet, and worked his way slowly up her body. He made her wait even though she was arching against him. She held his thick, dark cock in her hand and rubbed it against the inside of her thigh. He took her breast into his mouth and worked at her nipples with his dry, rough tongue, and still he took his time, pushing into her a little way and then out, holding her head in both his hands, watching the way her mouth moved. Afterwards they swam naked, the water on her body making Molly feel free and young again, and then sat close together wrapped in towels looking across the mountainside. There was a smell of jasmine and chlorine.

'Will you be sorry to go home? Are you dreading work?' she asked.

He turned to look at her and smiled.

'I'm not going back to my job. I handed in my notice five weeks ago,' he said. 'I'm having some time off. I've gone off accountancy. I think I'll try something else.'

Below them Georgioupolis, the small seaside resort three kilometres away, illuminated suddenly as if one giant switch had been turned on. She felt a chill even though her body was full of sun.

'When did you decide to do this?' she asked. 'How will we manage?'

Rupert pushed her aside as he got up.

'I knew you would be negative about it,' he said. 'That's why I didn't tell you.'

'I'm just surprised, that's all,' she replied.

Rupert stood with his back to her looking out across the hillside.

'Darling?' she said, getting up and walking towards him. 'Don't be upset, we'll work something out. You'll find something else. I just wish you'd said something . . . '

Without warning, he turned and lashed out at her with his fist. The blow was so hard she fell to the ground. For a moment she thought that she had been hit by something else; it seemed impossible that her husband had just struck her. And then she looked at his face and saw something that might have been triumph, a kind of glittering pleasure, and believed it.

13

Carrie and Jen spent the days leading up to Christmas getting ready for the sale. They knew that the things that glittered so brightly prior to the festive season would suddenly look tawdry as soon as the day itself was over, so in an attempt to counteract this post-holiday slump Carrie had ordered a lot of new merchandise that she thought would reflect the optimism and good intentions that the New Year brought with it. She had discovered a line of sportswear that would surely provoke even the most inactive to get physical. Made from soft towelling that bore no resemblance to the scratchy dressing gowns Carrie remembered from her youth, the retro-looking tops and jogging bottoms came in pastel hues. She was also expecting some bright gym bags with locker tokens attached, matching water bottles and some impractical but fetching sports shoes with wedge heels. For the less active, there were some journals and diaries covered in a selection of beautiful vintage floral fabrics.

Carrie was marking down a basket of glass baubles and remembering that her mother was due to arrive in less than five hours, when the doorbell went and Peter Fletcher walked in holding a parcel wrapped in silver paper and topped with a huge purple bow.

'I couldn't let Christmas go by without seeing

you,' he said, and gave her a hug. They had shared so much that Carrie always felt comfortable with him. He was one of the few people in her life with whom she didn't have to pretend.

'Can the shop spare you for long enough for some lunch?' he enquired and she thought that he looked tired.

'Are you OK, Peter?' she asked, knowing that it was a stupid question. Christmas is always the hardest time of year for people who have lost children. Everywhere you looked there were reminders of the years you had been unthinkingly lucky to have your child and a warning of all the years without them to come.

'Not really,' he said.

Jen was only too happy to have an excuse to stop tidying up the stockroom and marking down the sale merchandise and she came downstairs to look after the shop while Carrie was out. She gave Carrie a sly dig in the ribs as she put on her coat and gave her lips a quick gloss with raspberry-flavoured balm.

'What?' demanded Carrie, knowing only too well that Jen, with her mania for match-making, already had her signed, sealed and delivered into the arms of the widower, whose loss rendered him deeply romantic in Jen's eyes.

'He's keen. Mark my words he's keen,' she whispered, 'I think he's put on his best jumper.'

'Don't be daft,' said Carrie, shooting her friend a warning look through the window as she and Peter set off down the road.

They secured a table in the corner of the local

bistro that was tucked conveniently in a cul-de-sac behind *Trove*. They both ordered bowls of bean and chestnut soup with slices of brown bread and butter.

'I can't stop thinking about them,' said Peter suddenly. 'They're around every corner.'

Carrie knew from experience that she didn't need to reply. It was enough that she was there listening.

'And the actual day. I've not moved on like they say I should have by now. I play it and replay it in my head. The hospital, the way they were.'

Carrie placed her hand over Peter's and he clutched it.

'Sorry. I'm sorry.'

'Don't be,' she said.

She let him talk and they drank a bottle of wine and on the street outside the shop he held her very tightly. Carrie could see Jen through the shop window, capering to and fro like a mischievous, although rather hefty elf.

'Listen,' said Peter, 'I was wondering if you would like to come for dinner . . . I thought about inviting a few people from the old group, you know. Say if you don't fancy it.'

'That would be nice,' smiled Carrie. 'Ring me after Christmas. We'll talk.' She stood for a while on the pavement outside the shop and watched him walk away with the slight stoop that was characteristic of him. She wondered fleetingly whether grief had actually changed his posture for good. Perhaps in the days before she knew him he had walked straight as a die. Perhaps there was something about her too now, something visible, that allowed people to see that she was grieving.

★ ★ ★

Jen followed Carrie into the back room while she hung up her coat and scarf. She wanted details.

'What did he say? Did he admit his passion?' Jen asked gleefully, running feta-smeared fingers through her hair. She had eaten her Greek salad baguette on the move. Despite Carrie's frequent admonishments she had a tendency to touch the merchandise with greasy fingers.

'It's not like that,' said Carrie irritably. 'We just talk. He's still grieving for his dead wife.'

'I'm not saying he isn't,' answered her friend. 'It's just that I've seen him looking at you with those sad eyes of his. As if you might be the beginning of the cure.'

'Listen chum,' said Carrie, spraying Mr Sheen perilously close to Jen's eyes and attacking the surface of the huge framed mirror behind the shop counter, 'I'm nobody's cure. I'm still a mess myself.'

'Maybe you could be each other's salvation,' said Jen, moving swiftly away before Carrie decided she needed another spray of glass polish.

'It's not as if he isn't attractive. Needs feeding up a bit, but I noticed something that might have been quite a decent bum under that jumper he was wearing.'

'I think you should focus less on my love life,'

said Carrie, 'and think a bit more about your own.'

'Not that it is any of your business, but you are looking at a woman who this very night is meeting with an eligible bachelor of this borough,' replied Jen with a smirk.

'What!' said Carrie, astonished. 'You never said you were going out with anyone.'

'Well, strictly speaking, I'm not, yet,' said Jen. 'I met him online on one of those dating sites. I've seen his picture, but I haven't seen him in the flesh.'

Carrie was forced to cut short her questions, because the shop suddenly filled up with people. Half an hour later after a customer had asked to see pretty much every pair of earrings, agonised about each one and then left without buying anything, Carrie was finally able to resume her interrogation.

'Where are you going? What are you wearing? What does he do?' she asked, agog.

'Browns. What I've got on. Something in I.T.,' Jen replied economically, threading red ribbons through the holes punched in the *Trove* bags.

Carrie surveyed the sludge-green sack worn loose over fraying navy leggings that her friend was wearing.

'You are not seriously telling me that you are going out on a first date looking like that?' said Carrie in despair. 'Please let me choose you something else.'

After much begging and bribery, Carrie at last persuaded Jen to submit to a make-over. She was going straight to meet her date from the shop, so the transformation had to take place in the room at the back. Jen kept jabbing her elbows into the wall and swearing as she tried on dresses and Carrie had to keep darting out whenever she heard the doorbell ring.

After many visions and revisions and quite a bit of petulant behaviour, even Jen had to admit that the final product looked pretty damn good. She wore a beautiful skirt bordered around the hem with a pattern of boats and lighthouses and a shirt in exactly the same faded coral as the sails on the boats. The shirt fitted at the waist, making the most of Jen's ample curves, and the colour brought out the honey undertones of her skin and the amber streaks in her brown eyes. Carrie had forced her to bin her ragged ankle boots and replace them with beige fishnet tights and a pair of blue suede shoes with ribbon ties. She had also pulled back her unruly hair and fastened it with an elastic toggle adorned with a turquoise bird, leaving a few stray curls across her forehead. Finally, despite Jen's protestations, she had given her lashes three coats of mascara, dabbed a berry-coloured lip stain on her mouth and squirted Mitsouko down her cleavage.

'Knock him dead, girl!' she called out to Jen's departing back and her friend gave an exuberant shimmy as she walked away, almost knocking down a man in an overcoat who stared after her as if he had never, in all his life, seen anything so splendid.

* * *

When Carrie got home there was the usual dump of junk mail and adverts on her mat and she gathered them up wearily as she went through the front door. At the top of the pile of vouchers for free pizzas and menus for Chinese takeaways was a yellow leaflet advertising the services of a medium called Simon Foster. There was a poor quality photograph of him that was so blurred he could have been anyone. She took a dim view of those that preyed on the misery of others. In her opinion, pretending to hear messages from the dead in order to scam people out of their hard-earned cash was nothing less than a crime. Carrie threw the whole lot into the recycling basket in disgust and went into the kitchen. While she waited for the kettle to boil she looked through the window at the darkened garden and couldn't imagine that it would ever be anything other than the hard, clenched, wintery thing it was now.

By midnight, despite repeated calls to her mother's mobile, Carrie had been unable to track her down. Just when she had given up hope of her arriving that day, the doorbell rang. Cursing, she grabbed her dressing gown and put it on as she raced down the stairs. Pam was on the doorstep surrounded by bags and with a large, expectant smile on her face. She threw her arms round her daughter.

'My darling, you look wonderful! I've had a

journey and a half and am in dire need of a stiff drink.'

Carrie stacked up the numerous bags in the hallway and wondered with a sinking heart just how long her mother was planning on staying.

14

The post fell onto the mat with a dull thud and Molly scooped up a handful of Christmas cards. With a little jolt of shock she saw a brightly coloured postcard amongst the white envelopes and knew immediately it was from Rupert. She recognised the oddly flamboyant handwriting, which seemed so out of keeping with his character. She thought it was strange how other details about a person could fade, but their handwriting was always instantly identifiable. Molly quickly scanned the message, which described Rupert's job working on a holiday complex on the north coast of California that provided yurts as accommodation. Yurts, he explained for Max's benefit, were shaped like tents but were made of wood and had proper beds inside. He had drawn a tiny picture of one in the corner of the postcard with a stick figure of a man standing outside the yurt opening with an arrow saying 'me'. The postcard had a picture on it of fat leopard seals lolling on a beach by a hillside covered in some bright red cactus-like plant. After the initial shock of seeing it, Molly was reassured that he sounded positive, and she wondered if maybe the time he had spent away had done him some good. Perhaps he had been suffering some sort of extended breakdown and was now on the mend. Molly had a tendency to hope for the best in people. It was what made her a brilliant teacher, although it did nothing to protect her from the crushing disappointment she felt when people let her down.

★ ★ ★

Molly didn't tell anyone that Rupert had hit her. She spent the last night of their holiday huddled by the pool while Rupert drank himself senseless. On the flight back from Crete, she kept her foundation-covered face averted from his. She sat by the window next to Max who looked back and forth between his silent parents, knowing that something bad had happened but not really understanding what. His mother had explained her swollen and blackening jaw by saying that a wasp had stung her while she had been sitting outside having supper.

When they got back, Molly thought briefly about reporting what had happened to the police, but knew she wouldn't do it. She imagined what she would say on the phone and how they might answer her. She would be put on hold, with perhaps some soothing music to enjoy until she was transferred to a department where the officers were trained to ask the relevant questions. She imagined a room off the main corridor with a door that shut firmly and which had been decorated with a contrasting dado rail in a parody of home. She thought about the person they would send to sit with her in her own front room, knees neatly placed together, a cup held in a no-nonsense hand, the words kind, but the eyes looking around the room and at her, assessing her clothes, what she was saying. *What have we got here then? A vengeful wife who wants to get her own back on a faithless husband? A fantasist? A madwoman?* Or perhaps worst of all, a woman to be pitied. One who had the audacity to think that this wasn't the sort of thing that happened in marriages that started with tasteful throws and Umbrian honeymoons. Molly had always imagined, when she had thought about it at all, that women who let themselves be hit were creatures very different from herself. Becoming a woman whose husband hurt her was as strange and unlikely as becoming one of those shapeless forms under bits of boxes or in the doorways of office blocks that you saw in every major town.

Rupert's reaction to what had happened was to say nothing for the first few days and then get drunk and cry out his remorse in great big gasping heaves. He knelt at her feet, his face wet with tears, his mouth slack with contrition, and begged her to forgive him.

'It wasn't me. It wasn't me,' he cried. 'It was like there was someone else inside my body making me do it. And you know, Moll,' he said, rubbing his face with the back of his sleeve, 'you know how to push my buttons, you really do.'

Molly remembered him as the quick bright fox and held him in her arms, as if he was a wounded animal, until he stopped sobbing.

★　★　★

For a while afterwards she thought of the sound his fist had made against her skin and the way he had stretched the fingers of his clenched hand out afterwards, almost thoughtfully, as casually as if he had caught his hand against the edge of a window frame. Then as the days and weeks passed Molly began to think she had imagined the whole thing, or at least its impact on her began to lessen. The more time that passed, the more outlandish it seemed that such a thing had happened to the pair of them. *She* wasn't the sort of woman that got hit. *He* wasn't the sort of man who would do the hitting. What Rupert had done to her somehow became less about his violence and more about the state of their relationship and therefore partly her responsibility. In the end, what she did was redouble her efforts to please him and to ensure that nothing irritated or upset him. As long as she maintained the equilibrium, Rupert was the old, easy Rupert, full of charm and life.

Then when Rupert finally admitted two weeks later that he had been sacked from his job rather than left it voluntarily, this seemed to her to be a perfect explanation of why he had behaved in the way he had. He had been under enormous stress and he had cracked, as anyone would under that sort of pressure. When she then found out after a phone call with the bank that he had maxed out three credit cards due to an online gambling habit that had got out of control, Molly did her best not to show him the utter terror the news plunged her into. How were they to survive, with a sizeable mortgage on their house and Rupert finding it difficult to get another job, when all they had coming in was the money she made if she was able to sell one of her paintings? The obvious answer was that she had to go back to teaching, and despite Rupert's protestations that it was unnecessary because he would surely get another job soon, she approached her old school and they were only too glad to have her back.

Keeping a promise that he had made to address his gambling problems and determined to atone for his behaviour, Rupert joined a local support group for people with addictions. He paired up with a sad-looking man with a ponytail who had lost his house gambling on scratch cards. He would come and pick Rupert up for their meetings and, despite repeated invitations from Molly to come in and sit down, would insist on waiting in the hall, his hands firmly jammed into the pockets of his coat as if he didn't quite trust them to do what they were told.

★   ★   ★

For a while they managed to hold on to the house. Molly spent all of the money left to her by her mother on the mortgage arrears. She painted as much as she could at the weekends and managed to sell a few of her paintings to a gallery in town. She sat at the kitchen table writing lists of numbers onto clean, squared paper, feeling that by doing so she could somehow take back some control. But in the end, despite all her meticulous totting up, despite the small, careful economies and pleas for more time, their home was repossessed. On their last night Molly lay awake, thinking about all the things that they had done and hoped for in the house. She thought about the day they had moved in; Rupert carrying her over the threshold like something precious, the two of them sitting on the stairs, eating fish and chips, looking happily at the blank walls. She thought about the days it had taken her to strip all the paint off the banisters and the tiny rowan tree they had planted in the first month, which was now twice the height of the shed. She remembered the way she had stood at the back door feeling the rain on her face as the pain of Max coming pushed through her.

Rupert was sleepless too. 'I need you babe,' he said. He pulled her nightdress up and squeezed her breast hard. He held her by her waist, rubbing his erection against her belly. Although she wasn't ready for him he pushed himself into her with one swift movement. She shut her eyes and let him do what he wanted so that it would be over quickly. After he had fallen asleep she lay beside him, looking at his face half lit by the hall light. He moaned in his sleep and made restless movements with his hands as if brushing away flies. She felt something that might have been tenderness if she had been able to feel much at all.

★   ★   ★

A friend of Molly's had just inherited the house near Ely from an aunt who had died six months before and he was kind enough to let them live there for a nominal rent. He said he was planning on selling it when property prices looked like they were recovering, but until then they were welcome to it. Its isolated position meant that it was at least a twenty-minute walk from the nearest habitation, the small clutch of houses that made up the hamlet of Parson's Bridge. Its distance from Cambridge also meant an hour's drive into work every day, but Molly was grateful for a safe, affordable place to live while she tried to pay back some of the debt that Rupert had generated.

Although Molly's friend had cleared out most of his late aunt's belongings, it was still much as its previous occupier had left it. The kitchen had burn rings on the work surface and unclaimed keys hung from cup hooks which had been screwed into the Welsh dresser. One side of the house had a small lean to, roofed in corrugated plastic with a narrow shelf all the way round on which stringy geraniums balanced in yogurt pots.

The first thing that Molly did was make the attic room into as nice a bedroom for Max as she could manage. She scrubbed the old lino floor and spread his familiar duvet over the knobbly bed. She placed all his toys onto the shelves and hung some curtains with red airplanes and silver trucks at the small leaded window. He had been upset by the move, first refusing to go, and then bowing to the inevitable with a resignation that broke her heart. On the day they actually left their home, he waited until they had loaded up the last of their stuff and then ran back into the house saying he had left something behind. When Molly went to find him five minutes later, he was wandering from room to room, unable to say exactly what it was he was looking for.

Rupert seemed very pleased by the new house, saying that he was able to breathe out here in the Fens where the skies were so big and the land went on forever, in a way he hadn't been able to for a very long time. He decided to take up photography again, something he had given up years ago.

'I think that's why everything went wrong before,' he explained. 'I was never really happy hemmed into an office. I'm a creative person and I think I got frustrated.' He spent his days roaming the area, taking pictures, and then tinkering with them on the computer in the small wedge-shaped room at the top of the house. He also took up fishing and the activity seemed to calm him. He sometimes met up with an elderly man who had lived in the area all his life and he taught Rupert how to make eel traps out of willow. The pair of them would explore the canals and drainage ditches in a flat-bottomed boat that slid through the water almost silently.

'The landscape's beautiful, Moll. It's like it's waiting to be discovered,' Rupert said, and she was glad that he seemed happier. Her own happiness she didn't allow herself to consider. Every time she thought about her relationship with her husband her mind skittered away to hide in a shopping list or in how she was going to collect enough glass jars for everyone in her class at school to germinate beans. She thought that if she didn't dwell on it perhaps it would right itself like those drawings of Max's on plastic that you put in the oven that seemed, as they shrank, to bend in on themselves, to spoil, but which smoothed out miraculously when you stopped looking through the oven door.

★ ★ ★

Rupert seemed to be making a real effort to spend time with Max. At weekends he would sometimes take his son out and let him take pictures with his camera. Every evening after Max's bath he would read to him. Max's favourite was the poem 'The Highwayman' by Alfred Noyes and he made Rupert read it over and over again. She could hear them saying the words together, relishing the gore and the tragedy.

> 'Look for me by moonlight;
> Watch for me by moonlight;
> I'll come to thee by moonlight,
> though hell should bar the way!'

15

Jen was unnaturally quiet the day after her date. No amount of wheedling on Carrie's part could establish anything other than the rudiments of what had happened. Even strategic wafting of rose-flavoured macaroons failed to elicit a reaction. This was such uncharacteristic behaviour that Carrie suspected things had gone very wrong indeed the night before.

'What was he like then?' asked Carrie. 'Bit boring . . . ? B.O.? Lives with his mum . . . ? Obsessed with his collection of railway station signs . . . ? Kept his small change in a flowery coin purse . . . ?'

Jen shook her head pityingly at Carrie's blatant attempts to get a rise out of her, and carried on restocking the carousel with cards stitched with small silver charms to put into Christmas puddings. Carrie was concerned about the fact that Jen must have come into the shop at the crack of dawn — indicating either a disappointingly early night at home or a hasty first thing in the morning, pre-shower escape from his house. There was evidence of Jen's labours everywhere; she had filled a huge glass vase with berry-laden branches of holly and red and silver feathers, had built a teetering pyramid of bath cubes and had colour coordinated the rail of cashmere jumpers so that they now ran neatly from cream and the palest pink to chocolate brown and black via lilac, blue and burnt orange. Most worryingly of all, there were no signs of breakfast crumbs on the wooden floor that was redolent with lavender wax polish.

Giving up her attempts to get Jen to talk, Carrie decided to take advantage of all this silent industry and go into town and do some Christmas shopping of her own. Pam had indicated that she would grace them with her presence in the shop for a few hours and although all she ever did was fiddle with the merchandise as if she was in her own personal playroom, at least it meant that with someone else there the other person could go and replenish the stock or go to the toilet without leaving the shop empty. It only took Carrie twenty minutes to walk into the centre of Cambridge. The market square was illuminated by the somewhat sparse curtain of lights hanging down the front of the Guildhall and there was a seasonal smell of roasting chestnuts, pine-sap and urine. Two men who had hit Christmas early, or who possibly were simply drinking to forget the whole blasted thing, had settled on the step around the fountain and were heckling passing foreigners intent on buying union jack boxers or a plate adorned with Kate and Wills before they returned home. Carrie bought a bunch of mistletoe and four oranges studded with cloves, a book published in the fifties on how to make cocktails for Jen's brother and a little lime green jacket from the vintage clothes stall that she thought was perfect for her mother. She was just contemplating whether she should go in and try on the pair of patent leather boots that were glinting at her from the window of Office, when someone tapped her on her shoulder. Turning, she saw with a sinking heart that it was Rachel, a woman from Before Charlie, or BC as she thought of it to herself. She had met Rachel during the antenatal classes they had both endured in an overheated front room somewhere in Cherry Hinton. Carrie remembered that during the classes Rachel had been a harbinger of doom; constantly asking about worst-case scenarios and creating anxieties that had not been an issue before.

'What happens exactly when the cord wraps itself around the baby's neck?' she had asked on one occasion.

'Is it true that men are so repulsed by the vagina after watching their partners give birth that sex is never the same again?' on another.

Carrie and Damian used to snigger about her in the car on the way home, imitating the way her voice would go particularly high and posh whenever she mentioned body parts.

'Are you *one hundred per cent* sure that even a VERY large penis, will not harm a baby in the womb?' asked Rachel. Carrie remembered how at this point the whole class swivelled around to look at Rachel's husband whose too short fringe gave him the look of someone permanently surprised, who was on all fours and mid-pant at the time.

Carrie was pretty sure she hadn't seen Rachel since the party one of the group had thrown six months after the last of them had given birth.

They had lined their precious offspring up on a blanket-covered sofa and taken a commemorative photograph. Carrie could still recall the moment. Charlie had been in the middle, leaning against a cushion, his fists held up above his head as if in triumph.

'Hello Carrie!' said Rachel. 'I haven't seen you for years. How are you?'

'Oh fine, fine,' said Carrie wishing she could disappear. She knew this conversation could only end one way.

'I've had another since I saw you last. Got an eighteen-month-old little girl now too. We called her Florence. It took us a long time to get pregnant the second time. Turned out Pete's sperm was not crème de la crème. Evan's doing well, just started at St Faith's . . . how's Charlie? It was Charlie wasn't it?'

Carrie knew exactly how Rachel's face would look when she told her about Charlie. She had seen the same reaction in many other faces over the last three years. First, there would be incomprehension, which would be swiftly followed by stunned shock, then panic as the other person realised they would have to say something appropriate. Then finally, and lethally, the most crippling embarrassment would take possession. Along with the shock, the inability to know what to say and yes, the compassion, there would be relief. You had to know what you were looking for but once you did it was unmistakable.

'*Seven green babies sitting on a shawl, and if one green baby should accidentally fall, there will be six much safer babies sitting on a shawl.'*

Carrie didn't blame them for feeling like this. She knew that that was probably how she would feel too. She felt her heart hammering in her chest and she thought that she might be having a panic attack, like the ones she used to have soon after Charlie went. For at least six months, every time she found herself in a large, relatively open space the most agonising fear would engulf her. It was as if she had no control over any part of herself and she felt as if her heart would beat faster and faster until it exploded. All she wanted to do now was run, but she was held to the spot. She was sure the other woman was looking at her strangely. How could she tell this person that she barely knew that her heart had been broken? What would explain the fact that she had suffered such a grievous loss and yet, to all intents and purposes here she was amongst the Christmas crowds, lusting after boots, behaving as if nothing had happened? Nothing she could say would make sense to her or to Rachel. Trying to explain any of it filled her with a mixture of weariness and disgust.

'Oh, he's fine,' she said, her heart numb. 'He's just great.'

'We'll have to get them together one of these days,' said Rachel, rooting around in her capacious bag that no doubt held the requisite wipes and packets of raisins. The things mothers have in their bags, things that she used to have when she was a mother too. Rachel pulled out an envelope and a pen.

'Let me just write down my number, and we

can arrange to meet up in the New Year.'

It was amazing how politeness endured even in the most painful of situations. Carrie could feel her hand shaking as she took the proffered number. She could barely hold herself together enough to make the noises that were expected of her until Rachel at last released her and set off up the road. Carrie pushed blindly through the crowds, almost running in her haste to get away. She threw the piece of paper with Rachel's number into the next bin as if she was getting rid of the evidence. It was not simply the loss of someone you loved that stayed with you for the rest of your life, it was the loss of the person that you would have been if you had been allowed to have them forever. It was her fault, all of this. Her fault Charlie had gone. Her fault that her marriage had fallen apart. Her fault that she had become the sort of person who didn't even have the courage to name her loss out loud.

She stumbled on to King's Parade and despite the cold, felt sweat trickling down her back and gathering around her waist. She unbuttoned her coat and sat for a while on the wall outside King's College chapel where some men on scaffolding were cleaning the great windows in preparation for the Christmas Eve service that was broadcast around the world. Two women, their heads obscured by huge vases of white roses, were being led across the forbidden grass in front of the chapel by a third woman who was instructing them where to go in a loud voice. After she had recovered slightly, Carrie continued up the street. She had lost all heart for shopping and she knew she really should get back to *Trove* to relieve Jen, but some impulse drew her on. Her recent agitation had left her feeling disconnected and dreamlike and she walked in a trance along the pavement, oblivious to the chatter and the swinging bags of the people around her. She had the sense that she was out of step with everyone else, walking along a different trajectory. Amongst the usual small group of people who had gathered at the corner of Benet Street to look at the corpus clock, Carrie noticed a woman and a boy standing a little apart from the others. The woman was bending down, saying something to the boy who was staring with a kind of horrified fascination at the monstrous, time-eating grasshopper as it munched its way through another hour. Something about the way the boy held his mother's hand and listened to what she was saying to him made Carrie's heart shrink inside her. There was a quiet, unmistakable intimacy between them. It was the sort of closeness that she remembered with Charlie. She turned away just as the clock gave the terrible warning thud that marked the hour.

16

By the end of the autumn term Molly was completely exhausted. She had made cinnamon biscuits with her class and helped all of them to decorate the festive photo frames that were to be given to their relatives; she had dressed up as the smallest bear in the school Christmas production and had made everyone laugh by sitting on a collapsing chair; she had presented each child with a photo of themselves and written a special message on the back. She even found something kind to say about Grace Bennett who was a sullen girl who had never knowingly participated in any learning exercise but who had gloriously groomed hair.

'Happy Christmas Grace,' Molly had written on the back of her photograph. 'I have really enjoyed your hair accessories this term. You can do my hair any time you want.'

Molly was slightly late picking Max up, but when she arrived he was happily sitting on the floor playing with the childminder's youngest daughter Rosi. Kate Jefferies, who lived down the road in Parson's Bridge with her husband and two children, had become something of a lifeline for Molly. Not only was she an excellent childminder with seemingly limitless patience and a sure comic timing that children responded to, but the fact that she was genuinely interested in people meant that she not only knew what questions to ask, but more importantly, knew how to listen to the answers. She also thought nothing of having to keep Max longer than had been agreed if Molly got caught up in meetings at the school. Max had lined up all Rosi's soft toys and was making each of them dance in the hope that he would elicit one of the fruity chuckles she was famous for.

'He's been no trouble, as always,' said Kate, who was wearing a Father Christmas hat and a large net skirt trimmed with stars. 'We've been dressing up,' she explained unnecessarily.

'Have you time for a cup of tea?' Kate often had the sense that Molly was unhappy, but didn't feel she knew her well enough to find out why. There had been times when it seemed to the other woman that Molly had been close to confiding in her, but then at the last minute, almost as if she was catching herself on the edge of doing something wrong, she would change the subject. Kate didn't know exactly what had happened between Molly and Rupert but she had her suspicions, which she kept firmly to herself and her kind, bony, husband Dave, who ran a hardware shop in Ely.

'She turns really strange when you mention her husband, she said, easing her soft curves around his hard edges on their divan bed. 'I have a feeling he has done something really badly wrong.' And her husband, who wasn't one for talking in bed, said she was probably right, because she almost always was.

'Thanks, but I've got a million things to do at home,' Molly said, gathering up toys and clothes

115

and trying to locate Max's shoes in the chaotic front room. Kate took Molly aside and said in a quiet voice, 'I'm absolutely sure that it's nothing to worry about and it's practically standard in only children of Max's age to have imaginary friends, but he has been talking about that other little boy again. He hadn't for ages, so I thought the phase had passed, but this morning we were making flapjacks and out of nowhere he asked if he could make an extra one for his friend.'

'Yes, he's been doing quite a lot of that at home too,' said Molly. 'I'm quite worried about it actually. And it's not just the talking . . . It sounds really odd but the other day I had the strangest feeling that he was looking at something. Something that wasn't there I mean.'

'He's a child with a very powerful imagination,' said Kate. 'I think it's quite common for children to enter into elaborate fantasy worlds, but sometimes they react to a loss by creating companions. Could it be that Max is missing his father?' asked Kate tentatively, not wishing to pry. Before Molly had the opportunity to answer, the subject of their discussion emerged from the kitchen with a Tupperware box. With a smile of thanks directed at Kate, Molly ushered him out to the car and as always, Max waved enthusiastically at Kate who stood on her doorstep until their car was out of sight, despite the chill in the air.

As Molly and Max came through the front door, the phone was ringing. Max ran to answer it. He had become very fond of saying, 'Max Reardon here. How may I help you?' in his most

116

officious voice. Max held the receiver to his ear, looking increasingly puzzled.

'Who is it, darling?' Molly asked, hanging up their coats.

'I'm not sure,' said Max. 'I think it might have been Daddy.'

'What was he saying?' asked Molly.

'He wasn't saying anything,' said Max, 'but I know it was Daddy, because of that little noise he makes when he breathes through his nose.' When Molly took the phone from her son all she could hear was the ringing tone.

★　★　★

Four days before Christmas Molly took Max into Ely to do some shopping and show him the Christmas tree in the cathedral. Famously huge, it scraped the ceiling of the building and was decorated with white stars and candles woven out of straw. Underneath, a nativity with life-sized sheep and a life-sized baby with a frozen smile were in their allotted places. The temperature had taken another dip. The massive heaters in the corners of the cathedral were producing heat that felt substantial when you were standing right next to them, but which quickly became redundant as you moved across chilly stone. Molly looked upwards at the jewel-coloured octagon and felt the same vertiginous, slightly sick sensation that the height always produced. The building was almost empty, except for some children who were practising carols for the evening. An all-girl choir, they were lined up in white shirts and tiny, irreverent skirts and they were singing 'Once in Royal David's City' as if their lives depended on it.

Max was very interested in the statue of Mary that stood in the Lady Chapel. Dressed in a bright blue dress, she stood with her arms stretched up and her head bowed. She seemed out of place next to the worn stone of the floor and walls, and the unadorned windows.

'Has she lost Baby Jesus?' asked Max. 'Is that why she's begging?'

'I don't think so, darling,' said Molly. 'She hasn't had baby Jesus yet. She's showing how happy she is that she is going to be a mum.' In the emptiness of the chapel she again had that sensation of being un-anchored, set loose in a risky way and she touched a wall in an attempt to root herself. She remembered the feeling she had often had as a child, of things moving fast, freewheeling downhill. She had felt this most often at bedtime and the only thing that would make it go away was to come downstairs and sit for a while squashed safely between her mother and father on the sofa.

Molly and Max wandered back into the main part of the cathedral. She helped him to light a candle by the statue of St Etheldreda, otherwise known as Audrey, Fenland Queen, Abbess of the Cathedral and part of a long line of formidable female saints that had been venerated since the tenth century. She placed the candle on the spike next to the others and watched the flame flicker, almost go out, and then recover. Molly didn't go

118

to church and therefore felt she didn't have the right to a proper prayer but nevertheless she closed her eyes, and hoped the peace of the cathedral and some of Audrey's strength would transmit itself to her.

As they wandered back along the nave towards the entrance, Max noticed a group of people kneeling on the floor rubbing at pieces of paper taped to brass plates and pulled at Molly's hand, eager to join in. Molly was glad of something that would occupy them until teatime and got tape and paper and two fat gold wax crayons from the shop. Max chose a brass of St George and the Dragon, liking the curve of the dragon's tail and the stretch of its nostrils. Molly chose one of a lady with a wide forehead and patterned cloak and elegant pointed feet. At first it seemed as if nothing would come of their seemingly aimless scratchings across the black paper, but the shape of armour and lance soon began to emerge and then as they persisted, details like the patterns in the fabric lay burnished under their fingers.

'It's like magic,' Max said, his face shining. He sat back on his heels and held the finished product up for Molly to inspect.

'It's almost as magic as you are,' she said, and carefully rolled it up and secured it with a rubber band.

17

When Carrie got out of the shower and reached for the towel that she had left on the rail, she discovered it had gone. For about the third time that week she cursed her mother, who used towels as if they were tissues. The other day Carrie had found her turbaned and draped in no less than four towels, lying on Carrie's bed, boldly availing herself of Carrie's virgin copy of *Heat*. The only thing left in the airing cupboard was a small towel, which Carrie fastened around herself as best she could and went into her bedroom to dry her hair. Bending her head upside down, she turned her dryer onto full blast hoping that the hot air would drive away her bad temper. She heard a noise from downstairs so she switched the dryer off and went out onto the landing. There was a frantic screeching and the sound of running feet. Carrie ran down the stairs and was confronted by the sight of her mother standing on the sofa in the living room whirling a tea towel around her head, her face flushed and terrified, her eyes fixed with horror on a blackbird which was flying from one end of the room to the other, resting briefly on a curtain pole or on the edge of the table, and then taking off again, its wings loud in the small space.

'Catch it! Catch it!' Pam begged hysterically.

'Get down from the sofa and go into the next room,' Carrie said, 'I'll try and get it. How the hell did it get in?'

'I don't know. Maybe the door was open . . . aahhhhhh . . . ' Pam screamed again as the bird launched itself towards her.

'Just get down and walk slowly,' said Carrie. 'It can't hurt you. It's just afraid and all the noise you are making isn't helping.'

'It'll get in my hair,' moaned Pam as she got down reluctantly from the sofa and edged her way across the room, her eyes on the bird who had settled on the corner of the bookcase. When she reached the door, she practically threw herself through it. Once she had reached the safety of the kitchen she started shouting instructions, her mouth plastered to the crack in the door.

'Approach it from behind!' she suggested. 'Shall I pass you a colander?'

Carrie clapped her hands gently to startle the bird off its perch, in the hope it would settle somewhere more accessible, but it stayed where it was, its wings vibrating with a gentle tremor, its eyes bright with their distinctive yellow rim. Carrie made a waving movement with her hand, and at last it left the bookcase and set off wildly around the room again making a thin, high, anxious call. At one point it settled on the arm of the sofa and Carrie approached it slowly, but just as she thought she was going to be able to get hold of it, it rose again and flew away from her, towards the closed window at the other end of the room. It seemed to pick up speed at the last

121

minute, as if it thought it had found the way out, and she heard it hit the glass with a dull thud. It seemed to hover for a second before it fell to the ground. She approached it tentatively. Injured, the bird was far more alarming to her than it had been before. She felt a sudden repugnance but forced herself to pick it up, its form so much smaller than it had seemed in flight, its chest rising in tiny movements. What should she do with it? Was it in pain? Should she kill it? Carrie ran into the garden, holding the bird out in front of her. She went quickly down the alleyway. She could feel the bird's heart beating in her hands and although all she wanted to do was to throw it as far away from herself as possible, she knew she mustn't hurt it any more than it was already hurt. She looked around for someone who might be able to help and just at that moment, Oliver opened his front door. Carrie launched herself at him and held the bird out.

'What do I do?' she said piteously. 'I think it's damaged.'

Oliver took the bird from her and bent his head over it. She saw him purse his lips and for a moment she thought he was going to whistle, but instead he blew on it gently, his breath displacing its feathers.

'I think it's just stunned,' he said. 'I'll put it in a box for a bit and keep an eye on it, but I'm sure it will be alright.'

He looked at her and for the first time she remembered that she was dressed in the world's smallest towel.

'I'm sorry, I left the house rather suddenly,'

she said, feeling herself flush under his interested gaze.

'Don't apologise,' said Oliver. 'I think you look great.' She was aware of him looking at the slope of her shoulders, his eyes lingering on the swell of her breasts, which were barely hidden by the towel. She looked at his hands and the way that he was holding the bird so firmly and yet so gently as if it was the most natural thing in the world. She surprised herself by the wave of desire that ran through her at the thought of his hands holding her like that and, shocked into action, she moved away from him, her arms clutched around her chest.

'Thank you,' she said, 'about the bird. I hope it's OK,' and then she turned and fled. Oliver stood looking at her departing figure, his fingers absently stroking the feathers of the still unconscious bird.

★　★　★

After drying her hair smooth and sweeping up the feathers from the living room carpet, Carrie suggested to Pam that they get out of the house and make the most of what was left of the day. Both of them had done all the Christmas shopping they needed and Carrie suggested that rather than going into town they should drive to Ely.

'The cathedral is beautiful and I don't think I have ever taken you there,' Carrie said.

'Why not?' said Pam. 'I like a cathedral at this time of year, makes me feel all holy.'

She went upstairs and came down again wearing an outsized Russian hat, as if preparing herself for a trip to the outer reaches of Mongolia.

'It's chilly in the Fens,' she said in reply to Carrie's derisory look.

★ ★ ★

They found a place in the car park and walked the short distance to the cathedral. Carrie thought that her mother had made the right decision to dress warmly; the air seemed much colder here than it did in Cambridge, and the evening was gathering in, bringing with it a deep lavender sky and the prickle of imminent frost. On the grass in front of the cathedral two boys were sitting astride a cannon killing time. The beauty of the place always struck Carrie anew, even though she had visited many times. It didn't matter how many people were around, the cathedral absorbed them and the noise they made and stood magnificent and unperturbed. While Pam walked round, Carrie sat and looked towards the high altar with its intricate carving, the window behind it holding in its colours, the very last of the light.

She couldn't have said what made her turn at that particular moment. It was almost as if she heard something and felt compelled to move towards the direction of the sound although she wasn't aware of having heard anything specific. The woman and child that she had seen on the previous day by the clock in Cambridge were a

124

few feet from her. They were kneeling on the ground and at first it looked to Carrie as if they were praying, but then she saw that they were bent over crayons and paper. Something about the way the woman was kneeling with her face in profile seemed familiar to Carrie, but then the moment passed. It was a phenomenon she thought she had experienced before: seeing the same strangers in different contexts within a few days or weeks. It always left her feeling a little unsettled, as if she had noticed them for a reason or as if she had been shown a glimpse of the people she might have known if she had lived another life.

18

Suspecting that Molly might be feeling lonely stuck in the house with Max, who was clearly building himself up into a Christmas frenzy, Kate rang Molly and invited her over for wine and mince pies.

'I hope you don't mind that it's all a bit last minute,' she said, 'but I thought if you didn't have anything better to do you might like to come round. Give you a break from Max. There will be some other kids for him to play with.'

Molly heard the kindness in Kate's voice and felt quite tearful. It had been a while since she had allowed herself to get close to anyone. Rupert had spent so long instilling in her the idea that they didn't need anyone else in their lives, that she had almost forgotten what it felt like to be relaxed in the company of other people, let alone to trust anyone enough to tell them anything important about herself. She thought she might be able to trust Kate though. She was already halfway there allowing her to look after Max, and there was something sane and grounded about her that attracted Molly. She wasn't someone who would be blown off course and there was a tender toughness about her that inspired confidence. Molly still wasn't sure however that she would ever be able to tell her what had happened between her and Rupert.

She tried not to think about it but despite herself, the memories forced their way in. Although at first Rupert had seemed more relaxed in the new house, he began to get tense about not getting work. He had applied for several jobs but had not managed to get beyond the first interview stage for any of them and in the end this started to affect his mood. He stopped taking photographs and going fishing and spent a lot of time sitting on the sofa, brooding. He became hypersensitive to sound; wincing at the noise Max made running round the house and banging into the furniture, and shouting if Molly turned on any electrical appliances. Worst of all, he started to monitor Molly's movements again, wanting to know who she was with all the time.

★ ★ ★

The second time Rupert hit her was a Saturday morning, after she had been out swimming with Max. The water at the pool was tepid, the shower drains blocked with lumps of hair and an odour of sulphur hung over the place like a pall, but the big advantage of going there was that it was often empty. Most of the population of the town preferred the flumes and clean tiles and warm showers of the other, more recently refurbished pool. Molly loved Max in his swimming shorts. He looked so bony and clean, like something made specifically to move through water. He could already swim and ducked in and out, emerging with his hair plastered sleekly to his head. He was the shrimp and she was the crab and she held him close in her pincers, enjoying the slipperiness of him against her skin. Sound was muffled and the reflection of the water danced on the ceiling.

That Saturday it had taken her a long time to get Max out of the pool. He had pleaded for another and then another attempt to dive for the ring she had thrown to the bottom. Molly had been aware as she tried to towel him dry in the tiny changing cubicle that they were going to be back home later than she had told Rupert they would be. Max took what seemed to be ages choosing sweets from the machine in the swimming pool lobby. He was a boy who agonised about making even the smallest decisions. 'Do you think I chose the best thing?' he would often ask after lengthy deliberations over a comic or a toy. 'Have I made a bad mistake?' he would ask, his blue eyes anxious. She would always try and reassure him, pointing out the obvious defects in the rejected items, but he never seemed sure. When they got back, Max got out of the car and ran into the house and she followed with the swimming bags and the shopping they had got on their way to the pool. Rupert was sitting in the front room waiting for them. She knew he was waiting for them because he was so still.

'Sorry to have been out for so long,' she said, and she thought her own voice sounded strange and forced, as if she was talking to someone she didn't know very well.

'The traffic was terrible. It took us at least three-quarters of an hour just to get through town.'

He spoke quietly, almost casually, as if he was asking something that was of little importance.

'Where've you been?'

'The swimming pool. We said before we left that's where we were going. We always go to the swimming pool on Saturday morning.'

It was the way that she saw his hands moving on the arm of the chair that made her go over to her son and touch his head.

'Darling, why don't you go upstairs and start a game? Mummy will come up in a minute.'

Max looked at her almost as if he was going to argue, but went obediently out of the room. She heard his footsteps going up the stairs slowly. She imagined his hand holding on to the rail as he climbed. She saw him pushing his door open and the sun flecked with dust touching his head as he crossed the room. Rupert got up abruptly, as if he had just remembered something important.

'Give me the bag,' he said and it took her a while to understand that he meant the swimming bag that she was still holding. He took it from her and unzipped it, tipping the contents onto the floor.

'Show me your towel,' he said.

'What do you mean? It's there.'

'Pick it up.' He kicked the towel towards her and she bent to pick it up. He snatched it from her and ran his hands along the edges of the material.

'This isn't wet.'

'I didn't use it very much. I kind of drip dried while I was getting Max dressed,' she said and it felt already as if she was pleading with him.

'Where've you been?' he said again. She could hear Max moving in the room above them.

'The pool, darling. The pool. Where else would I have been?'

'You lying little slut,' he said, as if commenting on the weather. 'You lying bitch.' He swung his hand back and hit her full in the face. He hit her so hard she could feel the force of the blow in her teeth. She put a hand to her face and found that her nose was bleeding. She staggered and held on to the edge of the table, holding herself upright.

The door opened and Max came in. He looked at her face and ran towards her.

'Go out now, Max. Just go out and wait for Mummy,' she said, but he stood holding on to her arm.

'Get out, Max,' said Rupert, moving towards them. 'Me and your mother are just sorting something out.'

'No,' said Max. 'I'm staying here.'

'Do what you're told!' Rupert screamed the words close to his son's face, causing him to step back. It was this small movement and the quiet whimper of protest that the boy made that seemed to bring Molly to life. She got hold of Max and pulled him out of the room and up the stairs as fast as she could. She closed and locked the bedroom door and the two of them sat on the edge of the bed. She was half sobbing and

130

half trying to breathe. The blood was dripping off her chin and Max wiped her face with a tissue from the box on her bedside table.

'What did Daddy do?' he asked, his face white and surprised.

It was from a desire to protect Max, rather than Rupert that prompted her to make excuses for her husband. She couldn't bear the thought that Max should understand even a little of the ugliness of what Rupert had done. She thought that if she explained it away she could also wipe what had happened from his mind.

'It was an accident, Max,' she said. 'Daddy has not been himself because he is worried about not getting a job. He wants so much to look after us you see.' Her voice wavered. Max looked anxiously at her face and continued to dab at her nose with the tissue.

'You've got blood in your nose, Mummy,' he said, his mouth white and tight.

'He didn't mean to hurt me, Maxy. He didn't know I was standing there and he swung his arm round and it caught the side of my face.'

She comforted him and put him to bed and waited with him until he slept. When she went downstairs Rupert had gone out. He came back a week later. She never found out where he had been and although part of her hated him for what he had done, she couldn't imagine life without him. It helped her to think of him as sick and so she carried on perfecting the art of talking quietly; of becoming as close to a shadow as it was possible to be without actually disappearing.

When Max and Molly arrived at Kate's house a group of children were noisily decorating the tree and the grown-ups had taken refuge in the large kitchen. Molly took a glass of wine and Kate introduced her to the others. She was quiet at first and sat listening to the conversation, but soon began to lose her reticence in the face of their friendly chatter. There was a couple who lived in Cambridge who had both been to school with Kate, a woman who was also a childminder who lived on the other side of Parson's Bridge and Kate's sister Ruth who lived in London but who had come for a pre-Christmas visit with Kate's nephew and niece. Dave, Kate's husband, was also there pouring out drinks and warming up mince pies. Molly had another glass of wine and began to relax. Max had very happily joined the tree-decorating party and she could hear him issuing the occasional instruction. He was no doubt telling them to load up the lowest branches with the heaviest decorations.

The time passed very quickly and Molly had begun to feel pleasantly drunk. The couple from Ely left, closely followed by the other guests, including Ruth who wanted to get on the road before dark, but when Molly got up to go, Kate encouraged her to stay.

'I've just put *Ice Age* on the DVD player and Max is as happy as anything sitting there with my girls eating his body weight in popcorn,' she said. She must also have said something to Dave because after mumbling his excuses, her husband disappeared out to his very well-equipped workshop, where he was putting the finishing touches to the doll's house he was making for their eldest daughter's Christmas present. Kate poured Molly another glass of wine and put cheese and biscuits on a plate in front of her.

'Thanks,' said Molly, aware that she ought to eat something to absorb some of the alcohol.

'It's so nice just to sit here in your lovely kitchen.'

'I really hope you don't mind my asking; tell me to mind my own business if you want to, but what happened between you and your husband?' asked Kate, sitting back down at the table and loading an oatcake with a slice of brie. The habit of secrecy was so well ingrained that Molly's first impulse was to deflect the question, but her second impulse was to tell Kate the truth.

'I've never told anyone this before,' she began. 'I've been so ashamed for so long.' Molly hesitated again, but Kate was looking at her so kindly and anxiously that the last of her reserve disappeared.

'He hit me. Rupert, my husband did. He hit me many times.'

She looked at Kate to gauge her reaction to the words, but she was still looking steadily at Molly.

'He hit me when he was tired or angry or when it rained or when I rattled the cutlery too loudly.'

'I know people always ask this of women who

have suffered domestic abuse,' said Kate, 'but why didn't you leave him? Why didn't you tell someone and find a way of getting away from him? What about the police?'

'It makes me ashamed to say, but the more he hit me, the harder it seemed to stop what was happening. He always said he would find me if I ever left him. And I believed him.'

'Bastard,' said Kate. 'Where's the creep now?'

Now that Molly had started talking about Rupert, it was as if she couldn't stop.

'He's in America. I let him hurt me for a long time, but it was only when he hurt Max that I finally was brave enough to call the police.'

'What did he do?' asked Kate.

'I thought I'd managed to keep the worst of it from Max. Rupert tended to hit me when he was out of the room. He had that much control at least. I'd tell Max things like I'd fallen down or walked into something,' said Molly and Kate saw her hands on the table, clenched tight.

'Did he believe you?' Kate asked. 'He's such a sensitive little boy.'

'I thought he did, but one morning he passed by our bedroom door and he saw Rupert pulling my hair. He had wrapped it around the brass bit of our bed head and was pulling me tight against the metal. I tried not to cry out because I knew Max would hear. Max came running into the room and threw himself at his father and started punching him. It was terrible. He was crying with anger. I'd never seen him like that before. I tried to get him to stop, but he wouldn't. Even with what Rupert had done to me, I didn't think he would hurt Max, but he hit him so hard across the head that he ended up on the floor on the other side of the room.'

'Oh God,' said Kate, taking hold of one of Molly's tight hands and holding it.

'I waited for him to go out and I called the police. They came pretty quickly and were really good. They took pictures of what he had done to Max and me and they said there was enough evidence to arrest him, but before they could do anything, he disappeared. The next thing I heard was that he'd gone to America. His mother rang me and told me and she made it sound as if it was my fault.'

Molly started to cry, and Kate got up from the table and put her arms around her.

'Of course you know that none of this is your fault, don't you?' she said.

19

Jen invited Carrie and Pam over to her house for Christmas Day. The women decided to walk there rather than drive since Carrie was looking forward to a couple of Jen's lethal cocktails and Pam didn't do driving. There was a bit of a tussle in the hallway when Carrie caught Pam off-loading all the heavy items out of her bag into Carrie's bag, but they set off amicably into a crisp sunny day after Carrie had insisted on a fairer redistribution of presents and wine.

As they walked along, they could see evidence through windows of children high on sugar and excitement and many families were already out with new blades, scooters and bikes. Carrie remembered Charlie's third Christmas. It had been the first Christmas he had been aware that something exciting was going to happen. When she had crept up to his room on Christmas Eve he had been lying fast asleep, his mouth open and his arms stretched out flat, his empty stocking clutched in his hand. In his all-in-one pyjamas he had looked like the frog she had accidentally flattened on the patio when she had rolled out the rubbish bin. He had burst into their bedroom early the next morning, holding his miraculously transformed stocking against his chest, and had then spent a full hour going through every object. Unwrapping each one carefully, laying the tissue paper to one side, and examining each toy, each sweet, with reverence. She could see him clearly, sitting in the safe valley between their legs, chocolate around his mouth, his hair still sleep flattened, his eyes almost black with pleasure. People that seemed to know said that as time passed the grief she felt would incorporate itself into the rest of her life, like thread in a tapestry, but she was still waiting for that to happen. It sometimes seemed as if the pain would never leave her. Sometimes she was terrified in case it did.

★ ★ ★

Jen lived in a narrow house down a narrow street off Chesterton Road. Small but perfectly formed, it had one main living space and two bedrooms upstairs that were like cabins on a ship, with storage space cleverly engineered into every available corner. Even the treads of the tiny staircase had been converted into drawers to accommodate shoes. Jen's brother Paul, the owner of the house, had arrived the night before and had been alarmed by the number of ornaments the place had acquired whilst he had been away. When Carrie and Pam knocked on the door Paul was in the process of stoking up the log fire, while Jen was already dishevelled with the effort of preparing the dinner. Ensconced in pole position in front of the fire was a tatty-looking hound who Paul introduced as Enif, which apparently meant nose in Arabic.

'I called him that because he has a really good sense of smell. He was hanging around outside

King's Cross station and he kind of attached himself to me. I tried to lose him but he kept finding me. Enif is also a star from the Pegasus constellation,' said Paul as his new pet raised his head languidly and then settled back down with a weary air, as if he knew the accommodation wasn't up to scratch, but it would have to do.

★ ★ ★

Pam retired upstairs to one of the cabins for a rest at around the time when the issue of the washing up reared its head. In the lost hours between lunchtime wine and five o'clock cocktails, when Carrie and Jen were slumped on the sofa wishing that they hadn't eaten so much and wondering in a half-hearted sort of way whether they should perhaps venture out for a walk, Jen suddenly told Carrie that she was in love.

'I think I am. I am . . . I think,' said Jen, distractedly stroking Enif's ear. He opened one eye and looked at her disdainfully.

'The online man? The one you met for the first time on Friday?' said Carrie, looking at her friend's blushing face with disbelief. This was the woman, after all, who had sworn that the pair of them would do without men and eke out their last days in a fantasy Old People's Home, sitting next to each other in padded rocking chairs in a room with panoramic views, looking out at the sea, eating cream cakes and smoking lilac Sobranies.

'He's not even my type,' Jen said, as if she

138

couldn't quite believe it herself. 'He has a first-aid box in his car.'

'Have you slept with him?' asked Carrie, thinking that perhaps Jen, befuddled with Christmas booze and following a spell without a boyfriend, was suffering more from lust than love.

'We slept in the same bed. But we didn't do anything. Just held each other. It was nice.'

'He stayed all night?' said Carrie, knowing that if her friend had let this man wake up with her, it had to be serious.

'Yes. He brought me breakfast in bed. He put the last shrivelled winter pansy from the garden into a little vase. It was so cute.'

'Doesn't it seem a bit fast to you, Jen? I've never known you be like this before. So caught up. Since He Who Must Not Be Named in fact,' said Carrie, referring to Jen's philandering politician.

'He's nothing like that prat. When you meet him, you'll see,' said Jen and got up to prepare some of her deadly cocktails, the recipe for which she claimed to have got many years ago from a bar keeper in Spain who had told her the secret recipe after a night of passion on the roof of his house. One cocktail in, and Carrie found herself thinking about Oliver. She wondered how he was spending his Christmas Day. She hoped he wasn't spending it with the dark-haired woman she had seen him kissing so passionately outside his house. She hoped that he was spending the day with aged relatives who were keeping him trapped in an overheated house.

20

On Christmas Eve Max was so excited that he almost made himself sick. He positioned and repositioned his stocking, unable to make up his mind which place was the easiest for Father Christmas to get to.

'If I put it by the fireplace,' he explained earnestly, 'then he might not know that it's mine, but if I put it at the end of my bed, then he might be worried about waking me.'

Once the dilemma of the stocking had been resolved by hanging it on his bedroom doorknob, he then couldn't decide whether to leave Father Christmas a glass of milk or wine. This was followed by the trauma of what exactly to write in his letter.

'I want lots of things,' he said, 'but I don't want him to think I am greedy. If I ask for only one thing, will he know that I'm only being polite?'

After Molly had finally persuaded him to go to bed, she poured herself a glass of wine and started wrapping presents. An hour later they were all piled up under the tree and she went upstairs to check that Max had fallen asleep. His face was peaceful and showed none of the anxiety his awake self was plagued with. He had made a path of comics lined with marbles that led in a straight line to where his stocking was placed at the end of his bed. He must have had a last-minute change of heart and moved it from the doorknob. His bed was covered in the paper snowflakes he had spent the day painstakingly cutting out and then attaching to all the windows of the house with bits of Blu-tack. Molly sat for a minute, listening to the reassuring sound of his breathing, and then stuffed the stocking until it was bulging with small tissue-wrapped gifts. Downstairs, she ate the mince pie and drank the milk Max had left out for Father Christmas, then took a deep breath and rang her sister who lived in Sydney and for whom she presumed a sunny Christmas Day had already dawned. She had never been to Australia, never even seen pictures of her sister's house and couldn't visualise the space her sister occupied, or where the phone was located, or what the light was like that surrounded her. It was like talking to a phantom. The phone seemed to ring for ages and then she heard her sister's voice, which didn't sound completely her own but which had an adopted inflection that served to emphasise the distance between them.

'Hello Moll, Happy Chrimbo. What's the time there? Has it snowed? Is it even Christmas yet? I still can't get my head around it.' It was the usual rush of questions, designed to prevent the possibility of a pause.

'Midnight, so almost there,' said Molly. 'What time were you woken?' She thought of her two solid nieces with their hair in tight, neat plaits and matching zip-up tops, and couldn't really imagine them overcome with Christmas excitement.

'We've just got up. We're opening presents after breakfast and a walk. I'm trying to teach the girls about delayed gratification.' It struck Molly that learning to delay gratification could be a dangerous exercise. If you became too good a student you might forget what it was you wanted in the first place. Twelve-year-old Delphine and fourteen-year-old Daphne had visited England with their parents a couple of years before and had remained largely impassive when faced with the best tourist attractions London had to offer. A trip on the London Eye, ice cream at Fortnum & Masons and the best seats in the house for *The Lion King* left them unmoved. The only time they manifested the slightest animation was on the escalator down into Oxford Street's Topshop. There, they became briefly flushed over the selection of zip-up tops.

'I'm about to go to bed, just wanted to catch you before you went out. I hope you have a lovely day,' said Molly.

'You too sweetie!' said Susanna, already moving on into her version of Christmas, leaving her sister behind. As Molly put the phone down, she wished that they shared more than a sense of duty. The ten years between them had meant that they had had largely separate childhoods, with Susanna always tantalisingly ahead. She had blazed the trail with boys and broken hearts and babies. She had always done it all already. She was the professional and Molly the amateur. When their mother became ill, Susanna's guilt at being thousands of miles away and unable to help had widened the gulf between them. Her feelings of inadequacy had translated into criticism of the way that Molly was managing things. It seemed that now there was no way back.

Molly was just drifting off when the phone rang, shockingly loud in the hallway. Befuddled with sleep, she fumbled her way down the stairs and picked up the receiver. At first there was nothing but silence edged with what might have been the sound of distant traffic, but then he spoke.

'I just wanted to say Happy Christmas, darling,' said Rupert. 'Can I speak to Max?'

'It's three in the morning,' said Molly, peering at her watch. 'He's asleep. I can't wake him now.'

'Oh, yes, of course, I forgot,' he said, 'I'm on American time. I'm sorry. Tell him Happy Christmas from me.'

'I will,' she said, and then said nothing because she knew he hadn't finished. She sensed the same threatening quality in his silence as in the moments before he hit her.

'You,' he said, his voice low but conversational, 'you've ruined my life. You know that don't you? You've ruined my fucking life . . . '

Molly put the phone down on his voice, but carried its sound with her upstairs and into the bed which, despite assiduous daily airings, always felt slightly damp.

It was still dark when Max jumped onto her bed clutching his stocking. Molly wrenched herself from sleep and after tucking him warmly into the bed, made him promise he would wait

143

and not start investigating his stocking until she had made herself a cup of tea.

'You don't need tea on Christmas Day,' said Max, his fingers tracing the knobbly contours of the wool. 'You can have sherry, it's quicker.'

The kitchen floor was icy under her bare feet and for about the fiftieth time she wondered why she so resisted the concept of slippers. Their cat, Toffee, a refugee from their house in Cambridge, stalked across the floor with well-insulated paws. Never the most serene of animals, the move had upset the creature deeply. She now spent her time moving restlessly from room to room, tail twitching from side to side, ears held back as if continually preparing to throw herself through a hoop of fire. It was only during the moth season of early summer that she ever seemed to relax. Catching, tormenting and then putting to a slow and agonising death the biggest moths she could find seemed to bring her some sort of release. The next day Molly would find the poor creatures glued to the corners of carpets, their wings shredded.

Clutching her warm mug to her chest, Molly returned to her bed where Max, unable to resist temptation, had already started disgorging the contents of his stocking. After a cosy hour of wind-up toys and chocolate coins, they went downstairs and Molly put in the turkey and peeled some potatoes while Max sat by the tree, gloatingly counting and recounting the spoils that lay under it. The floor was littered with the snowflakes he had made — Molly had to tell him that she thought that it might be nice if at least a

144

bit of the carpet was visible. A teacher from Molly's school, a single parent, was coming over later with her two children and Molly wanted to be sure that everything was ready for the meal. Through the kitchen window she could see the sky, streaked now with pale light, the bushes and trees tipped white with frost. She put the radio on and the room filled with a choir and with Christmas and a sense that life, for all the obstacles it seemed to put in her path, was precious and worth celebrating. She cut neat little crosses in the bottoms of a bowl of sprouts so bright and green, they reminded her of spring.

Max loved all of his presents, particularly an electronic dinosaur fact file which gave the vital statistics of over a hundred of the beasts.

'Guess the power rating of an Alb-ert-as-aur . . . '

'Umm, don't know . . . '

'56!'

'Guess the intelligence rating for Mega-los-aurus . . . '

'Umm, don't know . . . '

'95!'

'Guess the . . . '

'Why don't you open another present, Max?' said Molly hastily, to stem the tide of dinosaur information. Max pulled out a parcel wrapped up in unfamiliar paper that was tucked slightly out of sight behind the tree.

'Is this one from Father Christmas?' he said, beginning to unwrap it.

'Oh, I don't know,' she said, 'I can't remember who sent you that. Maybe someone at school.'

A pair of shiny red boxing gloves fell onto the carpet, along with a piece of paper. Molly picked it up and instantly recognised the writing.

'Who're they from?' asked Max, trying to pull a glove over one sticky fist.

'I'm not sure, darling, maybe Aunty Susanna. It just says Happy Christmas on the note,' she said and crumpled the paper tightly in her hand. Max gave up trying to get the other glove on and began to punch the cushions on the sofa.

'Pow! Pow! Pow!' he crowed. 'It makes the BEST noise.'

It felt as if the floor was slanting away from her. She knew with sickening certainty that Rupert had to have come into the house last night. The parcel hadn't been there when she had put all the other ones under the tree. When he had phoned in the early hours of the morning, he hadn't been in America at all. He had been close by.

21

On the 27th December Damian rang Carrie and asked if he could come to Cambridge and see her straight away. His voice sounded strange on the phone, as if he was holding himself back from saying something, and although she asked him repeatedly, he wouldn't say what the matter was. He was with her an hour and a half later. She was surprised by how thin he had become. There was even a bit of grey above his ears and she decided that it suited him. He was wearing clothes that she hadn't seen before; a maroon jumper that he would never have chosen for himself. He has met someone she thought, and was surprised by how much the notion hurt her. He kissed her on her cheek and then gently sat her down on the sofa. She knew then, that what he had to say was important. For a moment she felt a surge of joy, but then almost immediately, her heart stilled. She knew that Damian would have told her on the phone if they had found him. She wondered how her heart could still be working when it had taken such a battering and imagined it inside of her, all black and blue with bruises. She was thinking of this when Damian told her that the police had rung him that morning. It seemed that following the arrest of a man who had been accused of abusing his stepson, the police had found some images on his computer. One of the boys in the photographs fitted the description of Charlie.

'They don't know for sure, of course. It's a description that would fit a lot of boys that age,' Damian said, seeing her face. 'It's almost certainly not him. You understand that don't you, Carrie? Don't you?' he said as she gathered her coat and bag and looked at herself in the mirror, running her fingers through her hair.

★   ★   ★

The only time that Carrie had been in the police station had been years ago to report the theft of a bike from outside the Grafton centre. Now she thought she would be happy if someone would take her present disaster of a bike off her hands so that she could buy a replacement that actually worked. She suspected that even if she left it unlocked with a note on it saying 'please take me', it would still be there when she returned a week later. She knew she was thinking of random things to stop her dwelling on what she was about to see. A detective who looked like the young Kevin Costner came out into the lobby to meet them. He was dressed in a dark, well-cut suit and was clearly unfamiliar with the doughnut. To her horror, Carrie heard the theme tune from *The Bodyguard* start up in her head.

Damian and Carrie were ushered into an office where a comfortingly traditional copper with big ears was sitting at a computer. Kevin Costner spoke in short sentences as if to forestall any possible manifestation of emotion.

'Now I don't want you to get your hopes up,'

148

he said. 'It's extremely unlikely that the images you are going to see are of your son. We have no idea where this young boy is from. He could be from anywhere in the world. We just need to check to be absolutely sure that it isn't Charlie. Would you like to sit down? Perhaps you would prefer it if your husband looked first . . . '

Carrie shook her head. She needed to see this and she could only see it if she stayed standing up. She thought that sitting down would in some way weaken her. Kevin Costner was speaking again in his cool voice. 'I need for you to look very closely at this set of images. I'm sorry, but some of them are a bit upsetting, although we have done our best to disguise what's happening.'

The policeman with the big ears apologetically scrolled down the screen and stopped when a set of five images appeared. He indicated awkwardly that Carrie and Damian should come closer, looking as if he would rather be anywhere than where he was. He kept rubbing his hand against his chest as if he had a pain there.

The first image showed a blond boy standing bare-chested in what looked like a hotel room. Behind him there was striped wallpaper and a wall light. The boy had huge, surprised eyes and his hands were closely pressed to his sides. In the second picture the boy was lying on a yellow covered bed and someone was holding him down. You could tell how small the boy was because of the size of the hands pushing against him. In the third image the boy was lying curled up on his side, naked, with a rope around one ankle, which led away and out of the picture. Carrie couldn't look at the fourth and fifth picture. There was no air in the room and she couldn't breathe.

'I need a glass of water,' she said, and it sounded to her as if her voice was coming from a long way away. She turned and walked out of the room. None of the pictures were of Charlie. They were of a boy about the same age as Charlie with the same pale skin and fair hair, maybe even the same rounded eyebrows that she loved so much, but it wasn't him. Some other mother somewhere was mourning this child with his tight little fists and his astonished eyes.

Carrie bent over the drinking fountain in the lobby and took several great gulping mouthfuls of water and then went and sat on the plastic chair that had been placed discouragingly by the entrance. She thought about the hands pushing down on the small, pale chest and she started to cry.

★ ★ ★

Damian and Carrie walked across Parkers Piece in silence. It had snowed during the night and children had already scooped up the meagre ground cover and fashioned diminutive snowmen that were pock-marked with mud. A few seagulls wandered between the figures as if they had lost their way and were looking for the shoreline. They went into the first pub they came to and sat at a corner table next to the fireplace.

'I'm sorry you had to go through that,'

150

Damian said, putting a large brandy down next to her.

'I feel ashamed,' said Carrie. 'I feel ashamed that I hated that pathetic little boy because he wasn't Charlie. Will they be able to find him?'

'Who?' asked Damian and took a long drink of beer.

'The boy in the pictures. Will they find him and take him home?'

'I don't know, Carrie. Maybe. He looked like Charlie a bit didn't he?'

'Fucking bastards,' she said and Damian stroked the side of her face gently. She leaned against him and was surprised that even after all this time it felt like a natural thing to do.

'Do you think of him still?' she asked.

'All the time,' Damian said.

'I think of him in the morning when I wake,' Carrie said. 'I think of him when I see something he liked or that made him laugh. I think of him when I feel sad or when I think I might be feeling happy. I think of him before I go to sleep and when I wake in the night. I think of him in every turn of a child's head. Every cry. Every laugh.'

★ ★ ★

Pam was out, otherwise the afternoon might have turned out differently. As it was, Carrie thought later that it was sadness that made her lead Damian up her narrow staircase and into her tiny bedroom with its balcony over the garden. She took off her clothes, dropping them

151

in a pile by the bed and got under the covers quickly, shivering slightly as her skin made contact with the chilly sheets. Damian knelt by the bed and kissed her on the mouth.

'I don't know if this is such a good idea,' he said. He lay on the bed next to her, his dressed body held away from her as if he was waiting for an answer. Carrie stroked him through his jeans until she could feel him harden against her hand. She sat up and pulled the unfamiliar jumper off his long body and kissed the base of his throat. They were careful of each other, as if sudden movements or too much haste would cause each other pain.

Afterwards they fell asleep, spooned together in the soft afternoon light.

22

A week after Christmas, Pam produced the leaflet as if she was presenting Carrie with a particularly wonderful surprise. Carrie had been rather grumpily making breakfast while her mother did what she usually did, which was recline upon the sofa, directing proceedings in a vague, but persistent way. Fond though she was of her, Carrie sometimes felt that being with her mother was akin to being trapped in a glass jar with a midge. She was also wondering how she might bring up the subject of how long her mother intended to stay without offending her. Pam had been talking rather ominously about the pair of them 'going somewhere lovely in the New Year', which seemed to suggest that she had no immediate plans to return home to Coventry.

'I wouldn't mind a little pancake,' said Pam, 'if you're making. One of those American ones with a drizzle of maple syrup.'

'I haven't got any maple syrup,' snapped Carrie, banging the frying pan down on the hob. Her mother was irritating, but the thing that was really bugging her was what she was going to do about Damian. When they had woken up from their shared afternoon sleep, he had seemed embarrassed and had dressed and left quickly, but since then he had texted her twice and left a message on her voicemail asking if he could see her again.

'It felt right, Carrie,' he said. 'Did it feel right to you too?'

She didn't really know the answer to that question. Being with Damian had been comforting and she had been surprised by how much she had wanted him, but she wasn't sure it was enough to start it all again and maybe cause pain, not least to the person who had been buying Damian expensive jumpers.

'I think we should go,' said Pam, breaking into her thoughts.

'Go where?'

'To this . . . haven't you been listening? I've always wanted to go and see a medium,' said Pam, waving a familiar-looking yellow leaflet in the air.

'It's a sign. Yesterday two women in the shop were talking about having gone to see him, and now I find this when I was putting the recycling out. We have to go.'

'No we bloody don't,' Carrie retorted.

'It might help . . . '

'I'm not going to see a con artist who uses people's suffering to make money.'

'You don't know he's a con artist,' said Pam. 'It says here that although he could fill large theatres, he prefers to work with smaller groups of people.'

'It's just exploiting people's stupidity. It's cynical and I hate it,' said Carrie, mixing the pancake batter rather too forcefully.

'He's hardly charging anything. Just a fiver. Apparently he has worked with the police.'

'I don't believe in all of that,' said Carrie, her

154

soft mouth pulled into a hard line.

'I never thought you'd turn out to be someone with such a shut mind. When you were a little girl you were so curious and enquiring,' said Pam sadly.

'Yeah, I was mostly enquiring about why my mum never seemed to be around.'

'You never used to be so cruel either,' said Pam with the special wounded face she used when she could smell victory.

*   *   *

That evening, Carrie found herself sitting in a small side room at a community centre in Romsey. Pam, dressed in sombre grey in honour of the occasion, with just a touch of pink in the scarf wrapped round her throat, was moving excitedly around in her chair.

'Stop wriggling,' hissed Carrie. 'I can't believe you've made me come here.'

Looking around her at the other participants, Carrie rather uncharitably thought they were exactly the kind of deluded and credulous people who would be interested in seeing a medium: the aged, the mentally challenged and the badly dressed. There was an elderly woman who was so thin you could have hung her on a coat rack by the back of her jumper, a mother and daughter who both had the slightly protuberant eyes of the terminally gullible, a man who kept blowing his nose who was clearly already close to tears, and another middle-aged woman who seemed held together only by the tightness of the fastenings on her clothes. She sat bolt upright, her coat buttoned all the way up to her chin, her neck wrapped in a scarf so tight it looked as if it was restricting her breathing. The last of their merry band was a young girl with a pale, narrow face and extremely long hair. Carrie thought sourly that she probably thought that having hair that you could sit on was a source of pride, rather than the sad and creepy state of affairs it in fact was.

* * *

Just when Carrie had decided she was going to bolt and leave her mother to it, the door opened and Simon Foster came in. For some reason Carrie had imagined that he might be fleshier, more theatrical, but this man was spare and slow in his movements. She guessed that he must be in his late fifties or early sixties. It was difficult to tell his age because although his body looked hard and well maintained, he had deep furrows between his eyes and along the side of his mouth and his skin was coarse, as if he might have spent a lot of time out of doors. His grey hair was cut very short, almost shaved, and he wore a navy sweater and dark trousers. He walked over to the circle of chairs and took his place at the one remaining empty seat. He smiled round at them.
'Hello everyone. I'm Simon Foster. I'm what is called a psychic medium.' His voice was soft, but slightly clipped, as if he hadn't quite been able to eradicate a former way of speaking.
'I thought I would tell you a little bit about

myself and also about what to expect from our session here today.' Carrie noticed his hands with their slim fingers were crossed in his lap, apparently relaxed, but that every now and again, his hands would move suddenly in a small jerking motion as if he was warding something off.

'I come from an army family,' he said. 'My father was a Major General and it was very much taken for granted that that was the way my life was going to go too. When I was seven I was involved in a serious car accident and I almost died. My heart stopped three times but somehow I survived. My mother wasn't so lucky. She died after being in a coma for a month. Soon after the accident, when I was still convalescing, I started to notice that I could tell when things were going to happen. They weren't important things. Just knowing when a door was going to open before it did, or guessing what someone was going to say before they said it.'

At this point in his narrative Pam jabbed Carrie excitedly in the ribs and the long-haired girl gave an audible gasp. Carrie, who had for a moment forgotten her impatience because she had been absorbed in his story, reminded herself of just what this man was claiming he could do. He might not be the sort of charlatan she had envisaged, but charlatan he obviously still was.

'By the time I was eight, my experiences had grown much more intense and in addition to my premonitions, I began to hear voices. The voices frightened me because I didn't know if they were coming from inside me or outside me. In the end

I told my father who referred me to a doctor who thought that perhaps the voices were a physical symptom caused by the head injury I had sustained during my accident.' Simon Foster got up and continued his story leaning on the back of his chair. Carrie was struck by the paleness of his eyes, which were such a light blue that there was hardly any differentiation between his iris and the white of his eyes.

'The voices didn't go away. Sometimes they left me for a while, but they always came back and as I got older I understood that the voices I could hear were the voices of the dead. By the time I came to this realisation, I was so used to living with it that it didn't come as the shock you might expect. The worst of it was that sometimes I got very little peace and during particularly intense periods I would suffer terrible migraines. Something that still happens to me at regular intervals. I followed the path that was expected of me. I tried not to let the voices intrude too much and the more active I was, the less I heard them. In the end I could control them to such an extent that it was only when I allowed myself to become consciously calm that I heard them at all. I went to boarding school, and then Sandhurst, and by the late seventies was serving as an intelligence officer in Northern Ireland. The work was by turns boring and terrifying because we were always waiting for something to happen and we were never sure what it might be. People I knew and worked with began to die. I found it harder and harder to control the voices. We were all contending with the danger of bombs and snipers and the sense we were not wanted, but I was also having to deal with the clamour of the dead.'

The man with the handkerchief blew his nose loudly and looked up at Simon with tears in his eyes. Carrie surreptitiously looked at her watch. It was all very well, all this talking, but when was he going to get down to business? The sooner he got on with it, the sooner she could get back to a glass of wine and a plate of the chicken casserole that was melting in the slow cooker five streets away.

'To cut a long story short, I couldn't cope with the pressure. I couldn't tell anyone what was happening to me. Hearing voices is not exactly compatible with an army career and in the end I left. My father was hugely disappointed with me and made his feelings so clear that I didn't feel I could go home. After years of knowing exactly what was expected of me, of having my every action mapped out for me, being in the outside world felt very strange. I didn't know what to do when I wasn't operating to a timetable and nor did I know what else I wanted to do with my life. I started drinking a lot. Friends who had been happy to put me up got fed up with me. I slowly ran out of favours. One night I was out drinking and realised I had nowhere to go, so I slept in a park in London. I stayed in that park and other parks like it for two years. Drinking stopped me facing anything and it also drowned out the voices. It will take me too long to tell you how I eventually got myself out. But I did. Part of what helped me was learning finally to accept that what I have is a gift. An irritating and inconvenient gift, sometimes, but something that I can use to make people feel better.'

Simon began to walk around the outside of the circle of chairs, almost touching people's backs as he passed. He walked slowly, and his voice became quiet, almost dream-like.

'I want you to know that everything said here is in confidence and I hope that you respect each other and keep to that rule. I don't always hear the people I want to hear. There are times when no one in the room recognises anyone that I am channelling.'

How very convenient, thought Carrie. He has set things up so that he can talk a lot of mumbo jumbo and then if no one can relate to anything he is saying, he has the ultimate get out of jail free card of saying 'Oops, wrong people, wrong time.' She felt impatient with herself for being even briefly impressed by this man. He had a certain presence, but then he would need to have a bit of charisma to get away with what he was doing.

'I want you all to be as still and as receptive as you can be. I want you to help me to hear the people who want to be heard here, today,' said Simon. He stopped walking, lifted his head up to the ceiling and what could only be described as a kind of ripple crossed his face; a rearrangement of his features that caused his mouth to slacken and the skin around his chin to soften. Despite herself, Carrie was quite startled by the transformation.

'There's a number of people with me,' he said.

160

His voice had become more of a monotone, seeming suddenly drained of the personality it had had before. 'They jostle for me. It's hard at first to pick out the ones that most need to be heard ... I've got a woman with me. Big personality. Loud voice ... she is saying something about someone in this room who is ill. Is there someone in this room who is worried about her health? She's quite insistent. Is she a mother? Has someone here had a mother who has died?'

'Pretty safe bet, Simon Foster,' muttered Carrie, earning a reproving look from Pam.

Simon looked around the room, his eyes coming to rest on the buttoned-up lady who had become flushed and who was rubbing her hands together in an agitated fashion.

'My mum passed over six months ago,' she said.

'That'll be her,' said Simon. 'Not a shrinking violet, this lady.'

'No,' said Ms Button and something that might have been a smile crossed her face. 'She had forceful opinions, to say the least.'

'She's saying that she knows you are worried about a health-related issue. Does that ring a bell? She is saying, and I quote: 'Tell the fool that she should stop worrying. There's nothing wrong with her that a bottle of tonic and a good night's sleep won't put right. And tell her to take off her coat.''

Ms Buttoned-up rubbed her eyes with curiously childlike fists.

'Thank you,' she said. 'I know that's her,

couldn't be anyone else.'

Simon moved on. There were a couple of voices that meant nothing to anyone in the room, a message that might or might not have come from the brother of the tearful man, but the mood in the room changed over the two-hour session. It was clear that the participants had found varying degrees of comfort. Even those people who hadn't received messages from anyone seemed buoyant. Carrie could see that Simon's influence was a positive one, but she still felt removed from the other people who seemed so ready to believe that their dead relatives and loved ones were hanging around waiting to pass on messages via some nut job ex-soldier. She was relieved when the session came to an end and made for the exit, Pam chattering behind her like someone who had just had gaffer tape pulled from her mouth. Simon was at the door saying goodbye to people as they left and as she approached him his strange pale eyes met hers. He held out his hand to shake and she was surprised by the strength she felt in the pressure of his fingers on hers.

'You are very resistant,' he said, in his almost prim, clipped voice. 'The lines are not as clear as you might imagine.'

'I'm just not a believer,' she said and pulled her hand away, but his unsettling gaze stayed with her for a while afterwards.

23

Driven into her bedroom by Pam, who not only showed little sign of going home, but had also taken it upon herself to advise in matters of interior design, Carrie decided to have a sorting session. The long indulgence of Christmas had left her feeling that it was time to take stock and streamline both her waist and her cupboards. Besides which, she knew she might well murder her mother if she stayed downstairs to witness the remodelling that was taking place in the living room. Through the floorboards she could hear the sound of wooden legs being dragged across a wooden floor and she gritted her teeth. She wondered, not for the first time, where her mother got her energy. Although the woman regularly became completely supine when it was time to prepare food or to wash up, Pam was a positive whirling dervish when it came to demonstrating her superior taste. The two of them had attempted to get Carrie a black coat in the sales the day before and the experience had left Carrie feeling exactly as she used to do when she was twelve and her pleas for a fashionable school skirt or for shoes without buckles met with scorn. 'It looks so very cheap, darling,' Pam used to say about her daughter's choice. Her mother never quite grasped that it didn't matter that a skirt was not lined as long as it was the right length and had correctly placed pockets.

* ★ ★

At the back of the cupboard, behind such disparate objects as hair curlers, expired diaries and half-completed cross-stitch tapestries (Carrie had a tendency to be seduced by the thought of nimble fingers flashing over bright strands of wool, but almost invariably became disillusioned by the length of time it took to complete even the smallest corner), she found her old camera. She had bought herself a digital one a year ago and hadn't needed this one any more. She picked it up and examined it, wondering if it might be worth keeping or whether she should take it to a charity shop. When she took off the lens cap, some sand fell into her hand and she felt the small sliding away inside her that always came when she thought of Charlie. It amazed her that this shock always felt new, always had the power to unsettle her. This was the camera she had with her on the day he had gone. The police, along with everything else she had abandoned on the beach, had returned it to her and she had put it away and forgotten about it. She saw that the film inside was finished and she opened the back of the camera to retrieve it. She had hundreds of pictures of Charlie; from the very first squashed-faced one taken minutes after his birth, to the pictures of his fifth birthday party where he was captured capering joyfully in a Dennis The Menace outfit. In the early days after his disappearance she had not been able to look at any photographs at all. She had been scared that seeing him would simply scratch at her pain, making it raw all over again. But as the weeks became months she realised, with quite another, much worse sort of fear, that his face had lost its clarity. She found she was struggling to remember exactly how his hair lay across his forehead or the creases in the corners of his mouth, and she had turned to her photograph albums with relief. Indeed, photographs of Charlie became a great comfort to her. She saw that there was no shadow in his face. She was the one who had been left to face the darkness. The years would pass and here he would remain, distinct and loved. Carrie knew that the film must contain pictures of Charlie and she wanted to see them straight away. This was a little bit of him that she hadn't realised she possessed.

★ ★ ★

A shop assistant delivered the blue packet into her hand and Carrie walked quickly across the road, down past the bus station and part of the way across Christ's Pieces, until she found a bench by an empty flowerbed. The council gardeners had taken out the frost-burnt chrysanthemums in wheelbarrows and turned the earth over. It wasn't the weather for lingering, the cold was making her face and neck sting, but Carrie found she couldn't wait. Her hands were trembling as she unsealed the packet. The first few photographs were of an evening out she had taken with colleagues to a restaurant. She could

165

vaguely recall that it had been a celebratory gathering, but she could no longer remember what was making them all smile. There was a picture of her with the cross-eyed face she often made when someone she didn't know very well pointed a camera at her. She thought she looked dumb, unmarked, like the 'after' picture in an advertorial for plastic surgery. Except this, of course, was before. Next there was a shot of the beach, with a line drawn across the sky by an absent plane and then . . . Charlie. Oh Charlie. His head back, his hands outstretched and full of sand. Charlie. Walking along looking downwards. A shot of him making a face with a piece of orange fishing net wrapped around his head. Her heart caught at his huge smile and two missing teeth. She thought of the teeth, which were still tipped with his blood and in a drawstring bag in her jewellery box. Plunder of the tooth fairy and now not the extra of him, just the all. There was a picture of him on his hands and knees, digging a hole in the sand with the boy he had met on the beach with his mother in the background sitting on a towel. One of him showing the camera a strange-shaped stick. And then nothing more.

★ ★ ★

That evening Carrie phoned Damian to tell him about the pictures, and only hesitated a moment when he asked her if he could come over and see them that evening. She peeled potatoes, seasoned some lamb chops and sliced orange

166

and red peppers ready for roasting. She opened a bottle of red wine and took a glass of it upstairs. She changed into a tunic-length black jumper and a pair of new dark denim jeans and put on a jet and pearl necklace that Damian had bought her years ago during a weekend they had spent together in Whitby. She remembered that it had been foggy and that they had spooked each other in a shrouded Abbey and eaten ice cream drizzled with strawberry vampire blood.

⋆ ⋆ ⋆

Jen had never been that keen on Damian, although she had attempted to hide her doubts about him, but then she had never been that keen on any of Carrie's boyfriends. Carrie had met Damian when she was twenty-seven, living in London and working as a researcher in the fundraising department of a cancer charity. He was three years older and worked in the communications department. He spent his days trying to persuade indifferent editors that they might like to write something about the importance of respite care for the families of terminally ill people. What reason is there for us to cover this story now? they would ask, eager to get him off the phone. Give us a hook. He had a slight stutter that became more pronounced when he was under stress. Carrie liked the way he ran his hands despairingly through his hair and the fact that he made coffee for the whole office.

★ ★ ★

They got together after the work Christmas party. A chilly affair in a church hall at which the staff, terrified of being seen to be spending money that could be better spent elsewhere, ate sausage rolls and supped on sweet red wine out of plastic cups. Carrie left early, driven home by hunger and the beginnings of a cheap-wine-induced headache. Damian spotted her leaving and followed her out. They went for a Chinese meal and although Carrie was seduced by the way he looked at her mouth all the time she was talking, they didn't kiss when he dropped her off at the door of her flat. The second date, they sat together in the cinema. She touched his thigh and he traced a line around her ear and down her neck with one finger. They missed the second half of the film to kiss against a wall in the alley alongside the movie house and she was surprised at the bold way he pulled up her skirt and pushed aside her knickers to feel her. The following weekend they stayed in a hotel in Hunstanton and got wet walking from groyne to groyne on a rain-lashed beach. She loved the feel of his stomach still chilled from wet wool and the fact that he didn't stutter when he said her name as he came.

'When we touched each other it just felt right,' she said the next day over the phone to Jen who was working in Paris at the time and tormenting her journalist boyfriend with her particular brand of indifference.

'What's he look like?'

'He's tall, about four inches taller than me. Dark red hair, not carroty like Ron Weasley . . . '

'Eyelashes?'

'Well . . . they are pale . . . '

'Boris Becker,' said Jen with disdain. BB was a loathsome figure in her eyes, not only because he had invisible eyelashes, but because he had been caught having sex in the broom cupboard of a restaurant. For obvious reasons she harboured a hatred towards men who liked to have sex in confined public places.

'No, much more like Damian Lewis, I promise you'll love him.'

★   ★   ★

When the two of them did eventually meet, it wasn't an auspicious beginning. Damian was anxious about meeting someone so important to Carrie and who had a lot of influence over her. Too much influence, in Damian's view, although he managed to keep the thought to himself. They had arranged to meet at an Italian restaurant off Tottenham Court Road where Jen and Carrie used to eat when they were students and had something to celebrate (and the funds to celebrate with). The two of them had toasted the end of exams, the finding of new flats and the acquiring of jobs at their corner table right by the bar, so as far as Damian was concerned, the place was heavy with history that he had had no part of. Damian had a tendency to sulk when Carrie mentioned any experiences that he hadn't shared with her. He thought that her life should be wiped clean until the moment when he first clapped eyes on her sitting at her desk with that soft mouth and the way she had of tucking her hair behind her ear. Prim, but also so sexy it gave him a hard on.

* * *

Jen was late for their meal, which enraged Damian. Unless the person had a bloody good excuse, like being tied up by bank robbers or swept up in a tsunami, he considered tardiness the height of rudeness. When she finally arrived in a plum-coloured coat large enough to house several small children, the first thing she did was to send him out with a peremptory wave of her braceleted arm to pay for the cab that was waiting outside. As the evening progressed, Damian decided that Jen was too fond of the sound of her own voice and Jen decided that Damian was manipulative and controlling and she didn't like the way he sucked up his spaghetti. Molly had never forgotten what Jen had said on the phone the next day. The memory of it still made her smile:

'He seems nice, really nice,' said her friend with her 'I'm being sincere' voice, 'although I'd say, if I'm being truthful, he's less Lewis and more Weasley.'

* * *

Carrie went out onto the landing and listened for signs of life outside her mother's bedroom door.

Pam had exhausted herself that morning during a relentless two-hour make-over session. She had taken down the white living room curtains, washed, dried, ironed and re-hung them. She had hemmed the edges of a piece of fabric that she found in a cupboard to make a throw for the admittedly rather stained cream sofa. She had stuck squares of opaque sticky plastic over the bottom sections of the sash windows to thwart the curious stares of passers-by. She had cleared the dark wood desk and placed pens and pencils in a couple of brightly coloured jugs. The cushions were plump, the floor had a polished gleam and the room smelt of the rose oil that Pam dabbed on her pulse points and which she had clearly sprinkled about the room with abandon. Privately and uncharitably, Carrie felt that her mother was now of an age when drawing attention to her pulse points was not entirely seemly. She felt a little embarrassed that Pam, who was entering her mid-sixties, was still convinced of her power to fascinate, and still refused to succumb to the elasticated waist and the comfortable shoe.

'The legs are always the last to go, darling,' she said, crossing her Wolford velvet touch stockinged legs complacently. 'The legs and the eyes. A woman can go a hell of a long way with legs and eyes.' At present it was clear that the aforementioned legs were horizontal and the eyes closed, because there was no sound from within. Carrie heaved a sigh of relief that her mother would not be around to cast quizzical looks over Damian's shoulder at her. On learning that Damian was coming round that evening, Pam had adopted her annoying 'I am a wise owl' face.

'Do you think that is a good idea?' she asked in meaningful tones.

'He's just coming round for dinner, Mum, that's all.'

'I know, darling, but I'm just saying, in case you were contemplating it, going back won't bring it back,' she said and she touched Carrie's face gently. If she didn't know her mother better, Carrie would have taken her expression for genuine concern.

★ ★ ★

Damian had come with flowers, as she had known he would. When they had been together he had bought flowers every Friday on his way back home from work. Having been told by her once, long ago, that she liked white flowers best, he never deviated from this rule. In summer there would be roses, iris and freesias, in winter carnations and orchids. She was, of course, grateful for this dogged application but sometimes she wished that his flower giving could be of the I-saw-these-and-thought-of-you spontaneous sort, rather than a habit. This evening he had brought a pot of cyclamen encased in a cellophane bubble, a flower, if ever there was one, designed to be hot pink, which looked somehow diminished in this snowy version. As she took the flowers and his coat she thought that he looked strained. He had the sort of thin, tight skin that showed his health and mood like a mirror. A couple of late nights revealed around his eyes as the purple of a fading bruise, a cold quickly rendering the space between nose and mouth a rough red.

'I've told her we're over,' he said almost as soon as he had sat down and she had handed him a glass of wine.

'Who?' said Carrie, knowing full well, but playing for time.

'Sarah. The person . . . the woman I've been seeing . . . ' he said. Carrie knew that he was looking at her as if he expected some response, but she didn't for the moment know what to say.

'It wasn't fair to her. Not when I'm hoping for you.' He paused. 'You do know I'm hoping for you. For us. Don't you, Carrie?' He got up then, and put his arms around her and she shrank against him, because there didn't seem to be any other place to go. He took their wine glasses and put them on the mantelpiece and he pulled up her jumper and put his hand under her bra and she felt so sad it took away the other feelings that she might once have felt. But then they were on the sofa and he pulled at the zip on her jeans and she felt his hardness against her and she felt the shape of herself blooming under him and for a while she forgot everything else, even the fact that Pam might walk in at any moment and object to what they were doing on the new throw.

★ ★ ★

After they had made love, Carrie made tea and Damian looked at the photographs of his son. 'There are still days I don't believe it,' he said and when Carrie looked at him she saw no blame in his face. Damian may have managed to forgive her but she would never forgive herself. She knew that there was nothing she could ever do that would atone for the way she had lost him.

'I love this one of him with the fishing net around his head,' said Damian, tracing the contours of his son with a finger. 'He was so full of life.'

'Yes,' said Carrie absently. Something in one of the photographs had caught her eye. The one of Charlie in the foreground and the people they had set up camp next to in the background. The woman kneeling on the towel in profile was the woman that Carrie had seen twice in as many days. The same woman and the same boy who had been brass rubbing in Ely cathedral. She felt a prickling sensation across the back of her neck and on the tips of her fingers. What were the chances of that happening? Was this more than a coincidence? Carrie thought again of the way she had turned to look at them, almost despite herself, as though she had been meant to see them.

A knock at the door brought her back to herself and, straightening her clothes and smoothing down her hair, Carrie went to see who it was. Oliver Gladhill was standing on her doorstep clutching a bottle of wine. Perhaps it was the faint flush that still lingered halfway up her neck or the fact her lips surely looked just a tad more swollen than they usually did, but something caused Oliver Gladhill not to press his suit when she said that she would love to invite him in but was too busy.

'Another time, perhaps,' he said, wondering who the lucky bastard was that had made her look so distracted.

24

Carrie woke before Damian and lay looking at his face as he slept. Although it felt strange to wake up with him after all this time, his face was still intensely familiar to her and she saw Charlie in the curve of his jaw and in the creases in his eyelids. Whilst Damian had clearly taken her response to his question about their future together as a yes, Carrie still wasn't really sure of her feelings. She wondered if perhaps much of what she was feeling was about her gratitude for his apparent forgiveness. On the other hand, how could she not love him after all they had been together? How could she not love a man with Charlie's eyelids? As if sensing her scrutiny, Damian opened his eyes and smiled at her.

'What's for breakfast?' he said.

'Bread in the bin, juice in the fridge, you'll have to get it yourself,' she replied getting out of bed and reaching for her dressing gown. 'I've got to be at the shop in twenty minutes.'

After a quick shower, she dried her hair and then pinned it up with two diamanté-embellished grips. She put on a navy wool skirt from Reiss, a cream polo neck, thick maroon tights and some soft ankle boots entwined with straps that she had bought in Spain several years ago. Still clutching a piece of toast and Marmite, she kissed Damian goodbye.

'When will I see you again?' he asked, wiping Marmite from his mouth.

'I'm not sure . . . I'm busy for the rest of the week,' she said, which wasn't strictly true, but she felt she needed time to gather herself, to try and work out what she really wanted. Damian heard the doubt in her voice.

'This is OK? Isn't it, Carrie?'

'Of course,' she said, stroking his face. 'I just need a bit of time to get used to it. It's all so sudden. I'll ring you . . . '

She left the house quickly, before he had a chance to ask her any more questions. Damian got up and went into the front room from where he could watch her unlocking her bike without being seen. He saw her arms go up to re-fasten her hair, the side of her breast in its soft covering, the way she swung her leg backwards like a boy to get on her bike, and he wondered how he could have ever let her go.

★ ★ ★

There was no sign of Jen at the shop, although she was usually first in. The day before Carrie had taken delivery of some more new stock and she needed to clear some space on the shelves to accommodate it. She put the kettle on and then checked the voicemail messages. There were two messages from the charmless Manchester artist enquiring about sales of his paintings, four messages from customers and one from Jen. She sounded out of breath:

'Hello Partner! Jen speaking. Just to say, might

177

be just a tad late in this morning . . . umm overslept . . . sort of . . . umm . . . will bring cake and coffee and abject apologies by eleven . . . at the very latest . . . ' Carrie could have sworn that she heard a muffled laugh and what could only have been bed springs creaking in protest.

⋆ ⋆ ⋆

Carrie made herself a cup of sweet chai purchased from Al Amin on Mill Road. She read the message attached to the string on the tea bag.

> *Those with an open mind will*
> *catch the butterflies.*

Humph, she thought, I don't want butterflies whirling around between my ears, I've got enough on my mind without that. The image of the woman and her boy on the beach rose up again but she shook the thought away, seized the scissors and began to attack the tape on the first of the boxes. Carrie was delighted with the new stock. There were cushions appliquéd with tulips, multi-coloured bird stickers to put up on blank walls, chandeliers made out of twisted gold metal and turquoise beads, wine goblets with stems like mini ice sculptures of angel wings and a consignment of old damask tablecloths fringed with cotton lace. There was also a whole box of party stuff; cocktail shakers, little plastic ballerinas to hang from the rims of glasses and strings of paper pineapples and tiny lanterns.

Carrie decided to make a cocktail party window display and as a centrepiece dressed one of the dummies in a beautiful strapless and fishtailed evening dress in the most wonderful rich claret colour. She was just stepping back to decide whether the dress was best accessorised with a black fake fur shrug or a silver cashmere stole, when there was a tremendous clattering on the window. She turned to see Jen grinning from ear to ear, two large coffees in a tray in one hand and a white beribboned box in the other.

Over frothy coffee and the most delicious butterfly buns topped with lemon cream, Carrie gave Jen the third degree.

'Did the online lover make the earth move then?' she asked a blushing Jen, who despite being transformed by love, had still managed to get lemon cream all over her face.

'I'm sorry about this morning, there was just a . . . a . . . miscalculation, time wise,' she said, wiping her face with the sleeve of an enormous jumper the same hue and texture as astroturf. It was clear that love hadn't improved her dress sense either.

'So, this Tom brings you cute little flowers on the breakfast tray, he has a responsible attitude towards potential emergencies and displays great prowess under the duvet. Anything else you have found out?'

'Yes,' said Jen. 'Plenty . . . He likes blackberries, blueberries and raspberries, but strawberries make him sick. He once got part of his ear blown off by a firework. He loves thrillers, *Hancock's Half Hour* and Emmylou Harris. He takes size nine shoes and can only wear socks without seams. He likes walks that go in a circle, not walks where you have to go back the way you came. He collects round stones on beaches and makes spirals of them on the windowsills in his flat . . . he . . . '

'OK, OK, I get it. He is an all-round wonder of epic proportions and you have fallen for him, hook, line and sinker.'

'Something like that.'

'He sounds great, not sure about the whirly stones though. What sort of man spends time arranging stones in little patterns?'

'A creative one,' said Jen, loftily.

★   ★   ★

During a busy afternoon that saw the back of three tulip cushions, two chandeliers and several other items, Carrie let slip that she had been seeing Damian again. Carrie could tell that the news had made Jen anxious because she had started to pull strands of wool out of the sleeve of her horrible jumper.

'So what's the deal then? Are you two back together?'

'Stop pulling your sleeve! I'm not sure. He seems to want it. I don't know what I feel. It's all tied up with Charlie and I don't know if it's such a good idea that we try and go back.'

'I'm not so sure either,' said Jen. 'I had high hopes for Peter Fletcher. He's going to be gutted,' and ducked as Carrie threw a pincushion shaped like a mushroom at her.

The bell on the shop door rang but because Carrie was on the floor trying to retrieve the pincushion she didn't immediately see who had come in. By the time she had got to her feet, still half laughing at Jen, Molly and Max were at the counter. She froze at the sight of them. It seemed extraordinary that the subjects from the photo should be here in the flesh in front of her, like a memory come to life. For her part, the other woman looked at Carrie as if transfixed. For a moment, it seemed as if she was poised to run, and she made a panicked turn to go but stopped when Max spoke. He put his hands on the counter and leaned towards Carrie as if he wanted to get a better look.

'You are Charlie's mum aren't you?' he asked.

'Now hang on, who exactly are you?' asked Jen, who was looking between the two women in surprise.

'Yes. I'm Charlie's mum,' said Carrie, looking at the boy.

'I know you from the beach,' he said solemnly. 'I'm Max, and this is my mum Molly.'

'I don't think this lady wants to talk about this just now,' said Molly, sounding embarrassed. She wished she hadn't come into the shop. She hadn't had any idea that the woman with the lost child worked in *Trove*. She had only come in because she had heard that they sometimes took in pictures from artists and she had brought two of her watercolours to show.

Max put out his hand to Carrie and she found herself shaking it.

'I'm really sorry,' said Molly. 'I wouldn't have

come in if I'd known.'

'What do you mean?' asked Carrie, puzzled.

'Well, because we were there on that day,' said Molly.

'I wouldn't want to remind you of it.'

'I expect you think of it all the time,' said Max. 'You don't need us to come in for you to think about Charlie.'

'Shhh Maxy!' said Molly, now flushed with mortification.

'What *did* you come in for?' asked Carrie.

'Oh, I won't bother you with it now . . . ' said Molly. 'I'll come another time.'

'No, please. Tell me,' said Carrie.

With great reluctance, Molly took out two small canvases from the bag she was carrying, and laid them on the counter.

'I'm a painter. I was just wondering if you might be interested in selling these.'

Carrie picked them up to look at them more closely. They were beautifully rendered land-scapes. The first depicted a ruined red brick building covered with ivy with a broken chimney, the sky above it full of clouds marked with a pattern that looked like snake skin. The second was of a figure in a wide fenland field, a spade in his hand, a ribbon of black birds above him.

'I used to do quite a lot, and I'm trying to get back into it,' said Molly. When the other woman didn't immediately reply, she said, 'Don't worry if they are not quite your thing.'

'Is this a real place?' asked Carrie, indicating the painting of the ruin.

'Yes, I always try and paint from life. It's a

strange building a few miles from where I live. We stumbled on it one day when we were walking.'

'They are beautiful. I'd be happy to take them,' said Carrie. 'There's quite a lot of demand for local landscapes.'

'Oh great,' said Molly. 'Let me give you my contact details. We can talk about prices and stuff later.' She put her card on the counter. There was another awkward pause.

'I'm so sorry,' said Molly. 'About what happened.'

'No one knows what happened,' said Carrie.

'No,' said Molly quickly, wishing that she could disappear and at the same time berating herself for her lack of courage and compassion. She knew better than most what it was like to feel isolated and there surely could be few things more isolating than suffering the sort of loss that made people wince away and avoid you.

'I remember you on the beach. I remember feeling so bad for you . . . ' Molly trailed off.

Carrie was in a state of shock. It was as if that day had come alive again. This little boy might have been the last person to see Charlie before he went. She wanted to touch him. To feel his skin. Charlie by proxy. She came round to the front of the counter and put her hand on Max's head. He looked up at her calmly.

'Charlie is my friend,' said Max.

Feeling her heart flood at his childish use of the present tense, no one referred to Charlie as if he still existed, indeed many people seemed to prefer not to mention that he had existed at all,

183

Carrie put her arms around him, looking over his head at Molly as if asking for permission and his mother smiled her assent.

'It's good to see you, Max,' said Carrie and for one sweet moment, as she held him, it was as if Charlie was back.

★ ★ ★

It was late by the time Carrie got home and as she approached the house she could see that someone was waiting for her outside. The lights were dim on her side of the street and she couldn't at first make out who it was, then he raised his hand in greeting and she saw that it was Peter Fletcher.

'Hello there!' said Peter. 'I hope you don't mind being ambushed like this, but I was passing and knew this is pretty much the time you tend to get back.'

'What if I'd gone out from work? You should have rung,' said Carrie, feeling slightly pissed off that she wouldn't now be able to get straight into the hot bath she had been planning. Despite the fact she had a lot of time for Peter, she wasn't fond of unexpected visitors, particularly on an evening when she was drained by the emotions brought up by Molly and Max coming into the shop. Damian was also preying on her mind. She was aware that she had been avoiding his phone calls.

'Come in,' she said, locking her bike up to the down pipe by the front door. 'It's a bit cold so I'll get the fire going.'

Peter put his coat and hat on the banister and she placed a firelighter behind the already set fire and lit it. Peter settled down on the sofa while she went into the kitchen to pour them both a glass of wine. Peter smiled gratefully at her as she handed him his glass.

'It's so homely in here,' he said, looking around her little living room. 'You've got so many beautiful things.'

'Rather too many,' Carrie laughed. 'I keep meaning to de-clutter, but when it comes to it, I can't quite bear to get rid of anything.'

'Have you kept all of Charlie's things?' Peter asked.

She didn't really want to talk about Charlie just now. Sometimes she didn't find it comforting to talk about what had happened. Sometimes talking about it felt like she was just torturing herself. Then there were other days when all she wanted to do was to talk, when the words came out of her and she couldn't stop them and with the words came the pain that scooped her out and left her empty.

'I've kept some special things. You know . . . his first shoes, some drawings, his favourite soft toy . . . ' she said.

'I've kept everything. I've not thrown anything away,' said Peter. 'His room is exactly as he left it the day he died, down to the pyjamas on the floor. I can't bear to change anything. The only thing I've taken from his room is the moose thing he loved. I took that to the place . . . you know . . . the place where it happened.'

Carrie thought of the little cellophane shrines

left by lampposts and road signs that punctuated almost every car journey. She had always thought them meagre monuments, a single shower leaching the colour from the cards and teddy bear ribbons, but she could understand the impulse to return to the place. She looked at Peter's desperate face and suddenly felt the burden of his grief too keenly. Carrie felt overwhelmed by it and she knew that she couldn't supply him with anything that he really needed. He needed to be loved and she couldn't do that. It was pure selfishness that prompted her suggestion.

'Peter,' she said, 'have you thought about getting some sort of help? You know . . . trying something different to see if it gives you comfort . . . ' She would take Peter to see Simon Foster because it might just make him feel better, although she wasn't sure how she felt about seeing the medium again.

25

Eager to finish the painting that she had started before Christmas, Molly had given in to Max's entreaties to watch TV, and he was now contentedly stationed on the sofa, while she had set herself up by the window. She had moved the hall table to the best vantage point and, with paint and brushes spread around her, was trying to translate the colour of the vivid streaks currently breaking up the blue of the sky to her canvas. It was an odd shade, somewhere between khaki and lemon yellow and she wasn't sure she would ever be able to capture it. She thought about the day before and how awkward it had been at first in Carrie's shop, but how Max had somehow made it all alright. He had a calm beyond his years and seemed instinctively to know what to say and do. Losing a child is every parent's deepest fear and although she thought she could imagine a little of the horror, she knew that the true extent of the pain was mercifully beyond the reaches of her imagination. What Carrie must have been through put Molly's own worries into perspective.

* * *

As soon as she had discovered the parcel from Rupert she had rung the police, and despite the fact that it was Christmas Day, the same officer from the domestic violence unit who had come round the first time arrived within ten minutes, only this time he came with another police officer. They seemed to take her concern that Rupert was nearby seriously, suggesting that she should perhaps move in with a friend or relative for a while until they could locate him. Molly thought that she would ask Kate if they could move in there but she decided against it in the end. Kate's house only had two bedrooms, and although she was sure that Kate would be only too happy to accommodate them, Molly knew they would be inconveniencing the whole family, particularly since it would have involved disrupting their Christmas Day. Although breaking into the house to leave his son a gift was alarming behaviour, it didn't indicate that Rupert meant them any physical harm.

'Mum, what does discrepancy mean?' Max asked now.

'That's a hard word to explain,' said Molly, still mixing yellows and greens on her increasingly muddy palette. 'It's sort of the difference between things but it is also about measuring the difference . . . What are you watching?'

'It's a programme about chemical reactions,' said Max.

Molly suddenly felt a draught across the back of her legs, despite the warmth of the fire. That's what came of sitting still too long. The house was impossible to keep completely warm. It had the odd cosy corner, and you were OK if you were sitting right up against the fire, but sit near a window or a door for any length of time and the

188

cold would creep in and around you. She was certain that she had locked the back door, but perhaps she hadn't. The recent wet weather had swollen the frame and it had become increasingly difficult to push it back into place. Just then her suspicion was confirmed when she heard the wind bang the door against the wall. 'Mr Wind, at it again,' Molly said, putting down her brush and getting up. 'I really must get that door looked at.'

★   ★   ★

It was only Molly's instinct to prevent Max coming in to the kitchen and seeing what she was seeing, that stopped the scream from coming out of her mouth. Hanging from a rope that extended from one side of the kitchen to the other were five or six dead rabbits. One had its ears hacked off, another, its feet, whilst a third had been disembowelled. The blood was dripping onto the tiled floor and had gathered in a pool at the far end of the room where the slight slope of the floor had taken it. There was a sweet, sickly smell in the air and in the cold kitchen she could feel the heat coming off the dead animals. Molly slammed the back door shut and put a chair against the handle. She came out of the kitchen, shutting the adjoining door behind her and prayed that the television programme about chemical reactions would keep Max glued to the screen for a while longer.

★   ★   ★

This time the police took a little longer to arrive, but they came with a photographer who recorded the grisly discovery before taking it down and disposing of it. While the clean-up operation was going on, Molly kept Max distracted in his room with stories and games, and although she thought he knew something had happened, he didn't ask her what it was. The police checked the garden and the shed and drove down the road to Parson's Bridge, but there was no sign of Rupert. Despite the strongest recommendation from the police that she and Max be moved to a place of safety, Molly found a stubborn streak that she thought Rupert had knocked out of her. She didn't see why she should have to leave her home and disrupt Max again. She had allowed herself to be beaten by Rupert, but she was damned if she was going to allow him to break her.

What she did agree with the police was that they would create a safe area in the house, a room Molly and Max could lock themselves into should Rupert come back and threaten them in any way. Within half a day a team had arrived, reinforced her dining room and kitchen doors and windows, and transformed the living room into a panic room with sealed-off windows, a barred door and a telephone that triggered an emergency police response. They talked her through what to do if Rupert turned up at the house behaving violently. They also helped her to explain to Max in words that were as reassuring as possible what he was to do if his daddy came to the house and scared them. Max listened intently to the instructions. He appeared calm, but Molly recognised his anxiety in the way he clenched his hands in his lap. After the police had gone, she discovered Max timing how long it took to get from his bedroom to the safe room and her heart broke. That night she sat with him on the sofa, holding him close until at last she felt his fists unclench and the little creases in his forehead smoothed finally into sleep.

★　★　★

Although a few days passed without sight of Rupert she didn't allow herself to relax. The two of them spent as much time out of the house as possible, but when they came back, Molly checked and double checked the doors and windows and as soon as it began to get dark she was careful to close the curtains to the very edges of the window frames. She tried not to think about the fact that maybe he was in the garden looking through the window at them as they moved through lighted rooms, as visible as fish in an illuminated tank. She thought of Rupert's hands and the way he had of holding them tight on the table and she felt her chest compress. His hands had been beautiful that first evening, the long fingers moving adeptly over the table, handing her things in bowls. She thought again of the way he had touched her leg, laying claim to her.

Not knowing where Rupert was and when he might next turn up began to torment her and she decided to ring his mother to see if she knew anything. Elizabeth answered the phone on the first ring, as if she had been hovering over it.

'It's Molly. I hope this isn't too late to ring. You weren't eating or . . . anything?'

'No.' Elizabeth managed to make the solitary word sound like a disappointment. Molly was sure she had been expecting someone else to ring. She knew the other woman had no interest at all in her grandson, but she had to say something, and Max felt like a safe subject to talk about. Something about the way Elizabeth withheld herself always provoked Molly to inane chatter. Some part of her still wanted this woman, who had always been so dismissive of her, to like her. She remembered the way Elizabeth had gone round a table Molly had laid in her own home, moving the pudding spoons from the top of the plates to the sides, and the way Molly had thanked her afterwards.

'Max is fine. Thanks so much for the book. He'll write and say thank you himself soon.'

'I'm so glad,' the older woman said coldly. 'Now, is there anything else? Because I really must . . . ' Not even bothering to give a reason for her impatience, Elizabeth allowed her voice to trail off, as if the thought of saying anything more to Molly at all was absolutely exhausting.

'Well, I was just wondering if you had seen Rupert recently?'

'No. He's in America. How would I have seen him?' Elizabeth replied, and Molly thought that for the first time ever, the other woman sounded rattled.

'I thought that perhaps he might have decided

to come back for Christmas,' she said.

'As you know he is managing a holiday resort in California. He wrote to me and said that he was spending the holiday period with some new friends,' said Elizabeth, who had recovered her habitual poise.

'Oh, never mind,' Molly said, 'sorry to have disturbed you. I'll let you get back to whatever it was you were doing.'

'I'd absolutely know if My Son was in the country,' said Elizabeth, and in that moment Molly felt sorry for her. Through the dislike in the other woman's voice, Molly could hear the pride and the loneliness.

'Of course you would. Don't worry.' As she put the phone down she thought of Elizabeth in her pale, carefully textured house, touching throws, arranging leaves, unable to settle.

26

When she heard that Carrie was taking Peter to a session with the medium, Pam insisted on going along too, saying that since Simon was her discovery she wasn't going to be left out. Carrie wondered why her mother, who manifested an unhealthy scepticism about most things, including the ability of her daughter to manage her own affairs, so readily believed in the possibility of an afterlife. Pam rushed upstairs to assume her grey costume, this time accessorising it with a powder blue silk scarf and matching kid gloves;

'Did you know that it has been scientifically proven that men are most attracted to powder blue above all colours?' she said, preening herself in the hall mirror while Carrie tapped her foot impatiently and thought longingly of her fire-warmed sofa.

* * *

As Carrie plodded wearily along over the railway bridge between her two companions, she heard the plaintive toot of a train pulling out of the station. The melancholy sound was like a lament and made her feel gloomier than ever. The trees by the bridge looked stark against the evening sky, the occasional ragged nest hanging between the high branches like a blood clot in an artery. Her life was not shaping up well. She was hurtling towards forty, her mother was apparently permanently ensconced in her spare room, she was sleeping with her ex-husband and wasn't sure she should be and on top of all this, her sense of duty towards her bereaved friend was so overdeveloped that she was willingly subjecting herself to an evening with the cardiganed and credulous.

The thought of Oliver Gladhill rose unbidden to her mind and Carrie wondered what he would think about what was about to take place in Romsey Community Hall. He would probably make Simon Foster into his mentor and then the pair of them could cut a swathe through the neighbourhood, hoodwinking the desperate and the big breasted. She wondered what had happened to him to make him so keen to continually prove his sexual credentials. He wasn't bad looking if you liked that kind of sexy, slightly rumpled thing he had going on. What was it he had said he did? She thought it was something in conservation and she remembered again the practised way he had held the bird. He had told her that it had made a full recovery after spending the night in a shoe box. 'He flew away like a bat out of hell,' Oliver had said, demonstrating the bird's trajectory with an exuberant swing of his arm. He was full of vitality, and yet his vigour was cut through with a certain reserve, as if there was a side to him that he kept hidden.

Heading towards the hall, Carrie saw that Peter was looking sideways at her and remembered why it was that she was putting herself through the next two hours. She could see that he was getting far too attached to her and she knew she was in no way the solution to what ailed him. He clearly needed to be given a focus other than herself. She wondered if there ever could be a solution for anyone who had lost something as precious as a child, or in his case, a whole family. How does anyone ever recover? The best you could hope for, surely, was that you learn to manage the pain; to stop expecting it to go away and instead find a way of living with it that was not too destructive to the life you had left. She hoped that one day she would reach a point when she could think of Charlie with more pleasure than pain. To see him more as the blessing he had been to her rather than the fact that that blessing had been so short lived. She thought of the way his hand had stroked her face that last time. Her flesh and blood. The very best of her.

★ ★ ★

The only familiar face in the group was the tearful man; the others were all new, although they shared the same expectant, hopeful look that she had seen on the faces before. Simon Foster looked tired when he came into the room. He had purplish shadows under his eyes and the lines on his face appeared to have deepened. After apologising to those who had been there the week before that they would have to hear it all again, he gave a potted version of his biography, and Carrie noticed that this time he

196

added a detail that he hadn't mentioned before, which was the fact that his father had been driving the car when it crashed. Carrie wondered why he had left the fact out last time. Was it an oversight? Or did the man embroider his story as he went along, adding new elements as they came to him?

The session went very much as the last one had, only this time the medium seemed to have adopted a more scattergun approach, claiming the voices were coming thick and fast and moving feverishly around the room as if there was nowhere to stop. At one point, his hands went up to his head and Carrie thought he was perhaps experiencing the beginnings of one of the migraines he had alluded to before. She also wondered if the voices he heard were some sort of prelude to the onset of an attack. A symptom of a disease rather than a so-called gift, like the visual disturbances and the feeling of dislocation that other migraine sufferers describe. Perhaps the man was even suffering from some sort of mental illness and really should be in a hospital being taken care of rather than in a room with a bunch of gullible strangers.

As she had suspected he would be, Peter was completely wrapped up in the whole experience. His eyes never left Simon and more than once Carrie heard him give a great intake of astonished breath. He looked at her in absolute amazement when Simon was claiming to channel the long dead brother of the tearful man, whose face was hidden in his handkerchief, his shoulders convulsing with . . . sorrow? Joy? It was hard to tell. Just when it seemed as if the session was winding up, and Carrie was already mentally out of the room and halfway home, Simon stopped stock still in front of her. Her heart sank. She was hoping that she might have made it through without undue attention. Pam gave a kind of subdued yelp and clutched Carrie's arm. Simon's face did that strange rippling that she remembered from before.

'He's talking to me about a flamingo,' said Simon in his odd monotone, his bleached eyes wide open.

Carrie froze. She felt the room turn about her. For a moment she couldn't speak.

'Who told you about that?' she said, her voice harsh. 'Tell me who told you.'

'He did,' said Simon. 'A young boy. Sweet voice. He says he went to feed the flamingo something pink.'

Carrie had the sense that Simon's voice was coming from a great distance. She heard it as a rushing sound funnelled through a narrow space towards her, so quiet when it arrived in the room that she could barely hear it. It had nothing to do with her, this noise. She reached for her mother's arm.

'What're you talking about?' said Pam, suddenly belligerent, seeing the effect of his words on her daughter. 'Are you OK, Carrie?' she said, alarmed at her pallor.

Without saying anything, Carrie turned and ran out of the room.

27

Lying rigidly in bed, unable to get to sleep, Carrie closed her eyes and conjured up her grandparents' house in a small Yorkshire village. She had not been back there for at least twenty-five years, yet every detail of it remained vivid. It was far clearer in her mind than other places she had been to more recently, maybe because she associated it with happiness; her indulgent grandparents, the summer stretching ahead forever. Thinking about the house usually made her feel relaxed enough to fall asleep, something she desperately needed to do tonight. She took a deep breath, rolled over onto her back and walked along a lane thick with fountains of hawthorn, through the green front door, across the terracotta tiled kitchen floor and past the larder, with its smell of earth-covered potatoes and sponge cake. Next was the dining room, where the long lacquered table was made up with place mats of Dickensian London and silver soup spoons smelling of the mildewed satin-lined box they were kept in on the sideboard. She saw the crossed swords on the wall above the fireplace and the two Chinese fishermen with real string fishing lines on the mantel. Down two deep stairs into the hallway and then the living room where her grandfather's glossy side table held his radio and spectacles and deck of cards, placed just so. Through the bay window there was a view of roses in lines and a sloping lawn down to a river. Try as she might tonight, her mind would take her no further through the house than this. She was left looking out of her grandparents' window, running and re-running what the medium had said.

★　★　★

She had walked home in silence, resisting answering her mother's concerned questions. After Peter had been more or less forced out of the house by Carrie's rudeness and clear unwillingness to offer him a drink, Carrie asked her mother if she had ever spoken to Simon Foster either before or after the first session they had attended, a suggestion that was hotly denied.

'What are you suggesting, Carrie? Are you saying that you think me and Simon Foster might have been in some sort of cahoots?' Pam pronounced it 'Carhoots' which would have made Carrie smile if she hadn't been so distracted. She didn't put it past her mother to have let slip relevant information. Perhaps she had met him in another context? It only needed the lubrication of a couple of glasses of white wine for her mother to become quite loquacious on the subject of herself, people connected to herself, and herself. The problem was that she didn't remember ever mentioning the flamingo to her mother in the first place. It had been a fleeting sighting, quickly superseded by what had happened afterwards and it had been forgotten until now. Carrie certainly hadn't consciously thought about it since.

Sleep was clearly going to elude her, so she wrapped herself in her dressing gown and went downstairs to sit at the kitchen table with a cup of tea, fighting the tears that kept coming, despite her efforts to remain in control. Nothing in her education, experience or temperament allowed her to believe that what had happened that evening had been genuine. It was impossible. The truth of it must surely be that the man was a con artist who had somehow managed to find out this piece of information about what had happened on the beach that day and used it to trick her. To suck her into believing in the sad lies he was peddling. She felt blazingly angry and found that she had bitten her lip and drawn blood. Could someone else have told him about it? She was certain that the only people who could possibly know what they had seen on the beach that day were Damian, herself, and of course, Charlie. She thought, with a twist of her heart, about the story of the lost bird she had never had the chance to tell him. Just one more untold story, along with all the hundreds of others she might have told him. Had she ever told him about the hawthorn in the lane at her grandparents' house and the wood nearby with fossils in the slate-filled banks? She couldn't remember.

Carrie fought to keep her mind clear and to focus on the facts. What were the alternatives? Simon Foster was obviously a trickster with a way of finding out things that seemed impossible for him to know. Perhaps he had somehow hypnotised her and caused her to reveal her memories? Had there been any point in the whole proceedings when she had felt altered in any way? Surely not. Perhaps he had met Damian in another context? Yes, that had to be it. He'd been in a pub and heard Damian tell someone about the flamingo. That couldn't be right either; the man would hardly base his whole act on random snippets of overheard conversation. Was it possible that Simon Foster had seen Charlie himself on the beach? Had he witnessed them as a family walking in the shallows? It was too elaborate a fantasy to imagine that he would wait all this time until she found her way to him and the community centre. Had he seen Charlie more recently? For a moment this seemed with terrible, sudden fear and hope to be a possibility. Simon Foster knew Charlie. Or he had Charlie with him. Carrie allowed herself to believe this for a moment, but she knew she was indulging herself. If he had Charlie he would hardly let her know that was the case by quoting her son's words to her. It was fantastical to imagine that he would have recognised her and decided to torment her in this specific and peculiar way.

But the only other alternative was too strange and outlandish to contemplate. If she was to allow herself to believe that this man was in communication with her son, this was surely tantamount not only to accepting that Charlie was indeed dead, but that it was possible here in this world to get messages from dead people. She unsuccessfully fought back sudden nausea and had to run quickly to the kitchen sink where she threw up so copiously her throat felt scratched and hot. She tipped half a bottle of bleach round the sink and returned to the table to see that the day was just starting to insinuate itself around the edges of the curtained window. Somehow the brightening light filled her with dread. *He says he went to feed the bird something pink*. And she remembered an uneaten iced cake and saw his small feet digging restlessly through the sand as he looked at the other boy. He took the cake to feed to the flamingo. *That is what happened*, she was suddenly sure. With the certainty came a pain so profound it felt like the end of her.

28

When morning finally came, Carrie rang the shop and told Jen that she didn't feel well enough to come into work.

'What are your symptoms?' asked her partner in that officious way she had when it came to medical matters. Jen was suffering under the misapprehension that watching *Holby City* was a good substitute for real medical training. She gave off a knowledgeable air which had fooled more than one person into thinking she knew what she was talking about.

'Oh, you know, headache, feel tired . . . probably a bug of some sort,' said Carrie, but Jen, herself a dissembler of the first order, smelled a rat. For a start, she had never known Carrie to take a day off before. A quick phone call to Pam, the world's least discreet person, told her all she needed to know.

'You take all the time you want,' said Jen, ringing Carrie back ten minutes later. 'I can manage here and if we get really busy, I know someone who will come in and give me a hand.'

Although exhausted, Carrie had just enough of a spark left in her to remind Jen of what happened when intimacies took place in confined spaces.

'I sincerely hope that you'll not be availing yourself of the back room and will keep your mind on the job in hand.'

Switching the phone off against her friend's protesting squeals, Carrie forced herself under a shower, feeling the water painfully hot against her skull. She dressed without her usual care, putting on some ancient jeans, a worn grey jumper that had pulled in several places and her wellington boots. She needed to get out somewhere where there was room to breathe and walk and where she could think about what was happening without interruption. The last thing she wanted this morning was her mother's attempts to cheer her up; Pam was at her very worst when trying to be maternal. Carrie much preferred her when she was being her unselfconsciously selfish self.

As she dried her hair she noticed that it was slightly static against the brush, a symptom that she had always associated with the coming of snow. A quick glance out of the window showed that the sky had that sulphurous, almost sepia-hued look that suggested that bad weather was on its way. She left a scribbled note on the kitchen table, saying where she was going and how long she was likely to be. She might be the centre of her own universe but Carrie knew that her mother worried that she wasn't looking after herself well enough, and in a way she was right. Since Charlie had gone, Carrie was all too aware of how happiness could be destroyed in a minute; but somehow this experience had made her less fearful and more careless of her own wellbeing. It was to do with feeling the very worst had happened already and that no disaster that followed, no pain, no absence could be as great.

She drove the five or so miles to Anglesey Abbey and parked in an almost empty car park. The garden wasn't exactly a visitor magnet at this deepest part of winter, when the orchids in the wildflower meadow were lying deep underground, the dahlias had been cut back, their origami blaze nothing but a memory, and the snowdrops had not yet started their pale spread across the earth. But Carrie loved the way the winter laid bare the bones of everything. The shapes of the trees were more distinctive in their structure, easier to compare against each other than they ever were at the height of their beauty. Without the softness of leaf or bud, the dark hedges stood out in sharp relief, making hard, clean lines against the sky. She walked across Temple Lawn to the stone lions set at the entrance of a hedged enclosure of classical statuary and frozen flowerbeds, and sat on one of the benches. She remembered a game that she, Damian and Charlie had played together here. Each of them took turns to guard the male lion and count to thirty whilst the other two hid until they found an opportunity, when the guard had his back turned, of running to the statue and laying claim to it. Charlie was predictably hopeless at the game; never learning from experience, he would again and again crouch down behind the lion, imagining that he was perfectly placed to rise up triumphantly the minute the countdown was completed. They gave up trying to get him to go further afield and would play along, looking around them in counterfeit bewilderment, saying to each other 'Have you seen Charlie?' 'Did *you* see which direction he went in?' then wandering just far enough away from him to give him the time to come gleefully up and throw himself onto the back of the lion, clutching the cool flanks between his legs. She could see him there now, arms round the neck of the beast, talking nonsense into its ear, but when she turned away and then looked back, he had gone.

She thought again of what the medium had said. If Charlie had taken the cake to feed the flamingo he would have taken it down to where they had seen the bird in the shallows. Perhaps by then the tide had turned, she couldn't remember, only that the whole world stretched out that day and took on a new shape and her son had got lost somewhere between the sky and the sea. Suddenly Damian appeared in front of her. Because she had been so deep in thought, it took her a couple of minutes to recognise him. His face swam in front of hers, coming only slowly into focus. She noticed he was wearing the kind of hat that she disliked on men, the sort with earflaps best left to the under-fives. He sat down on the bench next to her and put a gloved hand on her knee.

'When your mum said you had come here, I knew exactly where I would find you,' he said, putting his arm around her and drawing her close.

'You're frozen!' he said and she tried not to feel the little jolt of irritation she always experienced when she was touched before she wanted to be. Then the feeling went and she found she was glad that he had come. She didn't want to think about all of this on her own any more. She slowly told him what had happened the evening before. Indulgent and a little restless at first, Damian listened with increasing attention. Sometime during Carrie's explanation it started to snow, but both of them were oblivious to the slow drift and settle of the flakes.

'What do you think it means?' she asked him. 'I think he must be a fake, but how come he knew about that day?'

'There is only one way he could have known. Someone told him,' said Damian. His voice was so sure that she instantly believed him. Of course, that must have been what happened. How had she allowed herself to imagine anything different? But then, almost immediately, the doubts rose up in her again.

'But no one knew but me. Do you even remember what was in that picnic bag all that time ago?'

'I remember the flamingo,' Damian said, 'and I remember Charlie asking about how its feathers stayed that colour.'

'Yes, but have you ever mentioned that fact to anyone else?'

Damian shook his head and then both of them noticed at the same time the way the landscape had changed in front of their very eyes. They saw that snow had made ghosts of everything, giving the benches and the trees and the statues new shapes, making a continuum between things that had been separate before. They walked back to the car park arm in arm, the snow muffling sound and breath and conversation. Deciding to abandon her car until she could come back and get it once the snow was gone, Damian saw her gently to the front seat as if she was an invalid. As he pulled out of the car park he looked at Carrie and spoke as softly as he was able.

'If *I* didn't tell your medium and *you* didn't tell your medium, then the only other person who knew about that day was Charlie himself.' He paused. 'I think we need to tell the police about Simon Foster.'

29

The next morning, the view out of the window sent Max into paroxysms of delight.

'Let's go tobogganing! Let's build a snow-man!' he said, sitting on the bottom step, busily putting his wellingtons on the wrong feet. Molly was only too glad to escape the tension of being in the house. She had rung the police that morning and they still hadn't found Rupert. It was as if he had disappeared off the face of the earth. Perhaps this time he really had gone for good. They drove to the Gog Magog Hills, just beyond Cambridge, the site where the giant Gog and his cohort Magog are said to have indulged in some monstrous cavorting involving ripping up oak trees by their roots and brandishing them at unsuspecting travellers. The legendary giants must have done a good job of stamping all over the terrain since the place now offered the tamest of landscapes with the most modest of hills and a sprinkling of trees. The place was already swarming with people, anxious to make the most of the snow. The small slope down which children were slithering on red and blue plastic sledges was already streaked with mud. As Molly loaded Max onto his sledge she could feel his whole body quivering in the way it did when he was particularly excited. It wasn't a shiver of excitement so much as a vibration that passed through him.

'Keep your legs tucked in,' she said, 'and hold on to the rope so you can steer.' Then she gave him a little push and with the help of a series of small, convulsive forward movements, Max set off downwards, shouting with delight. She watched him go all the way to the bottom, narrowly missing a man who was standing with his back to the action and ending up sprawled in the snow, the sledge on top of him. Even above the general noise she could hear him, 'It's brilliant, Mum! It's the BEST feeling.'

Molly managed to finally persuade Max back into the car, only when the very last of the snow had been smeared into oblivion. Only the most dedicated of the sliders were still doggedly descending and ascending as if fatally addicted to the process. Looking at her son in the mirror, she could see that he would sleep well that night. He already had that half-transfixed look that indicated extreme tiredness. He rubbed his gloved hands across his eyes and then sat looking forward, eyelids heavy, his breathing slow, his face rosy with snow and exertion.

'Mum,' he said, his voice soft and sleepy, 'I had the greatest time.'

'I'm so glad, my love,' replied Molly.

'I saw Charlie there,' said Max.

'Did you, darling? asked Molly.

'He was there and he had a red sledge. I saw him.'

'You know Charlie wasn't *actually* there. Don't you, Maxy?' said Molly, looking at her son in the driver's mirror. His mouth was set in an uncharacteristically stubborn line.

'It was definitely him,' said Max. 'He made tunnels in the snow.'

She pulled up outside the house and drove straight through the open garage door. After collecting coats and boots from the back seat, she ushered Max through the front door. The enormous black cat that had taken to terrorising an already terrified Toffee, streaked brazenly across the hall and hurtled through the cat flap on the kitchen door banging it loudly behind him. Toffee was sitting on top of the bookcase in the hall looking like the victim of a flood, perched as far away as possible from the rising waters.

Molly sent Max upstairs to put the bath on and went into the living room to get the fire going. She sensed he was there before she saw him. It was as if the air in the room had been displaced and had been replaced by some other medium. He was sitting in the chair facing the door. His hands were placed on the armrests, legs were crossed neatly at the ankle. He smiled when she came in and she knew with terrified certainty that she had made a dreadful mistake by choosing to stay at the house.

'Here you are at last, darling,' Rupert said. 'I've been waiting for you.'

30

It was business as usual in Almond Street when Carrie went out on Saturday morning to the shop to get a loaf of bread and a tin of soup. Mrs Evans was standing at the corner, scrutinising the sky as if expecting the imminent arrival of an alien species, Emily Foxton, dressed uncharacteristically modestly in an all-in-one tiger suit, was lurking down the alley by the side of the family home having a sneaky fag and the orchestra at the Musical Prodigy House was in full throttle. Carrie got a glimpse of the pale face of Mr Musical Prodigy almost pressed against one of the bedroom windows. He had no doubt been driven upstairs by the sheer volume of his offspring and their fervent mother. She gave him a little wave and he raised his hand in response as if he was signalling goodbye from on board a boat sailing into a storm.

★ ★ ★

The police had rung the day before to report back on their interview with Simon Foster who seemed to have had nothing to do with Charlie's disappearance. It turned out that he kept meticulous records for tax purposes and was therefore able to establish beyond a doubt that he had been in Edinburgh that whole weekend. He had presided over an evening in a large theatre so there would presumably be hundreds of witnesses to the fact should one ever be needed. Although they said they were going to investigate further and check some of the information that had been supplied to them, Damian had got the distinct impression that they were not taking the matter seriously.

'They seemed to think I was making up the flamingo story,' he said. 'They kept repeating . . . *Norfolk beaches are not the usual stomping ground for your exotic bird Sir,*' and here Damian did a poor impression of a thick TV copper bent on obstruction.

'I'm going to find out where he lives and go and talk to him myself,' said Damian. 'He has to be hiding something.'

'Shouldn't we just make an appointment with him through the community centre?' asked Carrie. 'I'm sure he does one-on-one sessions.'

'I'm not giving him the satisfaction of treating him like a professional,' said Damian. 'The man's a cruel bastard and I'm going to get to the bottom of how he knows about Charlie.'

★   ★   ★

Despite Carrie's entreaties that he should cool down and think about it before he went ahead, Damian set off immediately for the community centre. At first all he managed to get was Simon Foster's work mobile phone number but in the end he persuaded the woman in the office that he really needed the medium's address too.

214

'I've already tried ringing his number,' said Damian, who, despite being an honourable sort of man was also adept at lying, 'but there is no answer, and I really need to pick my wife and sister up from there, they booked a session with him this morning.'

The receptionist knew that she really ought by rights to check with Simon, but it was almost lunchtime and she was more than a little ready for her tuna salad and besides which, the man really did have the most attractive colouring.

★　★　★

Simon Foster lived in a flat by the river, right next to the boathouse. Although it would have been much quicker to cycle or even walk across Midsummer Common, Damian was convinced that driving would be better. A couple of years living out of Cambridge had made him forget just how congested the roads were on a Saturday and he sighed and huffed and inched his way up East Road. In an attempt to divert him from his growing bad temper, Carrie switched on the CD player and was shocked to hear Ella Fitzgerald's familiar voice. She couldn't have contemplated listening to this record; just a few bars of it hurled her back to that car on that day, to the sight of Charlie in the mirror singing along. She looked at Damian in astonishment.

'When did you last listen to this?' she asked.

'I listen to it all the time. It comforts me,' Damian replied.

'There's a somebody I'm longing to see, I hope that he, turns out to be, someone to watch over me.'

As the words washed over her, Carrie felt her eyes fill with tears and she turned her head determinedly to the window. She thought it was sad that she and Damian had been forced to suffer alone what they might have helped each other with. It was true that loss was a great equaliser; it was how you dealt with the loss that set you apart from each other.

There was some delay before Simon Foster opened the door. They had clearly interrupted his lunch, because he was still chewing something as he looked at them impassively.

'Hello,' said Carrie, 'I'm so sorry to barge in like this. I came to one of your sessions a couple of days ago and we were wondering . . . '

'Exactly what sort of a scam you are trying to pull,' said Damian, interrupting her tentative introduction.

Simon Foster opened his door wider and stepped back.

'Would you like to come in?' he said, and led them through into a very spartan living room. There was a table, which clearly served both for work and eating. There was a pile of neatly stacked books and papers at one end and on the other the remnants of the meal they had interrupted. The only other furniture was the sofa upholstered in grey tweed and a matching chair alongside it. The walls were white and without pictures, but the lack of decoration

216

seemed simply to enhance the quality of the light that flooded in from a balcony overlooking the river.

'Please, sit down,' he said, indicating the sofa. He sat down himself in the other chair and looked at them calmly.

'I don't usually let people into my home without an appointment, but I was struck by the feeling in you when I saw you,' said Simon, looking at Carrie, 'and I'm glad you have made contact again.'

'How do you know about the flamingo on the beach?' asked Damian. 'Was sssomeone you know there on that ddday?'

Carrie could tell that Damian was rather thrown by the other man's calm demeanour. He was stuttering over some of his words, something he only did when he was agitated or tired.

'A boy came through to me who seemed to want to make contact,' said Simon. 'Sorry . . . what's your name?'

'Oh I'm . . . I'm Carrie Hudson and this is Damian Reynolds, my ex-husband.'

'The boy wanted to make contact with Carrie,' Simon resumed. 'I'm thinking that you must be his mother?' he asked gently, looking directly at her again.

'Yes. We are his parents,' said Carrie.

'Don't tell him anything,' said Damian. 'That's how these characters work. They pump you for information, and the next thing you know they are 'talking' to your long lost gran who has passed over. Isn't that the term you lot use? 'Passed over'? Bloody criminals with an obsession with euphemisms.'

'I've heard him since that first time,' continued Simon, taking no notice of Damian's outburst. 'Sometimes it's hard for me to recognise individuals. Some days I can't even hear myself think. But your boy's voice is very clear.'

'What else has he said?' said Carrie, unable to stop herself from asking.

'Don't give him the satisfaction,' said Damian, getting to his feet furiously. Carrie took him by the hand and pulled him back down to the sofa.

'You've somehow managed to fool the police,' said Damian, 'but you're not bloody fooling me.'

'I believe I answered all of their enquiries and they were satisfied that I had no part in your son's disappearance,' said Simon quietly, but with an edge to his voice that indicated that he hadn't been happy to be the focus of police attention.

'What else did the voice say?' asked Carrie again.

'We will have to arrange a proper time to focus on this. Would you like me to make an appointment for you? Would you both like to come?'

'Oh, and how much is that going to cost?' said Damian. 'This is a sting, Carrie.'

'I charge fifty pounds an hour for a personal consultation,' said Simon.

Damian got to his feet again, and this time Carrie couldn't stop him.

'I've heard enough of this crap now, thanks. No, I wouldn't like to make a fucking appointment. But I'll tell you what I *am* going to

218

do. I'm going to make sure I find out how you operate, and when I do, I'll shut you down.'

Damian left the room. Carrie heard the door slam behind him and got to her feet.

'I'd better go,' she said.

'Your boy is OK, Carrie,' said Simon, and the words pulled at her as she turned from him. On her way to the front door she caught a glimpse of his bedroom. The blanket was tightly tucked, his shoes placed neatly under the very end of the bed as if he was ready for an inspection.

31

Molly and Max stood frozen to the spot. After recovering from the shock of seeing Rupert, Molly's first impulse was to pull Max towards her and to start to walk backwards away from him. It was as if she had to keep him in her sights, keep him pinned away from her with her eyes; just turning her back on him felt like a dangerous thing to do. He was sitting between them and the safe room. There was no way that they could get to the door before he did. She felt for her mobile phone in her pocket and to her horror discovered it wasn't there. She frantically tried to remember where she had seen it last and remembered with a sinking heart that at one point she had thrown herself after Max's toboggan. She imagined the phone lying somewhere in the snow. Rupert got to his feet, smiling, holding out his arms to them both.

'Aren't you pleased to see me? Come and give your dad a hug,' he said and Molly could feel Max stiffen and look at her as if asking what she wanted him to do.

'I've been away, but I'm back now and I've missed you so much. I'm better now, Moll. I'm much better. Did you like what I left for you the other day?'

She stopped again and held on to Max's hand. In her mind she was rehearsing the route away, trying to shave seconds off their escape; the car keys by the sink in the kitchen, Max's shoes thrown off by the front door. The switch on the wall, the small delay as the garage door opened, the fumble in the dark to get the keys into the ignition. Why had she not fixed the light in the car? Would it be better to forget the car and try and get to Kate's house? She couldn't remember if her nearest neighbour's house was dark or whether she had seen their living room light on as she had driven past. She thought of the mud along the road by the house and of Max trying to keep up. She knew they couldn't make it. He was too fast for them. 'Go and give Daddy a kiss,' she said, ignoring the pale, fearful look her son gave her.

'Come on, don't be shy,' Rupert said, and bent down so that Max could kiss him on the cheek. He scooped the boy up in his arms and swung him up onto his shoulders. Molly saw with a shudder that he was strong. Wherever he had been for the last six months, he had been working out. Gone was the slightly stooping man who had left, and in his place was this man who seemed young again and full of vigour. Max looked down at her from his father's shoulders and it tore at her to see that he was trying to smile.

'Don't think much of the changes in interior design,' Rupert said, indicating the dining room door with a snigger. 'Took the opportunity of cutting the phone line. Seemed a little unnecessary, don't you think?'

Molly knew that it was important to try and stay calm and not to show Rupert how scared she was. She needed to try and convince him that she was glad he was back. She sat down on the armchair and smiled at him.

'Would you like some supper?' Molly said.

'If you're offering,' he said, patting his stomach. 'It's been a while since I've had a good home-cooked meal.' And he looked suddenly as he had looked all those years ago when they had first met; so sure of himself and of her. He bent over so that Max could slide off his back and the boy came over to his mother and sat on her lap.

'Still a bit of a mummy's boy I see,' said Rupert. 'Still, now that I'm back that will all change, won't it, son? Have you missed me?'

Max didn't speak, just nodded his head and then pressed himself against Molly. She could feel the tension in his arms and could hear the rapid beat of his heart. She gave him a reassuring squeeze and then told him to go up to his room to play a bit while she made them all some supper.

★ ★ ★

Over a hastily made spaghetti bolognaise, Molly ensured that Rupert's wine glass was always kept topped up and as soon as Max had finished his food she told him to get into his pyjamas and to wait in bed for her to come up and read him a story. After she had cleared the plates away, she left Rupert sitting on the sofa with another glass of wine and went upstairs. She quickly pulled a bag out from under her bed. Max was in the bathroom brushing his teeth and she went into the room with him and closed the door quietly. In a whisper, she quickly explained what she was planning to do.

'You and me are going to go away this evening once Daddy has gone to bed. You must pretend everything is normal. Do you understand, darling?' Max nodded at her, his eyes wide and solemn.

'Before you go to bed, get dressed in your jeans and a warm jumper and socks and put your trainers on. I will come and get you from your bed; we will have to be as quiet as mice and creep downstairs. We won't be able to go in the car because that will make too much noise. We are going to try and get to Kate's house, OK?'

'Shall I wear my trainers in bed?' he asked. 'I might get the sheets dirty.'

'Don't worry about the sheets,' she said.

'I'll get my torch too.'

'That's a good idea, my darling. Now go down and say goodnight to Daddy.' Molly gave her son a kiss on the forehead.

★   ★   ★

It felt funny being in bed with his trousers and shoes on. He had been clever and kept his pyjama top on over his jumper, even though his mummy hadn't told him to. His daddy wouldn't realise if he came into his room to say goodnight again that he had all his day clothes on. When he had kissed him his skin had felt all rough and he smelt funny, not like his daddy used to smell. He felt scared, but he wasn't sure why. He could

223

hear his mummy downstairs laughing and he could tell that she didn't really think it was funny. When his mummy thought something was funny she laughed a bit like a machine gun and her eyes went really small. He wouldn't go to sleep. He would stay awake until his mummy came and got him. He sang quietly under his breath to make the minutes go by.

★　★　★

After drinking more than a bottle of wine, Rupert had been ready for bed quite early. Molly had only been able to shove a few things into her bag; some warm clothes, their wash things, Max's inhaler, her purse, and their passports. She put the bag in the hall cupboard and she spent as much time as she could without arousing suspicion on brushing her teeth and combing her hair, hoping that he would be asleep by the time she got to bed. She had no chance of getting dressed without waking him up so she wore her warmest pyjamas and hoped that her Wellington boots and her winter coat which she placed by the door would keep her warm enough. She had stuffed Max's gloves and scarf into her coat pocket.

With a sinking heart she saw that Rupert was sitting up in bed when she went into the room. She made sure not to shut the door behind her because it made a grinding noise when the handle was turned. He looked at her substantial striped pyjamas and raised one eyebrow in what she knew he fondly imagined was a rakish way.

'Got your passion killers on, eh?' he said in the pretend lecherous voice he put on when he was referring to sex. She wondered if she had ever found it funny or endearing. She must have done in the early days, now it just made her flesh crawl. He patted her side of the bed.

'I've missed you, my darling, have you missed me?'

Molly made an acquiescing noise and got into the bed beside him.

'I expect you're tired,' she said hopefully, lying as far away from him as possible. She thought that she would not be able to contain her revulsion if her feet were to touch his.

'Not too tired to show my appreciation for being back home,' he said, and it was all she could do not to cry out when he bent over her, his breath winey and hot against her face.

'I'm not sure I want this just yet, Rupert,' she said, pushing against his chest. It was as if she hadn't spoken. His fingers unfastened the buttons on her pyjamas and he took her nipple into his mouth and bit hard on it. She cried out, she wanted to fight him, but she knew that it was safer to let this happen. He would sleep afterwards and Max and she would be able to get away. Rupert pulled her pyjama bottoms down and forced himself into her quickly. She felt her whole body convulse. He thrust twice, shuddered and lay on top of her for a while, heavy and still, before rolling off. She pulled her pyjamas up and turned her face away from him so that he didn't see that she was crying. She could feel his semen trickling out of her and she desperately wanted to rub herself clean, but she didn't want to do anything that would keep him awake any longer than necessary. She lay rigid, listening to his breathing, which slowed and then finally changed tone, becoming resonant.

After lying still for at least fifteen minutes, she was sure that Rupert was in a deep sleep. She inched herself slowly to the edge of the bed and got up without a sound. She stood for a few moments holding her breath watching his face for any signs of change, but he was completely still, his arms above his head, his mouth slightly open, so she crept out of the room. Max was already awake and fully dressed, with his torch clasped in his small hand. Her heart burned at the sight of his determined face, hair sticking up on one side, trainers on the wrong feet. Molly retrieved the bag from the cupboard and they crept down the stairs, wincing at every creak. Molly put on her coat and boots, dressed Max in his anorak and hat and scarf, and slowly pulled back the sliding lock on the front door. Outside, the sky was studded with stars but it was dark and it felt as if they were stepping out into the unknown. Molly took hold of Max's hand and they started walking.

32

Carrie spent the next three days in bed, gripped by some sort of flu-like fever. For whole sections of the day she slipped in and out of consciousness, only vaguely aware of the people around her. Pam became a surprisingly assiduous nurse, hovering almost continuously by her bedside, offering her sips of water or sprinkling eau de cologne on cool flannels and placing them across her forehead. She persisted in doing this even when Carrie irritably told her to stop. During her fever, Carrie seemed to be tossed by agonising hallucinations. Pam could make no sense of her ravings and became very alarmed when she came into Carrie's room to find her sitting up in bed apparently conscious, but completely incoherent. When she finally came out of the fever she was so weak that she could barely lift her head. She didn't even have the strength to tell Pam to stop fiddling with curtains and blankets and drinks. Jen had been nobly managing the shop single handed, helped occasionally by Tom and her brother Paul.

⋆ ⋆ ⋆

As she got better, Carrie lay on her bed and tried not to think about Charlie and Simon and what it all meant. She knew that if she allowed herself to dwell on it too much she would lose her bearings. She felt that she might even lose her mind. She tried to explain to Jen who had come round after work, bearing glad tidings of amazing sales and six cupcakes sprinkled with glitter, how she felt.

'I don't know what to think about Simon Foster. I can't believe he can do what he claims to be able to do. But there is something about him . . . he seems so sure. Part of me can't bear to hear what he says about Charlie, the other part of me feels broken hearted to turn my back on it,' she said as Jen stroked her hand. 'If this is what I can have of him now, shouldn't I take every little bit of it? Does it really matter how it comes to me? Does it even matter if it's true? And even if the man is a fraud, shouldn't we keep talking to him to see if we can find out anything about what happened to Charlie? Damian just refuses to involve himself at all. It's like he has pulled the shutter down on the possibility of it. What if we are rejecting Charlie by doing that?'

Jen didn't know how to advise her friend. She had no experience of such matters and the whole subject gave her the creeps, but she sat with Carrie and let her talk and fed her bits of cake and hoped that one day her friend's heart would heal. She promised that as soon as Carrie was better she would go with her to the medium's house although she was very much of the opinion that the guy was probably a swindling arsehole and that she was going to fix him with a beady eye and then expose him for the charlatan he was. She had, after all, a bit of experience in destroying reputations. Just then the doorbell went and Jen discovered a diminutive Musical Prodigy at the door clutching a flute saying that his mother had heard that Carrie was unwell and had sent him over to provide some healing sounds. Jen sent him packing. Hadn't the poor woman suffered enough?

★ ★ ★

It took Carrie five days to feel strong enough to get out of bed. She wobbled her way on weakened legs through a shower and her first cup of coffee in several days. Her time out of action had given her the space to think and she had decided she was going to book a session with Simon Foster. She knew that Damian wouldn't be happy with her decision. He had rung her a couple of times over the last week, ostensibly to find out how she was but also to tell her about his progress in getting to the bottom of Simon Foster's perfidy. During their last conversation he had gone on so long about private detectives that the only way she had been able to stop him was to say she was too ill to talk and needed to get some rest.

She got through to Simon straight away and arranged to see him in the afternoon, then spent the rest of the morning trying to get the house straight. Pam may have been vigilant with the cold flannels, but she hadn't done the laundry and the kitchen floor was sticking to the soles of her feet. Carrie cycled to Simon Foster's flat, but she left herself plenty of time to get there, aware that she wasn't yet back to her full strength. This time he was expecting her and took her into the living room, which looked exactly as it had on the previous visit. He sat her on the sofa and offered her a cup of tea.

She thought that Simon looked rather ill himself; his skin was grey and the bruised-looking skin under his eyes was darker than usual. She wasn't sure how you were supposed to behave with a medium. What exactly was the etiquette? Was it like being at the doctor when you weren't supposed to ask them anything personal about themselves, especially when they were doing very personal investigations into you? Or was it like being with a hairdresser when an exchange of holiday information or titbits about your sex life was more than acceptable?

'Have you had one of your headaches?' she asked.

'Yes. A pretty bad one this time as it happens,' said Simon, handing her a mug of tea. 'Seems to be an occupational hazard. The more clamour the voices make, the worse my migraines.'

Simon sat down on the chair next to her and she waited for him to speak.

'I can't promise to hear who you want me to hear,' he said. 'But I'll do my best. It helps if I can just sit in silence for a while and let whoever is out there come to me. My head sometimes feels like it is full of static and it can take me quite a long time to tune myself into the right frequency.'

Despite the fact that part of her still refused to believe him, Carrie felt her heart hammering in her chest. She was aware of feeling something that might have been hope. Exactly what she hoped for she wasn't sure. She hoped for an answer, certainly, but she also hoped that she might feel better, forgiven, healed. It was very quiet in the room. The door out onto the balcony was shut and through the glass Carrie could see the opaque green river disturbed every now and again by a passing rowing boat. Simon appeared to be meditating, his peculiar pale eyes seemingly looking inwards, and there it was again, that extraordinary disturbance of the flesh on his face, like feeling made visible in waves. He did that impatient shifting of his hands that she remembered from before.

'I've got him,' said Simon at last in his peculiar monotone. 'He's waiting so patiently to talk to you . . . He's saying something about how sorry he was he didn't wait. He knew he should have waited, but his daddy took so long . . . He wants you to stop being sad . . . '

Carrie felt her heart swell. She felt it might be a weakness to even listen to this. Just days ago, she had scorned it and now here she was letting it in.

'He says he knows you won't believe it. He says you will have the face you used to have when he had told you he had washed his hands when he really hadn't . . . Now there is something about a story . . . a made-up boy and a dog called some funny name beginning with C and a kennel with cups and chairs . . . '

Carrie made a gasping sound as the realisation of what this must be hit her.

231

'It's *Mister Dog*,' she said. 'It's his favourite story. It's about a dog called Caspian who likes strawberries.' Carrie suddenly knew how it felt for all those people in church halls and theatre auditoriums. This was love and comfort and a line that you could hold on to for dear life.

Simon came out of his trance with a little shiver, as if he was cold.

'He was there for you, Carrie,' he said.

'I don't know what to feel and think,' said Carrie. 'There seem to be too many things between me and being able to believe it. And if it is true, that means he's dead doesn't it?'

'I can't make you believe it. It is something you have to come to or not for yourself. All I can do is tell you what I hear.'

'It's just so strange,' said Carrie. 'I know none of my friends and family do, but I still think he's alive.'

Simon got up and took her cup from her, signalling that their session was at an end. Carrie stood up too. For a minute the room swung around her and she thought she might faint. Simon saw her falter and put a hand out to help.

'I'm alright, I've just been ill and I think all of this is getting to me,' she told him.

As he saw her to the door, Simon said, 'Don't be worried by it, Carrie. It's not scary. It's just worlds overlapping.'

33

Molly knew that they only had about another fifteen minutes' walk before they got to Kate's house. She hoped to God her friend hadn't chosen this weekend to go away. Max was shining his torch up ahead, picking out the tops of bushes and once what might have been the eyes of a fox. He was beginning to shiver. The Fenland wind was particularly sharp, with nothing but low hedges to dispel its strength, and tonight it was blowing so hard it seemed to pass through their bodies as easily as it passed across the dark landscape. Molly wondered if the ghostly Fenland farmer was out there somewhere, crouched over his fields, cramming his mouth with lumps of frozen peat. She suddenly remembered Max as a smaller child stamping on an icy garden in his wellington boots, asking her why the ground was stale. She held his hand even more tightly. To the side of them the narrow stream of water glinted. There were very few roads in the area that were not lined with drainage channels. The fight between water and land seemed to be quite evenly matched, with only a few centimetres between the two adversaries. A few days of rain and the land softened easily, its edges blurring into marshland. She wondered if one day all of this would revert to water, making Ely an island as it had been in the Middle Ages. Sometime, maybe not too far in the future, this land under her feet would be hidden by the writhe of eels and the sway of dark reeds.

He appeared so suddenly that Molly barely had time to react. She felt Max's hand being wrenched from her own and heard his frightened gasp. His torch went up, the beam briefly illuminating Rupert's figure and the gleam of the knife he was holding against his son's throat. Then the torch fell out of Max's grasp and landed on the path, its light shining into the dark water. She instinctively moved towards them.

'Don't . . . ' said Molly. She was so terrified, she couldn't speak. Rupert sounded almost amused.

'Where were you two off to then?'

'Let him go. Rupert, let him go.' Molly could feel her voice rising in panic.

'Bit late for a walk isn't it? Not really the weather for a midnight stroll . . . ' Max tried to wriggle out of his arms, but his father's grip on him tightened, the knife moving closer to the white skin above the collar of his anorak.

'Max, just stay still, darling. It'll be alright.' Rupert was fully dressed. He had even found the time to tie a scarf neatly around his neck. It was the sight of this that frightened her more than anything else. He had known all along that they were going to try and get away. All the time he had been pawing her, he had known that she was just lying there waiting for him to finish. Molly felt sick.

'Why are you doing this? What do you want,

Rupert?' She did move towards him now, her arms out for Max.

'All I want is for us all to be together.' Rupert said the words in an aggrieved tone, like a small child who had been cheated of a treat. 'I just want what's mine.'

'OK,' she said soothingly. 'We'll come back, just give me the knife.'

'Do you promise?' he asked.

'Yes. Yes. I promise.'

'OK, I'll walk with Max, you walk next to us,' said Rupert, his face suddenly cunning. 'And I'm keeping the knife. I'm taking no chances,' he said with a kind of strange giggle. 'You two are as slippery as a pair of eels.'

She reached out and gave Max's shoulder a squeeze. She could see that his teeth were chattering convulsively.

'Don't worry. It will be OK,' she said, trying to smile at him. The three of them started walking back towards the house.

34

Carrie rang Damian to talk about what Simon had said, but found him unresponsive, even cold on the phone. He still refused to countenance the fact that the medium could be communicating in some way with Charlie and was impatient with her for even thinking of it as a possibility.

'Come on, Carrie, this is me you are talking to. This is the real world, not some parallel universe generated by hysteria and misery,' he said, not even listening to what she was saying.

'But Damian, he was talking about that story Charlie loves . . . you know, the one about the dog he used to make me read him twenty times a night.'

'There's any number of ways he could get hold of that sort of information. You probably told him yourself. I think you should stop this right now, Carrie, before you get any more involved. Promise me you won't have anything more to do with him. I'm really worried by what is happening to you. Getting ill and everything. I've been really tied up with work, but I'll be there at the weekend. We need to talk about things. Real things, I mean, not this rubbish.'

'Won't you just come and see Simon with me once? It would really help me if you would come too.'

'No Carrie. I won't. I think you are going to end up hurting yourself with all of this. We need to talk about us and where we are going. That's what I am interested in.'

After Carrie had rung off she felt the same kind of loneliness she had felt when Charlie had first disappeared and she and Damian had faced their loss so differently. Whilst her grief had been messy and all encompassing, his had been no less keenly felt, but he had managed to re-channel it into useful action. She knew Damian would never allow himself to believe in the possibility of Simon having communicated with Charlie. He was a man who liked to know the limits of things and to be clear about where he stood in relation to the rest of the word. Carrie had escaped the isolation of being an only child by inventing a city that existed beneath her bedclothes. It had been an extraordinarily well-realised place that could be conjured up by the simple action of pulling the sheet over her head and although as a woman she had long given up creating imaginary places, she had remained a person who was open to the possibility that what she knew was only a fraction of what there was. It was surely in keeping with the splendour of what she *could* see, to believe that there was much more of it out there, beyond the boundaries of her imagination. Charlie had been so vivid in the world, had filled so much of it for her, that it didn't take too much of a leap for her to believe that he couldn't just have ended like a road tipping off a cliff or a bird silenced mid-song. He must be somewhere, shining, her love made manifest.

Despite her doctor's instructions to stay away

from work until she was a hundred per cent better, Carrie decided to go into *Trove* for a while to give herself something else to think about. In any case there was no peace to be had at home. Her mother was reclining on the sofa in an inappropriately tight powder blue polo neck, the only thing moving one languid hand that dipped periodically into a carton of chocolates. Nothing was more guaranteed to make Carrie feel restless than watching her mother at rest. A couple of hours of soothing stocktaking would at least offer some relief. She felt guilty that she was so easily irritated by her mother, particularly since Pam had been very kind to her the night before. Nursing a large brandy that she had poured for herself without asking Carrie if she wanted a drink, she had sat on the armchair by the fire, her legs tucked under her in a supple, girlish fashion.

'Men are such prosaic creatures,' she had sighed when Carrie had explained that Damian seemed angry with her for seeing Simon Foster. 'They mostly just want to follow the path of least complexity. You can't expect him to be able to make the leap. He just doesn't have it in him.'

'What do you think about what Simon is saying about Charlie? Do you believe it?' asked Carrie.

'Why not? I've always felt close to the shadowy side of life,' Pam said. 'I think I have a touch of the psychics myself. I have stopped at least twelve watches absolutely dead. Your F.A.T.H.E.R. used to be convinced that I did it on purpose so that I could get myself a new one, but I think it was my magnetism interfering with the mechanism.'

'I can't believe you still spell out the word father after all these years,' said Carrie.

'I may be of the opinion that there is only a thin veil between life and death, Carrie, but there is a rock-hard wall between right and wrong.'

Carrie forestalled the inevitable conversation that she knew would follow by offering her mother another drink. She knew every detail of her short and unhappy marriage to Carrie's father and wasn't keen to hear it all again. He had left them when Carrie was four and all that she could remember about him was walking around the room with her small feet on the top of his enormous boots and the way he threw his head back once so hard when he was laughing that his hat had sailed off and landed in a river. She had never seen him again. As an adult she could look back on her childhood and understand Pam's almost frenetic activity in the years after he had left. She could see now that it had been grief that had made her mother so unreachable, but as a child she had simply felt abandoned.

'I wasn't a good mother,' said Pam as if she was reading her thoughts. 'You were a much, much better one, my darling,' she said and her face suddenly crumpled into grief at the memory of this loss and others. Carrie felt her eyes fill with tears at her mother's words. She was so used to her brisk selfishness that she felt this unexpected tenderness catch in her throat. Pam sobbed, childlike, into her cupped hands. When

Carrie bent over to comfort her, she noticed that her mother's scalp was visible through her hair.

★   ★   ★

As she came out of her front door to head for the shop, Carrie saw that Oliver Gladhill was just coming out of his. Because she was still feeling less than robust and because he tended to have an unsettling effect on her, she tried to duck out of sight behind the hedge, but she wasn't quite quick enough and he saw her and crossed the road. She noticed that the royal blue scarf he was wearing went uncannily well with his eyes. She found herself torn between admiring his dress sense and castigating him for his vanity.

'Hello Carrie!' he said. 'I haven't seen you for ages. Where have you been hiding?'

'Nowhere . . . I've been ill for a few days . . . ' She trailed off, suddenly inexplicably close to tears. He looked closely at her.

'You do look very pale,' he said, his voice unexpectedly gentle. 'Where are you going? Will you let me take you for a coffee? I've finished work for the day.'

Carrie wasn't sure if she really wanted to go with him or whether she simply was too exhausted to think of a credible reason not to, but she found herself walking with him down Mill Road and into a little café that sold wonderful coffee and generous slices of cake. There were bright paintings all round the walls and a window too clouded to see out of. Sitting there with her hands cupping the warmth of her coffee, Carrie felt more relaxed than she had for days. Oliver meanwhile was thinking what a beautiful mouth she had, curved in just the right place and fuller in the bottom lip than the top.

'I know you've told me, but sorry, what is it exactly that you do? I think it was something to do with wildlife . . . ' said Carrie, aware of his scrutiny and wanting to find a neutral topic of conversation.

'I'm a wildlife consultant,' he said, 'which is a grand way of saying that I spend a good proportion of my time crawling around in the mud and getting cold feet.'

'Do you work locally?' asked Carrie, looking at his hand, which was resting on the table — long fingers with clean fingernails despite his avowed claim to roughing it in the countryside.

'I work all over, but just at the moment I am working for a private wildlife trust who are trying to establish a population of bitterns in an area of wetland near Ely.'

He anticipated her question. 'Bitterns are birds that have become almost extinct because the type of terrain that suits them best isn't as available to them any more. I'm trying to get that right and hopefully have ten more male bitterns in the next couple of years.'

'Your job would explain how easily you handled the hurt bird,' she said. Carrie could see no trace of his habitual flippancy in the passion with which he talked about his work. The man might be a womaniser, but he clearly had hidden depths, not to mention very blue eyes, a firm chin and the physique of a man who was no stranger to the gym or at least to exploring inhospitable terrain.

'But listen,' he said, 'the bitterns can wait. Will you tell me what is making you so sad? If you want to that is, you can tell me to piss off if you would prefer.'

Carrie hesitated because she knew that what had happened to Charlie affected the way people treated her. Even Carrie's close friends avoided talking about their children in front of her, even though she had told more than one of them that hearing about their children wasn't going to make her feel worse about the loss of her own. It was Charlie she wanted back, not anybody else's child. But for some reason, she didn't mind telling Oliver. There was something about him that made her think he would be able to handle it and so she began to talk about what had happened and found, to her surprise, that the words came easily. He sat in silence, only occasionally making the sort of encouraging 'tsking' noise that she imagined he might employ with his bitterns.

'It's only very recently,' she said, 'that I have even begun to countenance the fact that he might be dead. I think for the last three years a big part of me has been expecting him to be found. And every news story I read of families discovered in bunkers, or children turning up on the other side of the same town in which they disappeared, just reinforces the hope.'

'So what's made you accept the possibility? What has changed?' Oliver asked, making no move to console her or to commiserate. She appreciated his restraint. It made her think that he had had experience himself of grief.

'This is going to sound completely off the wall, and believe you me a month ago I would have dismissed it as the ravings of a lunatic,' she said, 'but this man I went to see seems to be getting messages from him.' She looked at Oliver, fully expecting him to laugh or worse, patronise her, but his expression didn't waver.

'How does it make you feel?' he asked, and Carrie wondered why Damian hadn't thought to ask her that, and then felt disloyal for thinking like that about him.

'I'm not sure. It makes me feel scared and confused. It makes me think I must be going mad. But I want to have everything that I can have of him. I know that people who are grieving latch on to every scrap of comfort. I've seen people swallow stuff that clearly makes no sense because they want to believe and I'm probably no different from them, but this man knew things. Things he just couldn't know any other way . . .'

Carrie noticed that it had become dark outside. They must have been sitting there for a couple of hours but she hadn't been aware of the time passing.

'God is that the time? I've really got to go. I need to go to the shop and see what's been happening in my absence,' said Carrie, gathering her coat and the scarf that had ended up on the floor under the table.

'Could I take you out to dinner?' asked Oliver.

243

'Wednesday night perhaps? I've enjoyed talking to you so much.'

For a moment Carrie hesitated, thinking about Damian and how things were tricky enough already without adding a further layer of difficulty, and then she thought about spending the evening alone endlessly going over what had happened with the medium.

'I'm actually seeing my ex-husband at the moment, it's all a bit complicated,' Carrie broke off awkwardly.

'It's just dinner, Carrie,' said Oliver. 'Not a date . . . unless you want it to be.'

'OK thanks, that would be nice,' said Carrie, and she was surprised to see the pleasure that her acceptance clearly gave him. They parted company outside the café and as she hurried to get to *Trove* before closing time, Carrie reflected on how much better she felt for having been able to talk honestly to someone who would just listen and not feel bound to take a point of view. She was astonished that it was Oliver of all people that she had chosen to unburden herself to.

35

Daddy doesn't look like my daddy any more. He looks all tight and angry. Once when we were sitting outside a pub we put some beer at the bottom of a jar and caught five wasps in it and they made so much noise you could feel it on your hand when you touched the glass. That's what my daddy sounds like when you shut your eyes. My mummy is as quiet as can be. Quieter than a mouse when Toffee is sniffing near. I think she knows that Daddy would not like sudden moves. Sudden moves will make Daddy lash out. Lashing out is what people do when they are angry and surprised. Lashing out is what people do when they are in a tight corner and afraid. Euoplocephalus — Power Rating 96, Intelligence Rating 53 — used the bone in its tail to lash out at its enemies. It had a kind of bommyknocker at the end of it. That's what Daddy said it was called. He showed me a picture of a knight in armour with a bommyknocker at the end of a chain.

Daddy used some string from the kitchen drawer to tie Mum and me to chairs. He used the dining room chairs from the safe room. He put the string around our ankles and the legs of the chair and also on our wrists and tied them behind us. He tied my leg ones really, really tight and I can feel the string digging in through my socks. I don't think I am bleeding though which is good because if I start bleeding I will need a plaster to stop the blood coming and I don't think my daddy knows where the plasters are kept. Mum is very still but I can see that she is trying to smile at me with her eyes because she can't use her mouth. I think she is trying to keep my spirits up like she does when we have to go on long walks and I'm really tired. When we are on long walks she sometimes sings the song about soldiers marching and gets me to swing my legs and that helps time pass. I feel very thirsty. Daddy put some soft stuff in my mouth and then used a tea towel to keep it in. I can smell chicken on the tea towel. My mummy has some torn-up sheet around her face but I can see her eyes. Daddy is making lots of noise around the house. I think he is packing for a trip. He has two big bags and he is putting things into the bags and I am counting all the things that go in like I do in the car when we play aunty goes shopping. My aunty went shopping and brought back a cow. And then you say my aunty went shopping and she brought back a cow and a turnip and then the next person thinks of something else like a hat or a globe and adds it to the list. Once I got up to twenty-three things before I got confused. I think my daddy has put more than twenty-three things into the bags. He put a hammer in and some nails and the silver tape from the garage and some candles and lots of other things I couldn't keep track of. I don't think things are going our way. *Something tells me things are not going our way.* That's what the Colonel said in a film I watched. The enemy

246

were approaching and they were trapped against a cliff and the Colonel said: *Something tells me things are not going our way*, and he said it in a voice that sounded very sad but firm, then in the nick of time he quickly remembered a tunnel and they rolled a rock away and there it was and they ran down it and it had bats in it but they didn't mind because they were free. I'm not mad on bats. Charlie doesn't like bats either. Charlie told me bats were bad luck and creepy because they slept hanging upside down and there was a sort of bat called a vampire bat that fastened itself to a pig's bottom and sucked all the blood out. Daddy knocked over my mum's chair because she tried moving it when he was upstairs getting the towels. Now she is lying on the floor and I can see that her arms behind her are hurting her because she is on top of them. But she is not crying because she is brave like the Colonel. It's very late which means I have stayed up all night without hardly going to bed at all because I don't count that first bit when I had my day clothes on under my pyjamas to fool my dad but I think he knew all along.

36

When Carrie woke the next day her first thought was of Charlie. It was perhaps the last vestiges of a dream lingering on, but as she lay there half asleep, she had a sudden strong sense that he was with her. It wasn't that she saw anything, it was more that there was a kind of vibration in the room; a disturbance of air, nothing more. She had heard other bereaved people describing moments when they had felt their loved ones around them, but she had never experienced it before. She stayed in bed for a while and thought of him. She had recently discovered that it hurt less if she let herself remember. Battling against the pain only made it more acute.

After a quick coffee she dressed in a pale pink silk shirt, a teal cardigan and black jeans. She twisted her hair into a knot and fastened it with a slide and put on crystal earrings and a thick silver cuff. As she put on her make-up with quick strokes, a swirl of peach blusher to combat her paleness and a smudge of dark grey on her lids, she noticed that her face had changed. She thought it was partly her recent illness that had hollowed out her cheekbones and altered their shape but there was also something new around her eyes, a tightness and wariness that she had not noticed before. She thought she looked older, or at least as if something she had seen or felt had left marks of damage on her.

She arrived at *Trove* at the same time as Jen who was wearing a leopard skin beret at a jaunty angle. Jen gave her friend a worried look.

'Are you sure you feel up to being here?' she asked, bringing her face three inches from Carrie's and scrutinising it as if looking for evidence of wrong doing. 'Blusher's all well and good, my girl, but it doesn't fool me.'

'I'm fine,' said Carrie. 'Honestly. I want to keep doing stuff, it stops me brooding and anyway, I can't leave you looking after the shop on your own forever.'

The truth was that being at the shop soothed her. When the rest of her life seemed so out of control, here at least she could take the measure of things. She could shape the shop according to her own ideas and desires. It restored in her the same sort of calm that she used to feel as a child when she played in the garden, placing leaves and flower heads and bits of bark on the rickety nature table she had made out of two planks of wood and some bricks.

The sale had left various areas of the shop depleted, and as her first job of the day Carrie set about moving all the reduced items to the back of the floor and ensuring that the non-sale merchandise was set out in enticing piles. She folded some soft, grey woollen blankets threaded through with thin purple stripes the colour of heather and stacked them onto the shelves of an old cupboard that Jen had found at a junk shop and revamped by papering the inside with antique maps. On the back of one of the open doors she hung a yellow leather satchel and a bright blue hat with a peacock feather. She enjoyed playing with colour and creating small displays, and *Trove* was laid out in a series of distinct areas, each with its own character. She was particularly pleased with the central table that showcased their latest range of body lotions and room fragrances all sold in old perfume bottles and glass medicine jars and stacked up in seductive profusion around an array of silver-backed hairbrushes and big floral jugs full of those old-fashioned, heavy headed chrysanthemums the colour of old gold.

The shop was unusually quiet and the morning passed without much incident. There were, of course, visits from the regulars; the man who walked around for some long-forgotten reason with a shepherd's crook. They had named him Little Bo Creep because of his somewhat disconcerting habit of stroking the merchandise, particularly the silkier items. Then they had the usual full weather report from HBC, so named because of her uncanny resemblance to Helena Bonham Carter, who let the cold air into the shop by standing with the door open and intoning the shipping forecast in doom-laden tones. The Wire Man never came in but passed by the shop at the same time every day on his constant and never ending quest for stray bits of wire. By lunchtime Carrie had sold two tea lights and Jen had stood precariously on a ladder and festooned the chandelier with green velvet bows and tiny glitter balls. She was still balanced at the top when the phone in the pocket of her enormous red sweater started to emit a just-about-recognisable *Carmen*. Carrie held her breath and ran for the bottom of the ladder as her friend attempted to answer and not fall off all at the same time. Carrie knew something was wrong immediately because of the way that Jen hunched her shoulders, as if preparing herself for a blow. She came down the ladder slowly, the phone clutched in her hand, the person at the other end still talking.

'What's happened?' Carrie asked. Jen could hardly get the words out. 'It's Tom, he's been in an accident. His bike . . . '

Carrie took the phone from her friend's unresisting hand and spoke into it. 'I'm sorry, are you still there? . . . Yes, I am her friend. Of course . . . of course . . . I'll bring her.'

When they arrived at the hospital they were taken into a small room and offered tea by a nurse with her hair tied back so tightly it set Carrie's teeth on edge. She sat holding Jen's hand, only leaving her once to try and find out if anyone had any information yet about what was happening. After an hour that felt much longer, the door opened and admitted a shambolic figure who looked like Boris Johnson's less-groomed brother but who turned out to be the doctor. Carrie could feel the whole of Jen's body stiffen into dreadful attention. It was as if some invisible force was holding her upright against her chair. Her nails dug into Carrie's palm.

Boris had bad skin and a gentle voice. 'I know it's not what you want to hear, but I can't tell you anything definite yet,' he said, looking straight at Jen as if taking the measure of her ability to endure this.

'He is critically hurt and I'm afraid his head bore most of the impact when he was knocked off his bike.'

Jen stared at the doctor, aghast. 'Wasn't he wearing a helmet?' she asked, through lips so pale they had disappeared into her face. 'I don't think so,' Boris said. 'At least he didn't have it on by the time he got here.'

'It's because I told him he looked like a toadstool in it,' Jen said. 'I laughed at him.' And she put her face in her hands and Carrie held her while she wept.

★   ★   ★

After a while they allowed Carrie and Jen to go into Tom's room. He was so still it seemed for a moment that he was play acting, as if he was holding his breath until the last moment when he would surely sit up shedding tubes and smiling. But the only sound came from the machines surrounding him and a hoover clattering against a wall in a nearby room. Jen approached his bed with what was almost a look of wonder on her face. She touched his hand on the place where the needle of the drip had pierced his skin.

'Carrie, meet Tom,' she said. 'He's the man I'm going to marry.' And she smoothed the wrinkles out of his sheet, making it lie straight over his legs. It was hard to see through all the bandages and the wires, but Carrie was pretty certain that Jen's Tom was the man she had seen

252

outside the shop who had stared at Jen with such wonder. She suspected that even without the make-over, even in her unravelling leggings, Tom would have thought that Jen was the most beautiful woman in the world.

37

Molly was not sure how much time had passed. Despite her discomfort, she had tried to remain as quiet as possible. Max's even breathing from across the room indicated that he had fallen asleep at last and she wanted him to get as much rest as possible. She could no longer feel her arms because they were crushed beneath her, tied at an awkward angle over the back of the wooden chair in which she was lying. She had been trying to loosen the string that was bound around her ankles by rocking the chair slightly from side to side and she thought that the fastening was a little slacker than it had been before. She wished that Rupert had at least left the light on because she might then be able to see something that she could use to cut her way through the string round her wrists. She thought if she could perhaps get her feet free she would be able to roll herself upright and the rough edge of the radiator might be sharp enough to at least saw some of the way through.

★ ★ ★

After he had knocked her over, Rupert had snickered and said something about her being like a beetle on its back. His face was flushed, intent. He bent over her, and for a moment she thought he was going to hit her. She tried to stop herself flinching. She knew that if she showed her revulsion and fear it would only stimulate him into further cruelties. It seemed to her that her senses were more heightened than they had ever been before. She could smell his breath, which was hot and foul. She could see where his hair at the front was thinning, each follicle distinct, emerging slightly damp and erect from his scalp. He untied the strips of sheeting he had wrapped around her mouth and face, and slowly traced a finger round her mouth. He watched her closely as he pulled down her pyjama bottoms. She could feel him fumbling, pinching her hard and then thrusting his fingers into her, the effort making him grunt, his teeth pushed into his bottom lip which was purplish and slightly swollen as if he had been biting repeatedly on it. She was glad that the chair that Max was tied to was turned away and he couldn't see.

'Why are you doing this, Rupert?' she said, keeping her voice as calm and even as possible. Trying not to make any sudden movements, as if she was in the presence of an animal that would not react well to being startled. He pushed his face even closer to hers.

'You're making me,' he said.

'I don't understand,' she said trying not to plead, but knowing that her voice had risen, despite her attempts to control the pitch. 'What have I done?'

'You. Brought. This. On. Yourself,' he said, punctuating each word with a twist of his fingers inside her and although the pain was sharp she tried not to cry out.

'I need to go to the toilet. I need you to untie me.'

He pulled his fingers out of her, stood up and rubbed his hand with an exaggerated movement down his leg, his face registering disgust.

'Piss yourself for all I care,' he said and then he went over to the door, unlocking it with a key from his pocket.

'Rupert . . . could you just let Max go? Just Max. Take him to Kate's. Please. Please.' She couldn't stop herself from begging but he had ignored her. He flicked the light switch off and walked out, locking the door behind him. She had heard the front door opening and closing, then the sound of the car starting up in the garage and reversing down the path, and then there was a silence so deep and so profound that she felt suffocated by it.

She thought he had now been away for about four hours, but she wasn't sure. She had no watch and this room didn't have a clock and because the window had been boarded up she couldn't even see how light it was outside. She wondered how long it would be before anyone came looking for them. She thought that Kate would probably come round to the house if she hadn't seen them by the end of the day, and the thought consoled her. Max shifted in his chair and made a gentle moaning noise. She knew he still had the gag across his mouth and was trying to say something to her.

'I'm here, darling,' she said to him. 'You've been asleep.'

Max shifted his chair from side to side causing the legs to scrape against the floor. She could feel his agitation and fear.

'Don't worry. We'll get out of here. Your father has gone. I don't think he's coming back and I'm sure Kate will come soon, or the police.'

Molly wondered why the police hadn't already been since they must be aware by now that the phone line had been cut. That in itself should surely have triggered some sort of an alarm.

'I've loosened the string around my legs a bit. If I can just get it a bit looser I might be able to slip it off the chair leg.'

★　★　★

For another hour Molly continued to pull her legs up and away from the chair until she thought she was too exhausted to move any more. The muscles in her stomach were straining. The string had rubbed her flesh raw and she could feel her ankles burning. Max had been crying on and off into his gag and as she rocked and wriggled she had done her best to console him. She had run through her repertoire of stories and poems and had even resorted to a selection of feeble knock knock jokes. Just when she had decided that she would never get free she managed to slide one of the bindings off the leg of the chair. Heartened by her progress she worked away at the other until at last, both legs were free. She rolled over onto her side and then over again until she was lying against the wall. She used the wall to lift herself up, pushing against it until she was standing upright still attached by her arms to the chair. Because she had been lying for so long at a strange angle the pain in her legs was excruciating. She leant against the wall for a while, feeling the blood starting to circulate around them again, the stinging sensation of pins and needles receding.

Bracing the side of her body against the wall, she moved along slowly until she hit what she recognised as the edge of the radiator. She bent herself to the right height and scraped the chair and her wrists against the edge. Through the noise of the chair banging against metal she could hear Max whimpering and rocking from side to side. At last she felt the string give and with one wrist free was able to work away at the other one until it too came loose.

She went over to Max, put her arms around him and then pulled his gag off. He spat out the lump of sodden cotton wool and took a deep, gasping breath.

'I wet myself,' he said piteously. 'I couldn't hold it in any more.'

'It doesn't matter, Max. I'll get you free and there's a change of clothes in the chest of drawers.'

She turned the light on, both of them blinking in the sudden brightness, and went over to the chest of drawers that was stocked as the police had recommended with some basic supplies; a change of clothes for Max and herself, some biscuits, a torch, a couple of bottles of water, some antiseptic cream, some bandages and a small pair of scissors. She was very glad that she had taken their advice since at the time she had felt vaguely ludicrous taking what seemed to be a wildly unnecessary precaution. She quickly cut through Max's bindings and got him carefully to his feet. As she pulled off his wet trousers she could feel his body trembling. She dressed him quickly in the dry clothes and sat him on the sofa with a biscuit and a bottle of water while she rubbed cream into the sore places on his ankles and wrists where the string had made angry raw patches.

'You are such a brave boy,' she said, stroking his hair off his eyes. 'I don't think any boy could be braver than you are.'

'You're a brave mummy too,' he said, and he put up one gentle hand and stroked the hair away from her eyes. It was such a tender, almost adult gesture that it made her eyes fill with tears. She got up, took a long drink of water and then looked around the room to see what she could use to pull the nailed wood away from the window.

38

Carrie stayed at the hospital until very late. Jen kept up a constant stream of chatter from the chair by Tom's bed, getting up periodically to touch his face and stroke his hands or to walk from one side of the room to the other. By three in the morning there had been no change in Tom's condition and Doctor Boris, who at this hour, and after a double shift was beginning to look as if he might slip into a coma himself, suggested that the women go home.

'I'll get someone to ring you if there is any change,' he said, rubbing his eyes and then straightening his back with a jerk as if readying himself for the next five, pallid hours until he was finally released back to his flat and a narrow bed that never got made. Carrie tried to persuade her friend that she was serving no useful purpose remaining at the hospital and that it would be more sensible to get some rest so that she would be better able to cope with whatever the next day would bring. But Jen wouldn't be moved. She had the same stubborn look she got when Carrie told her to brush her hair, and Carrie finally gave up the fight and crept out, leaving her curled up on the armchair in the corner of the room, her eyes fixed on Tom as if the sheer force of her vigilance would keep him alive.

Carrie left the hospital and walked across the

frost-slicked car park. Looking back at the bulk of the building with its vaguely sinister chimney she saw that many of the rooms were still lit up and thought about the stories unfolding behind the regulation blinds. All the everyday miracles and the everyday tragedies played out time and again. All that joyful and sorrowful breath filling up the corridors. On the way home the roads that were so well known to her seemed unfamiliar and threatening, dimly lit in most places and then suddenly brighter, discolouring a wall or catching a stretching cat on the edge of a roof.

At the last minute, just as she was turning into Mill Road, she changed her mind and drove on. She knew she was unlikely to go to sleep now and the prospect of sitting flicking through late-night TV wasn't appealing, although she had a soft spot for those channels selling cheap jewellery. For some reason she found it soothing watching the glitter-dusted hands pointing the fake diamonds to the studio lights, trying to generate a counterfeit sparkle. It seemed to Carrie that however miserable she might be, there was always someone much worse off, sitting in a studio, having to keep her voice enthusiastic whilst selling ugly rings to insomniacs.

It only took her a couple of hours along deserted roads to get to the beach. She parked in the empty car park and walked past the cement block toilets and the shuttered kiosk that sold plastic spades and cans of Coke in the summer.

The night was only just holding the day at bay and she could sense rather than see the dim beginnings of light. At the opening in the dunes she turned right along the beach, the way they had always walked. She knew her way in the dark as well as she might have done in daylight. She judged the tide to be high because she could hear the sea shifting restlessly. She walked for an hour or so, until the sky had lightened enough for her to make out the dunes and the jagged stumps of rotting groynes. Pulling her coat around herself to protect against the damp sand, she sat down facing out to sea, her arms wrapped around her knees. When Charlie first went, his absence tormented her so much that she didn't have the space to think about anything else. She was filled up with the pain of losing him. But as time had passed she had become increasingly aware that she had nowhere specific she could go to mourn him. There was no gravestone or ashes sprinkled in a well-loved spot. She had not been given what was left of him to lay to rest in safety. He had slipped through her fingers; faded out like a dream. Carrie thought about what Simon Foster had said about worlds overlapping and she had the same feeling she had had when she had woken the day before that he was near her. She had a sudden dizzying sense of the world flattening out and of sound and sensation being vivid and loud. She could feel the wind on her skin and her heart was light and beating with something that might have been joy. He was in the fresh breeze and in the salty spray. He was running as he had that day, with his hand holding up his shorts. He was in the moment she had first seen him after his birth, with his wrinkled, starfish hands over his face. He was in the man he would have become, walking down a dusty street away from her.

★   ★   ★

When she got home she listened to her messages. There was one from Jen saying that Tom had not yet come round. Her voice sounded muffled as if she was talking through cotton wool. Carrie phoned her back and left a message saying that she was to take as much time away from the shop as she needed. She had an hour before the shop was due to open, so on an impulse she rang Simon Foster and asked if she could come and see him straight away. She had a rudimentary shower, dressed in a tightly fitting maroon jumper and bottle green pencil skirt and pulled on brown stack-heeled boots. After a slice of toast and cup of strong black coffee she navigated her bike out of the shed and along the alleyway. She noticed that the phantom vodka addict was back. Always at his most prolific at this gloomiest time of year, the path was littered with empty half bottles. She wondered about the identity of the secret drinker; one of her neighbours perhaps, slipping out for swigs in between making the beds and arranging tea for the scouts, or maybe it was the local greengrocer, who always smiled at Carrie a little too much. Perhaps he hid the half bottles in his waxed jacket pocket to swill on the sly between the narrow fences. She gathered the bottles and put them in her bicycle basket to put in the first bin she came across.

She cycled quickly, taking advantage of the fact that the rush hour was yet to hit. Little Bo Creep had started his perambulations, and the bench outside the Co-op was already occupied by Fred who operated on the same principle as German holidaymakers and made sure to spread his skanky mac over the seat before anyone else could get there. The Wire Man had already been hard at work, his open rucksack bristling with his finds and his fists full of copper bouquets. What was left of the snow had gathered in slushy brown lines in the gutters and Carrie knew that the back of her coat would soon be splattered with dirt. The roads and sky had the leaden, lowering look that she associated with the deepest part of winter. There was nowhere else to go now but up again on the long climb to spring.

★ ★ ★

Simon made her tea and sat her in the usual place on the sofa. She almost smiled as she reflected how quickly she had become accustomed to this little ritual. He sat down in the chair and looked at her carefully.

'I've broken two rules this morning,' he said in his precise, low voice. 'I don't usually see people before nine o'clock and I never see people more than once a week. I think it's too much.'

'Thank you for breaking your rules for me,' said Carrie, noting that even though it was early, Simon had dressed with his habitual care, white shirt collar over dark sweater, and trousers ironed into sharp creases.

'I think you are at a point when you need to be able to move on,' said Simon, 'and I want to help you if I can.'

'I don't know if this is something that you do. But I thought I would bring this,' said Carrie, and she opened her handbag and took out Charlie's yellow shorts. They were still in the cellophane bag that the police had sealed them in, but she opened the bag, took them out and handed them to Simon. Without saying anything, he took the shorts and held them. Being in this flat always gave Carrie the sense of time standing still and today that impression was reinforced by the view through the balcony window of two boats stationary on the river. Presumably they had stopped to begin a race or perhaps to get instruction from the man on the bank, but they looked frozen in the undisturbed water.

'He's here. Carrie,' said Simon, 'He's singing . . . *and I seem to find the happiness I seek, when we're out together dancing cheek to cheek* . . . he says that he loves you more than anything. He wants you to be strong . . . I'm sorry, his voice fades out from time to time . . . he says he wants you to know that the sea came quicker and deeper than he thought it would. It went faster than a galloping horse . . . he couldn't run fast enough . . . it pulled him

265

under and it wouldn't let him go . . . there were cold bubbles and he breathed them in and then for a long time it was dark.'

* * *

Carrie stood up and walked over to the balcony door. The boats set off down the river suddenly, as if released. That was it then. He had drowned. He was nowhere in the world waiting for her or wanting her or beginning to forget her. Not missing. Not taken. No chance that he might on some unmarked morning walk through the door. She would never again feel the touch of his hand on her face or hold him in her arms. The best of her was gone and all that was left was this interminable pain. She felt the little heart she had left break, and everything twisted and bent under her and she fell to the floor. She came to with Simon bending over her, looking anxiously into her face.

'Are you alright?' he asked. 'Let me help you up.' And he led her back to the sofa. Carrie looked at him in bewilderment.

'I'm sorry for your loss,' said Simon with an oddly formal intonation.

'He really was the most perfect, beautiful boy,' said Carrie.

39

Sometimes when I'm going to sleep I get this really hot tight feeling in my head. I feel like a big puffed-up ball spinning down a hill. I get faster and faster until I can't stop. I feel like that in the day now too. Mummy almost got the cover off the window but then my daddy came home. We heard the car coming. My mum tried to lean against the window so he wouldn't see, but he saw just the same. She worked and worked to get it off. She used some scissors to get under the wood and she tried so hard her hands got blood all over them, but we had plasters so that was OK. When we heard my daddy coming we got quiet again and I sat on my chair. My mummy had the scissors in her hand and when he came close to her she tried to jab him, but he is a Wise Old Fox and he caught her hand really, really tight. He squeezed her hand until she dropped the scissors on the floor. I tried to put my foot over them, but he saw and kicked them away. I don't know what has made my daddy so angry. He even smells angry. He smells like our green bin does after hot sun has been on it and you open it just a tiny crack and let the smell out. Toffee sits on the green bin because it is the cosiest place in the house or garden. That's because rotting vegetables and fruit make gas. Bananas make the most gas of all. I was a bit sick in my mouth when my daddy hit

Mummy. I told him to stop but Mum said to be quiet with her eyes so I did. She can do lots of talking with her eyes. When he hit my mum her eyes went empty. He hit the talking out of her. It was almost morning when he took us out. I could see the shapes of things and the ground was hard and glittery. I would have shouted really loud like they told us to at school if a stranger asks us to come and look for his puppy or if he offers us sweets, even if he is a person we think we know. But there wasn't anyone to hear. I left a message though. Charlie told me where to put it and so I did it quick while Daddy put Mummy in the car. He put some string round Mummy's neck and tied it to the metal bit where you put your head. He drove so fast I was scared we would go into a ditch. It makes me feel funny in my tummy when I think of the car going into the water. The way we would be moving around on the inside trying to get out and outside would be still and dark and wouldn't notice us. I would get Mummy's string off first before anything else, even if I only had a tiny bit of breath left. We drove for a long time and then we went off the smooth road and onto a very bumpy road. I think it had some stones in. The car stopped suddenly and Mummy cried out because I think the string strangled her a bit. But my daddy cut it off and he got us out of the car and we walked for a long time and then he put us in a building, which is where we are now. It's not a house. It has no furniture and it has wet bits on the floor and on the walls. It has no lights. He locked us in the dark. My mummy asked for some food and a torch and my asthma puffer but he said no. I sat very close to Mummy on the floor. It's so cold. Mummy gave me her jumper but I'm still cold. I think there might be rats. I can hear noises. I'm trying to think of something happy. I'm trying to think of Three Reasons To Be Cheerful. One. Mummy is here. Two. We didn't go into a ditch. Three. I can escape into my head because Charlie showed me how.

Oh I love to go out fishing in a river or a creek, but I don't enjoy it half as much as dancing cheek to cheek . . . Heaven, I'm in heaven . . . And my heart beats so that I can hardly speak and I seem to find the happiness I seek, when we're out together dancing cheek to cheek.

40

Carrie left Simon's flat in a daze. He had tried to make her stay for a while and recover from what she had heard, but she was adamant that she wanted to leave. She pushed her bike over the nearby bridge and then started walking along the path by the river. She didn't really know where she was going but was possessed by the need to keep moving, to be alone so that she could think about what had just happened. After wandering along unseeingly for a while, she remembered with a start that she was supposed to be at the shop and phoned Paul to tell him she would be late in.

There was no longer any doubt in her mind that her son had been talking to her through Simon. If someone had told her a few weeks ago that she would find herself accepting this most outlandish of notions, she would never have believed them. It seemed to her that if she could have come around to this, then what everyone believed in and chose to act on was simply decided by what they happened to stumble on, a sheer accident of circumstance.

She heard her boy singing and listened to his words again, and for an agonising moment felt the fear he must have felt as the sea took him. She had spent five years attending to every graze and bump, soothing fears and explaining puzzles and yet she hadn't been near when he had needed her the most. She had to stop and lean, winded and sick, on the handlebars of her bike as the reality of it hit her. She hoped harder than she had ever hoped before that he hadn't suffered and that the end when it came had been quick. She shook away from her the image of his body in the water. She couldn't let that in for now. She had trained herself to shut down beyond a certain point. It was the only way to survive. She allowed herself the first tears she had ever shed for his death. Mixed up with the pain was a kind of release and the sense that at last she could mourn him without feeling she was letting him down.

★ ★ ★

At the shop, Paul took one look at her face and made tea. Even Enif seemed to sense her mood and was less supercilious than usual, condescending so far as to put his head briefly on her shoe.

As she moved around the shop, glad to be busy, Carrie felt as frail and tender skinned as if she had been in an accident. She was due at the hospital to see Jen in the afternoon so she was keen to get the place straight before she went. She hoovered the floor, dumped the wilting golden chrysanthemums and replaced them with pink tiger lilies and after grabbing a sandwich, apologised to Paul about abandoning him for the second time that day.

'It's fine. I'm glad you are going to see her. Send her my love,' said Paul to Carrie as she was getting her coat. 'Tell her that Enif and me have got our fingers and paws crossed.'

'I will,' said Carrie, 'I'm going to try and persuade her to go home and get a bath and some rest. They put a camp bed up in the room for her. But I don't think she is sleeping much at all.'

Carrie had packed a soft, brushed cotton nightdress, a change of clothes, a pot of silky face cream, some magazines and an enormous bar of Cadbury's Fruit and Nut and she hoped that the items would give Jen some comfort. At least gathering them up had given Carrie something to do. She felt so helpless in the face of Jen's misery. What had happened to Tom had shown her that enduring your own tragedies did precious little to equip you to deal with the tragedies of others. She was as hopeless at saying the right things as Jen had been when Charlie went. All she could do now was turn up bearing chocolate and be there in case she was needed.

*   *   *

Jen was sitting in almost the same position as Carrie had left her in. She looked up as Carrie came into the room, her face white and drawn, her make-up smeared around her eyes and down her cheeks, and gave a watery smile. She got up and put her arms around her friend and Carrie could feel that she was only just keeping herself together.

'There's been no change,' said Jen and her voice was unrecognisable. Carrie was so used to sarcastic, bawdy, noisy Jen, that it was a shock to hear how small and dull her voice sounded.

'His left hand sort of gave a twitch about an hour ago, but the nurse said that limbs often twitch and it isn't necessarily a sign that he is going to come round.'

'What have they told you?' asked Carrie.

'They just keep saying it's too early. He could wake up and be fine. They just can't tell until he comes round.'

'But he will come round, right?' asked Carrie

'I don't know. I don't know anything,' said Jen, sounding like a bewildered child. 'I won't be able to bear it if he dies.'

'Why don't you come home with me, just for a while? Give you a chance to get freshened up, have a bit of a rest. If you prefer, you take a taxi back and I'll stay with him.'

'What if something happens . . . and I'm not here?'

'It won't be any help to anyone if you get ill . . . ' said Carrie. 'Have you actually eaten anything at all since you have been here?'

Jen shook her head. 'I can't eat. I can't put anything in my mouth.' The fact that Jen hadn't eaten anything alarmed Carrie. Jen usually started to feel faint and talk about sinking blood sugar levels if she went without cake for longer than two hours.

'Please go home for a rest. I promise I will ring you the minute there is any change,' said Carrie, stroking her friend's hair off her face. 'You look terrible.'

At last Jen was persuaded into her coat and

Carrie asked at the desk if they would call a taxi for her.

'I'll be back soon, my darling,' Jen said, and kissed Tom's forehead. Carrie hustled her out of the room before she could change her mind.

★ ★ ★

An hour into her vigil and Carrie had eaten half of the bar of chocolate and attempted, and failed to divert herself with a piece in *Closer* magazine about dogging for the over-eighties. The combined effect of excessive chocolate and the thought of octogenarians having it off in Nissan Micras had started to make her feel sick. Tom hadn't moved at all. She thought how strange it was that she was with him when he was at his most vulnerable and yet she had not even met him. Being there felt a bit like an invasion of privacy and she wondered how he would take it if he suddenly woke up and saw a stranger sitting beside him. Just then a woman in a green uniform put her head through the door and asked if she wanted a cup of tea and Carrie, who was feeling thirsty in the dehydrating atmosphere of the hospital, was grateful for the offer.

'There's always hope,' said the woman as she handed Carrie a cup of milky liquid. Her face was a mass of small scars, as if her skin had been pitted by a shower of burning rain.

'Oh, he's not my . . . ' Carrie started to say, but the other woman put her hand on her arm.

'Just don't give up, my dear,' she said and smiled at Carrie as she dragged her trolley out of the room.

After drinking her tea in one thirsty gulp, Carrie decided that she needed ten minutes of air away from the persistent clicks and whirrs of the machines. She slipped out of the room, telling one of the nurses on her way out that she would be back very soon. She didn't want to let Jen down by missing anything crucial. She walked through the hospital concourse with its shops selling gifts no one had any use for, least of all those propped up in hospital beds — cuddly toys, bunches of stiff flowers and empty picture frames. As she went past the hairdressing salon she saw a line of ladies, all surely within a whisker of death, all with their hair in rollers. She wondered at their dedication to grooming even at this late hour. Perhaps it was easier to meet your maker with a tidy wash and set. Outside, on the tiny patch of grass between the car park and the place where the ambulances pulled up to disgorge their casualties, were the inevitable clutch of diehards. Dressed in hospital gowns and hooked up to drips, they stood smoking defiantly. One of them was really pushing the boat out and had a can of Special Brew in one hand, a burning twist of tobacco in the other. He raised his drink in Carrie's direction when he caught her eye and then bent double with a cough that sounded as if it was coming from the bowels of the earth. Carrie walked a short way out of the hospital grounds, sat on a bench and rang Oliver to find out what time he was expecting to meet up.

* * *

Jen managed five hours away from the hospital but at least seemed to have taken the opportunity to get some rest and to change from one pair of leggings and a jumper to a slightly different coloured version of the same ensemble. She put her arms around Carrie and held her tightly.

'You are the very best friend I could ever possibly have and I love you dearly, but this is my watch,' she said, giving Carrie a little push towards the door.

'Ring me if you need anything,' said Carrie. When she looked back, she saw Jen bending over Tom. Gone was the exuberant woman that Carrie had known for so many years, and in her place was this tender character, almost a stranger to her, her shadow long in the dimly lit room, her stillness full of waiting love.

* * *

When she got home Carrie ran herself a bath and poured a hefty slug of something that smelt of lemon under the hot tap, keen to get rid of the hospital odours she was sure were still clinging to her person. She wasn't sure if she was in the right frame of mind for going out to dinner, but felt she had left it too late now to cancel without seeming rude, and besides, there was something very seductive about the way Oliver listened to her. After the heightened emotion of the last couple of weeks and while she was still feeling so conflicted about Damian it would be a relief to spend a few hours with someone who didn't associate her with sadness and loss. Anxious not to dress as if this was a date — she had an uncomfortable memory of the way Oliver's eyes had lingered on the bits of her body not covered by the towel — Carrie chose a simple navy dress from Jigsaw, with a scooped neck and gathered at the front and matched it with red tights and some elegant black platforms.

★ ★ ★

Oliver was waiting for her outside the restaurant and because she was walking on the other side of the street, she had the opportunity of observing him before he noticed her. He was leaning against the wall with his arms crossed and she was struck both by his air of confidence and the length of his legs in burgundy chinos. He smiled his slow, *I'm very sexy* smile, and leaned over to kiss her on the cheek. He smelt clean with just a trace of some citrus aftershave and that slightly woody smell she had smelt before, as if he had been rolling around in bark chippings. The restaurant was decked out to look like the inside of a Bedouin tent, with draped ceilings and walls and was dimly lit by hanging coloured glass lanterns. Carrie was glad to see that they were not expected to loll around on floor cushions and that the waiters were not costumed in baggy trousers and waistcoats. Oliver had been to the restaurant before so she left it to him to order a selection of the mezze while she chose the wine.

'What sort of a day have you had?' he asked.

'I can't even begin to tell you,' said Carrie. 'It doesn't make for particularly good dinner conversation.'

'Try me,' said Oliver and leaned towards her. His shirt was slightly unbuttoned and she could see the skin of his chest which looked surprisingly tanned, considering it was the middle of winter.

'Well I spent the afternoon with my friend in hospital because her boyfriend was in an accident and is now in a coma and this morning I discovered what happened to my son, so it's been a bit of a day, all in all.'

'Did you see the medium again?' asked Oliver, and Carrie was so grateful for the matter-of-fact way that he asked her the question that she could have wept.

'You don't think that sounds mad?' she asked.

'What matters is that *you* believe it. I can't judge it because I wasn't there and I never knew your son, but if what this person is saying to you makes sense, then why wouldn't you go with it?' said Oliver, pouring her another glass of wine. 'Is it making you feel better about losing your son?'

'I'm not sure . . . It's like it's loosening something in me. Something that I have kept very hard and tight inside me ever since he went,' replied Carrie.

Carrie told him what Charlie had said to her about what happened on the beach. Oliver didn't

278

attempt to touch or console her, nor did he offer tissues in that panicked way that men often do at the sight of tears; he simply sat and absorbed everything she said with calm sympathy. Then they drank some more wine and talked of happier things. Oliver made Carrie laugh with a story about Mrs Evans coming to his house in the night saying that she had an intruder.

'I had to get dressed and everything. When I got there it turned out that she had forgotten she had left the radio on in the kitchen,' said Oliver.

'Hmm . . . I wouldn't be surprised if Mrs Evans was harbouring carnal thoughts,' said Carrie.

★　★　★

When they got back to the house, Carrie didn't know whether to invite him in. She didn't want him to think that she was expecting or wanting anything more from the evening than they had already had. Seeing the indecision in her face, he made it easy for her.

'You've had a hell of a day,' he said. 'And I've got an early start tomorrow . . .'

'Yes,' said Carrie feeling absurdly crestfallen. 'You're right . . . it's been a lovely evening. Goodnight.'

Before she could turn away, Oliver bent to kiss her goodnight on her cheek. The kiss lingered and then moved to her mouth and Carrie's whole body leapt in response. She wasn't sure if it was due to the turmoil her strange day had unleashed or the bottle of wine she had drunk, but she was astonished by how much she suddenly wanted him. She opened her mouth under his, her hands twisting in his hair. She wasn't sure who made the first move, but they found themselves in the alleyway by the side of her house, their bodies pressed against each other, their breath coming hard and loud. She felt him kissing her neck, his hand on her breast, her nipple hardening at his touch so that he could feel it through the fabric of her dress. She ran her fingers across the front of his trousers and stroked him until he groaned and pulled away from her. His eyes were dark as he looked at her.

'I want you. I think you can feel how much I want you,' said Oliver, 'but it doesn't feel right . . . '

Carrie gaped at him. Was Oliver, the shag king of Almond Street, really turning her down?

'You've been so sad today. A lot has happened,' said Oliver, tracing a finger along the side of her face. 'You are so gorgeous and I'd give anything to . . . but I want you to be really with me, and not doing it because I'm a distraction from what else is going on in your life.'

'What's wrong with distractions?' asked Carrie, furious that he had turned all decent on her. 'Don't answer that. Goodnight then. I don't want to keep you,' she said sharply, and let herself into her house and shut the door, already feeling mortified by his rejection. Oliver Gladhill, the seducer of a hundred frail blondes, had just ruined his reputation.

41

After Rupert left them Molly had felt her way along the damp walls of their prison, but found no way out other than the door which Rupert had locked behind him. She tried pushing against it, even throwing her whole body weight behind the endeavour, but the wood barely registered the impact. She and Max had spent the rest of the night huddled together with their backs against the driest bit of wall. She had watched the light gather in the one small, barred window set high up, almost at the roof. It cast some dim light across the room, enabling them to at least see in more detail where they had been imprisoned. Even in the dark, she had recognised the building when they had first arrived as being the derelict pumping station that they had stumbled upon all that time ago. On that occasion they had not gone inside, but had walked a little way beyond it and sat on the ground and eaten the lunch they had brought with them. It had been one of the good days with Rupert. He had left her to sketch the building while he had taken Max exploring in the nearby wood. The room they were locked up in was very tall and rather narrow. The place smelt dank and mouldy and there were a series of green marks of varying depths along the walls that indicated that the place had been flooded several times. There was some old farming paraphernalia in one corner, and three large metal drums or boilers of some sort set up on their sides with hinged lids that opened at the front with a grinding noise.

Molly was concerned about Max. His breathing was ragged and he had developed the cough that he sometimes got when his asthma was taking a turn for the worse. He looked pale and despite the fact that she had given him her sweater, he was still shivering uncontrollably.

'How long are we going to be here?' asked Max.

'I don't know, darling,' said Molly. 'Come and cuddle up to me. We'll keep each other warm.'

'What's Daddy going to do to us?' asked Max, his eyes wide and afraid.

'I'm sure he won't hurt you, Max,' said Molly with as much certainty as she could muster, although she was far from feeling certain. It seemed to her that Rupert had lost control completely. She no longer knew what he might be capable of.

'I'm hungry,' said Max wretchedly.

'I know darling. Be brave. I'm sure Daddy will come back with some food.'

'I don't want him to come back,' said Max.

'Shall I tell you a story?' asked Molly.

'Tell me about when I was born,' said Max, settling against her. She felt his bony little shoulder pressing into her side and she put her arm around him to hold him as close as she could.

'Once upon a time,' she said, 'there was a mummy who longed and longed for a boy of her very own. But she didn't want any old boy.'

'Oh boy no,' muttered Max, already soothed by the sound of his mother's voice telling him this familiar tale in this familiar way.

'Oh boy no,' echoed Molly, who was trying to be as calm as she had the strength to be. 'This mummy wanted a very special boy. A boy who was clever and kind and very, very handsome and who knew the words to all the best songs. This mummy knew that in order to get the very top-notch boy that she wanted she would have to do something brave and good to earn him. But she wasn't afraid. She was ready to fight crocodiles and fire and floods and even eat worms to get her heart's desire.'

Molly told the story until she could feel her son's shoulder relax against hers and she knew that he had fallen asleep. She sat as still as she could and watched the light at the window and waited for what might come next.

42

Carrie spent the next day licking her wounds and trying to recover from the most awful hangover by drinking tomato juice liberally laced with Tabasco sauce. In the afternoon she finally summoned up the energy to haul some of the rotting pots in her garden over to the flowerbeds into which she tipped their soggy contents. She stamped down the mush of roots and strange curling centipedes with her booted feet and then tackled the holly tree that had thickened in all the wrong places. The phone in her pocket rang, and pulling it out with a muddy hand, she saw Jen's name flash across the screen.

'He's awake. Carrie, he's awake,' said Jen. 'He opened his eyes. Stared around him for a bit and then noticed I was there and gave this big smile.'

'Oh my God, I'm so glad. How long ago?' said Carrie.

'Just half an hour ago,' said Jen. 'And Carrie . . . we're engaged. I struck while he was still befuddled with medication. Say you'll be my Best Woman.'

'Only if I get to choose the dress,' said Carrie, shuddering inwardly at the thought of what Jen might pick if left to her own devices. 'No trailing sleeves. No empire lines. No attempts to look like an extra in a fifth-rate film of the legend of King Arthur.'

'It's a deal,' said Jen and rang off.

Carrie had a bath to wash off the mud and dressed quickly in a long white shirt over skinny black trousers, pulling her hair back into a simple ponytail. She had arranged to meet Damian in a nearby pub, thinking it might be easier to say what she had to say on neutral ground. When she arrived he was already there in a corner seat. There were two glasses of red wine on the table in front of him. He knew her so well. There had been other people who had been there during their story, but it was only the two of them that had felt the full force of the joy and the pain. He was the only other witness. The only one she would never have to explain it to.

'Jen's Tom has come round,' Carrie said, taking off her coat and putting it on the end of the bench.

'That's great,' he said. 'Is he going to be completely OK?'

'I think so. Jen sounded so happy. They are getting married. A spring wedding.'

'I hope you are choosing the dress,' he said, and she laughed.

'Do you remember what she wore to our wedding?' he said.

*   *   *

It had been so hot. There had been a kind of hazy shimmer on the path leading up to the registry office. Damian had looked pale in a new, dark suit, too heavy for the weather. She had worried about sweat patches under the arms of her silvery grey dress, her hands clammy around the bunch of cream roses. Jen had worn a hat — some sort of boater decorated with daisies and a floor-skimming gown of almost neon pink. She remembered the evening party in a hotel and the anonymous room that they had made their own by decorating it with ivy and silver ribbon and tea lights in baked bean tins with hearts punched through the metal. Outside, in the sudden thunderstorm they had stood so close that it had felt as if their bodies had fused together in the rain.

'She looked like a giant prawn,' said Carrie.

'There was one moment,' said Damian, 'when we were standing in the rain. I tried to hold it still in my mind so I would be able to go back to it. I still go back to it.'

She saw that he was making his case and in that moment she loved him more than she had ever done.

'It's still what sustains me, Carrie.'

'Damian . . . ' she began, but they were interrupted by the arrival at their table of Greg who had been at university with Damian, and whose friendship they had managed to dislodge a few years ago, despite some fairly dogged persistence on his part. Despite her irritation, Carrie felt sorry about the rip in the pocket of his jacket, the smell of old fried breakfast that hung about him, and she pulled out a stool.

'Come and join us,' she said. 'We're staying for another quick one.'

In a grateful flash, Greg's jacket was off, his

sleeves were rolled up and Damian was making his way to the bar.

'What's the story?' asked Greg, having found Damian's half-eaten bag of crisps. 'I thought you two were all washed up . . . . '

It was another hour before Carrie and Damian were able to escape. They walked down Mill Road, which although never as aromatic in winter, still sent out the odd pungent gust of air as doors opened and closed. They selected a noodle bar on the basis that there was a free table in the window and it sold crispy duck. Carrie watched while the waitress pulled the duck off the bone, expertly shredding the soft meat with quick movements, placing pancakes in their bamboo steamer and little cups of dark sauce within easy reach. The orange gerbera on their table had given in to the weight of its head and drooped over the edge of the glass vase.

'Poor old Greg . . . . ' said Damian.

Carrie busied herself rolling the meat, shredded spring onion and sauce into its floury pancake.

'What's to become of him? He wanders round the pubs of Cambridge until he finds someone willing to put up with him for half an hour. It's so sad.'

Carrie didn't know how to tell Damian about what her latest visit to Simon had revealed. She knew that he didn't believe the man could tell them anything, but all the same she thought that this latest message would come as a shock, if only because it showed him that she now believed that Charlie had drowned. She had the feeling that although deep down Damian knew that Charlie was gone forever, Carrie's own dogged belief all this time that he was alive had allowed him a little hope by proxy.

'Don't be angry,' she said at last, not wanting to hurt him, but unable to think of another way of saying what she had to say. 'Simon has had another message from Charlie.' Damian shifted impatiently and looked down at the food on his plate as if he didn't want to listen.

'He said, that he drowned,' said Carrie gently. For a moment she thought she saw something shift across his face; a look of bewilderment or shock, and then he seemed to recover.

'I know this means something to you, Carrie,' said Damian, 'but I just don't get why. It's not like you, not really.'

'I believe that he's in touch with Charlie. I know we won't ever agree about it,' said Carrie. 'I felt as if something ended when he told me.' She looked at Damian's face to see if her words had had any impact on him, but he seemed not to be listening properly to her.

'Let's get married again,' he said. And he looked just as he had all those years ago when he had asked her to marry him on a wind-lashed beach.

'We know we love each other,' he had said. 'What's the point of waiting?' He held her hair away from her face in a bunch at the back of her head and kissed her eyelids.

He had always been so sure about everything. His feelings as clean and true as the slice of metal twine through clay. She thought that perhaps there had been a time when she had been as certain as he was about what he felt and what he wanted, but nothing seemed straightforward to her now. She knew nobody would ever again give her the easy peace he had been able to give her.

'I can't,' she said now. 'I'm sorry.'

'Please,' said Damian. She saw he was holding on to the edge of the table, as if letting go would cause him to rise up and drift to the ceiling.

'I lost Charlie and I lost us. There's no getting any of it back,' Carrie said and saw in his face that he had expected this.

'Couples go through all sorts of things. We were too caught up in the pain. We didn't know how to help each other. We can now,' said Damian.

She put her hand over one of his clenched fists.

'We didn't manage it. It wasn't your fault. Or mine. It's just what happened,' she said.

She touched one of his Charlie-shaped eyelids with her finger. Outside, the moon was high and bright. The lights wrapped around the branches and trunk of the tree outside Mick Flynn's poolroom had been switched off after the proper post-Christmas period had been observed, but they would remain in place for the next seasonal illumination, growing into the fabric of the tree, making grooves in the bark.

★ ★ ★

When Carrie got back to her house she checked her phone and there was a message from Simon Foster. His voice sounded softer, more tentative on the phone than it did in real life.

'Could you give me a ring when you can,' he said. 'I'm having messages from Charlie. Lots of them. I can't filter them out. He seems very upset, Carrie. I think he is trying to tell you something really important.'

43

Although she was anxious to hear about the latest messages, Carrie waited until the morning before she called Simon. The phone only rang three times before he answered it. She imagined him sitting on his bed with its hospital corners or moving across the empty floor to his neat table. All around him quiet and orderly, but inside him all the pleading, the justifications, the explanations, the inane and the mad, the cruel and the kind, the anger, the sorrow, the secrets and even, still, the lies. All the wandering souls looking for anchor, trying to ensure they had meant something.

'Hello Simon, it's Carrie . . . you left a message for me last night . . . '

'Oh yes, Carrie. I didn't really know whether to ring you or not,' said Simon. 'It's just that he seems so very anxious. So unusually present.'

'What has he been saying?' asked Carrie.

'He just doesn't sound like the boy he was when he came through before. He sounded quite calm before. But he seems quite changed now. I explained before that if I think that what has been passed to me is going to upset someone or puzzle them, I try to edit the messages . . . '

'Tell me what he's saying,' said Carrie, her heart in her mouth, part of her wanting to know this, the other part of her wishing she didn't have to hear. But she had let him down before. She couldn't again.

'His voice is different. I barely recognised it. He seems frightened of something or someone. He keeps talking about being wet and cold and not being able to breathe properly.'

'Is he describing being in the sea?' said Carrie, unable to bear the images Simon's words were conjuring up. She wanted so much to know he had not suffered, but it sounded as if he had been spared nothing.

'I'm not sure, but I don't think so. He said something about being locked up and a strange smell . . . I'm sorry this is so vague. I'm sure it's not helping you. The reason I phoned is that he was so very insistent that he needed you to know, he said he needed you to help.'

'What does he want me to do?' asked Carrie, her voice breaking.

'I don't know, Carrie,' said Simon. 'I promise I'll tell you as soon as I know any more. I can't always hear him that clearly.'

'Will you ring me again?' asked Carrie.

'I will. I really hope I haven't upset you too much,' he replied.

★ ★ ★

When she got to the shop Carrie was grateful for Jen's chatter. She badly needed to be distracted from hearing Charlie's words, which were turning round and round in her head. Fully restored to her former ebullient self, Jen was full of news and plans. Apparently Tom was expected to be in hospital for at least another week until the doctors were sure that he had recovered sufficiently to spend the rest of his convalescence at home. He had concussion, extensive bruising, various grazes and scrapes and a broken arm, but this hadn't stopped him and Jen starting to plan what was clearly going to be the wedding of the century. In fact, Jen was taking further advantage of the fact he was not yet quite the full quid to push through some of her more extravagant suggestions. She was pretty sure he wouldn't have agreed to swans on stilts if he hadn't been a little under par.

Carrie was amused to see that Jen had acquired a velvet-covered ring binder from *Trove* and had drawn up lists for everything and then colour coded them. She had been transformed in a short space of time from someone who used to mock the weddings of friends to bridezilla extraordinaire, given to examining at length the relative merits of chiffon ribbon over satin. The very woman who used to claim that buffets and bubble machines were the work of the devil had now drawn up a list of possible wedding venues within a ten-mile radius of Cambridge and was systematically working through them all, giving them a star rating system in the process. Carrie didn't want to curtail her exuberance by talking about what Simon had told her about Charlie, so she kept it to herself. Jen had had the most terrible few days and she deserved a break from misery.

'Looks like I'm going to be alone in the Fantasy Retirement Home, after all,' said Carrie, who was ironing some silk playsuits that had arrived in boxes and were too crumpled to display, while Jen leaned on the shop counter, too absorbed in a magazine spread of wedding party favours to answer.

'I don't really care. All the more Sobranies for me,' Carrie said.

'What?' said Jen, looking up sharply. Dazzled though she might be by the sight of a feature on a hundred and one ways of decorating wedding tables, she wasn't so distracted that she missed the clanger of a clue Carrie had just lobbed at her.

'Has something happened with Damian?'

'I told him last night that it was over,' said Carrie.

'What made you do that?' asked Jen. 'I thought you said it was going well between you.'

'I don't know. It's complicated. It was something to do with how you were with Tom at the hospital. And also the fact he didn't really want to talk about the medium stuff — it reminded me of how we were when Charlie first went. I don't know. A lot of things really. He asked me to marry him again and that kind of forced my hand.'

'OH MY GOD . . . We could have had a double wedding!' said Jen, convincing Carrie, if she needed any further convincing, that her friend had truly gone over to the dark side.

Carrie hung the pink and blue suits on padded hangers, placing ribbon-trimmed over-the-knee socks and pale blue suede t-bars on the floor underneath the rail. The playsuits were strictly for the under twenty-fives, but there were some twenties-style drop-waisted dresses in dark green with a pattern of acorns and leaves in a lighter green, and some in cream with a pattern of dark brown curled-up cats. These, teamed with some soft, woollen tights in vivid purples and blues would suit the customers who felt that their playsuit days were over. Although Carrie wouldn't put it past her mother to try and squeeze herself into one. The woman was becoming more skittish by the day. It really was time to ask what her plans were; she couldn't stay with Carrie forever.

'I can't imagine you wanting to share your day of glory with anyone else, and besides, it was never going to happen,' said Carrie, casting a critical eye over her efforts.

'Does this mean that Peter Fletcher with his romantic, troubled brow is back in with a chance?' said Jen slyly.

'No. Definitely not. Although ... ' Carrie trailed off.

'What?' demanded Jen. 'Tell me.'

'Don't go blowing it out of all proportion, but there might be someone else ... '

'Who?' said Jen, turning astonished, round eyes at Carrie. 'You never said anything about anyone else.'

'Just because we run a shop together, doesn't mean I'm contractually obliged to tell you every detail of my life.'

'Yes, but this isn't just a minor detail is it?' said Jen indignantly.

'Do you remember me mentioning Oliver

Gladhill?' said Carrie.

'What? The bloke with a high opinion of himself? The serial shagger?' said Jen.

'Yes.'

'I thought you said you couldn't stand the sight of him.'

'Well, we went out the other day and he wasn't at all how I expected him to be.'

'What do you mean?'

'He was really nice. Listened . . . you know . . . and seemed to understand when I told him things . . . '

'Let's get this right in my head. The last and only time you have mentioned this bloke to me, you said he had different women coming out of his house at all hours and that he had shifty eyes. Now, he's suddenly Claire Rayner reincarnated . . . '

'I don't know. I just thought he was nice. That's all. He has a way of talking about things that makes sense,' said Carrie, adding bold gemstone pendants to the dresses and standing back to judge the effect.

Just then the shop doorbell sounded and Oliver came in. Carrie was so surprised to see the subject of their discussion suddenly in front of her that she turned round too abruptly and knocked over a basket of enamelled brooches. After an undignified scrabble on the ground and helped by both Jen and Oliver, the basket was put back in its place by the till and Carrie turned a flushed face to her friend.

'Jen, this is Oliver Gladhill. Oliver, this is Jen,' she said only too aware that Jen had turned on the full force of her scrutiny and was inspecting Oliver from top to toe. Her eyes lingered particularly on his shoes. Oliver, although somewhat taken aback by the gimlet looks that Jen had fastened on him, was gratified to see Carrie's reaction to his arrival in the shop. She really did have the most beautiful skin, particularly when she was a little flustered as she was now. Her gaze was as clear and direct under those dark brows as he remembered it.

'Nice to meet you,' said Oliver, shaking Jen's hand and giving her the full benefit of his charmingly lopsided smile.

'I came in to find out if you were doing anything tomorrow, Carrie. I wondered if you might like to come out to the reserve with me. You mentioned you would be interested to see the work?'

Carrie was tempted to tell the cocky bugger to piss off. She was still smarting from the humiliation of having practically thrown herself at him and been rejected. All that guff about wanting her to be sure; she clearly just wasn't blonde enough.

'I'd like that,' she heard herself say, to her surprise. 'All I had planned for tomorrow was food shopping and cleaning the house.'

'Great. I'll knock on your door at around one. Dress warm and waterproof.' And, after giving both the women another of his devastating smiles, he went out.

'Handsome and knows it,' said Jen. 'Also, his shoes are just too trustworthy to be trusted. It's like he has read some manual and found out what women like.'

'I know,' said Carrie. 'That's what I've been saying to myself too.'

'Very nice smile though,' said Jen grudgingly and returned to her magazine.

'It might be useful,' said Carrie, 'if certain parties put aside wedding plans just for a moment and helped me to put price labels on these dresses.'

'I'll just make us some tea first,' said Jen, 'and perhaps I'll just nip next door for a packet of Jaffa cakes, and then you can give me your initial ideas for wedding dresses. I've been thinking pale green, off the shoulder. *A Midsummer Night's Dream* kind of vibe.'

'It'll be *Midsomer Murders* if you don't stop talking crap,' said Carrie. 'Pale green will make you look anaemic and I've told you before that off-the-shoulder dresses don't make you look like Jennifer Beal in *Flashdance*, they just make you look dishevelled. I'm thinking along the lines of something quite structured. Perhaps some lace. Elegant.'

Jen rolled her eyes and went to put the kettle on.

44

Molly felt Max waken, and then stiffen in her arms as they heard the key turning in the lock. The door swung open and Rupert came into the room, shutting and locking the door behind him and putting the key in his pocket. He was carrying a small holdall and was dressed in the clothes he used to wear when he went out fishing; his weatherproof anorak and trousers. Molly stood up, her legs stiff with the cold and the position she had been forced to keep for the last few hours in order not to wake Max. Rupert stood looking at them from the other side of the room.

'Rupert, Max isn't well. He's cold. His asthma is getting bad. Please let us out,' pleaded Molly.

Rupert didn't reply. He came towards her and she couldn't stop herself from shrinking back against the wall. As he stood over her she felt an immediate and quick revulsion. He smelt of alcohol and of something rotten and musty, like a wet towel that had been left at the bottom of a swimming bag. He had a red, sore patch on the side of his face, as if he had been rubbing at his skin repeatedly.

'Daddy, I'm hungry,' said Max and he started coughing and couldn't seem to stop. Molly crouched down beside him and stroked him on the back.

'You can see. He really isn't very well, Rupert.

Even if you don't let me go, take Max. Take him to Kate's or the hospital,' said Molly.

'Your friend came round yesterday evening,' said Rupert. His voice sounded calm, the tone light and conversational. 'I told her you and Max had taken a little trip away. I said that Max hadn't been very well and that you had taken him off to recuperate. Silly bitch wanted the address of where you were staying . . . '

'What did you tell her?' asked Molly, wanting him to keep talking since then there might be more chance of him seeing how ill Max was.

'I told her you had gone to a hotel in Norfolk. I said I had written it down somewhere but didn't know the name off the top of my head. She waited for me to go and get it, but I pretended to forget.' Rupert looked suddenly crafty. 'I think I fooled her. I'm not going back to the house anyway.'

He put the holdall on the floor and unzipped it.

'I brought you both a little present.' He pulled out something covered in newspaper and unwrapped it carefully, holding a snake-like creature up for their inspection. It was olive coloured and wet looking and hung straight down from his fist as if it was pouring from his hand.

'Only the third eel I have ever caught. Quite a catch, considering it isn't even the season.'

He placed the eel on the floor in front of Max, who shuddered and averted his eyes. Rupert returned to his bag and this time took out a bottle of water, which he put down on the floor next to the eel.

'No plates, I'm afraid,' said Rupert and patted Max on the head. 'You'll just have to make a picnic of it, eh? A little adventure.' Max flinched away from him and in response Rupert grabbed hold of him by the front of his sweater and pulled him upwards so that his feet were barely touching the ground.

'Don't, Rupert. Please don't,' said Molly desperately, moving towards her son.

'She's turned you against me hasn't she?'

Max shook his head and Rupert released him so suddenly that he fell back down onto the floor and banged his head. He cried out in protest and pain.

The sound seemed to stop Rupert in his tracks. He raised his head for a moment as if scenting the air and then looked about him in bewilderment. He seemed to have forgotten what he was supposed to be doing. He swayed slightly on the balls of his feet and then sat down with his back to the wall as if suddenly and overwhelmingly exhausted. Although he appeared to be looking straight at Molly, his eyes were unfocused and empty. He began rubbing at the raw patch of his face so hard that he scraped his skin with his fingernails and drew blood.

Molly got up and walked slowly towards him. She thought that if she moved smoothly and quietly she might avoid startling him out of his strange reverie. If she was very careful she might even be able to get into the pocket of his coat.

301

She placed her hand on his shoulder but he didn't acknowledge the gesture in any way. He continued to stare straight ahead and continued to worry away at his wounded face. Emboldened by this, she crouched down beside him. It took a real effort of will for her to put her arm around him since her instinct was screaming at her to get as far away from him as she possibly could. She spoke gently as if to a small child or frightened animal.

'I don't think you are feeling very well yourself,' she said, stroking his shoulder. 'Shall we just try and get you back to the house?'

She manoeuvred her arm so that it was just resting over the pocket of his anorak. She tried to remember if it had a Velcro fastening or not. She attempted to keep her breathing even, her voice low and soothing, the words repetitive.

'Why don't we just get up together. We'll get you home and into a lovely warm bed. Get you a lovely hot drink. Put all of this behind us . . . .'

She managed to get her hand into the top of the pocket of his coat and her fingers fastened around the cold metal of the key. If she could just pull her hand out in one smooth gesture she might be able to get the key without him even noticing that it had gone.

All of a sudden she was aware of a savage grip on her wrist and then a blow across her face that knocked her sideways. In an instant he was up. All sign of weakness was gone and had been replaced by that unnatural strength, that gleam she had seen in him before.

'D'you think I didn't know what you were

doing, you stupid bitch?'

Rupert paced up and down the floor in front of her. She could feel the spittle from his mouth as he spoke.

'I might have let you out. I was going to let you out. Then you try to trick me and so you've only got yourself to blame. You're forcing me to keep you in here.'

'Can I have a coat for Max? Please give me something to keep him warm,' Molly begged. She tried to stop herself from crying, because she knew it would upset Max, but she was so very tired. All the bones in her body felt soft and her head ached. Rupert walked to the door, unlocked it and went out and slammed it shut. They listened as the key turned once more in the lock.

45

The day was bright and clear but as they drove past the wide fields traced with lines of green like balding corduroy, tatty corrugated iron edifices and the occasional ranch-style building that wouldn't have looked out of place in Texas, Carrie thought that even the blue sky did little to give this landscape any beauty. It had nothing of the soft or picturesque. It was all serviceable, practical lines with nothing extra to requirements apart from one punch of colour supplied by an abandoned, deflating Santa, bent double as if in pain on the roof top of a glowering bungalow.

Although he was skilled and clearly very familiar with the road, Carrie felt that Oliver was an overconfident driver, given to one-handed and reckless overtaking. When he suddenly swerved out beyond a tractor to assess the road ahead, Carrie clutched the sides of her seat. She may also have made an involuntary noise although she hoped she hadn't. She didn't want him to think she was feeble spirited.

'Don't worry. You're in safe hands,' he said, smiling at her. She wished he would keep his eyes on the road and his mind on what was a busy and tricky dual carriageway. She was very aware of his close proximity in the car and of his hands, the wrists strong and flexible, his fingers just resting on the leather of the steering wheel.

She couldn't help a glance sideways to assess his legs encased in dark denim. Neither of them had made any allusion to what had happened at the end of their evening out together, but Carrie was determined that she wouldn't make the same mistake twice. She wouldn't have made it the first time if she hadn't drunk so much wine.

They arrived in a small empty car park and after walking a little distance across a field of sedge and past some willow trees, their odd pronged branches emerging from thick trunks, they came to a series of raised boardwalks that had been constructed to access the watery terrain. Ditches and patches of black water were surrounded by dry reeds, pale and bleached of colour at this time of the year. Standing on a small bridge, Carrie could see both the reflection of the reeds on the trembling, wind-agitated surface, and then clear through to the place where they grew out of the dark ground in their secret underwater bed. Being on the walkway gave the illusion of floating above the surface of the land, separated from what teemed below in amongst the reeds and the water. In an adjacent field two Highland cattle lay under a tree and breathed out great gusts of white air.

Oliver explained that he had spent the last three years ensuring that there was a flourishing reed bed and a good supply of the right-sized eels populating the waterways, and at the last count he thought there were at least nine bitterns now making this patch their home.

'They are really hard to spot because they are very well camouflaged by their surroundings and they are pretty secretive. In the mating season they make a weird booming noise and that gives us a clue as to where they are, but at this time of the year the only way to count them is in the couple of hours before dusk, when they fly in to roost,' said Oliver, leading her into a small wooden hide.

Inside, the hide was surprisingly cosy with a wooden bench across the length of it, and an aperture that looked out across a stretch of water surrounded by the startlingly white trunks and branches of silver birch trees. Carrie was amazed by the sudden sound that assailed her. Whereas outside the hide, all had been relatively quiet, here in this sheltered spot, well serviced with a variety of feeders, the place was suddenly loud with the song of birds. Yellowhammers and bluetits and chaffinches jostled for space amongst a gang of pushy squirrels and a solitary muntjack deer that had wandered into the enclosure, drawn by the prospect of food.

It felt to Carrie that life was vivid and teeming around her in a way that she had not expected in this desolate place. She sat with her head resting on her hands, elbows propped up on the sill watching the action outside. Oliver saw her face in profile, her hair tied back from her lovely face, and had to control the impulse to reach out and touch the dark curl that rested against her ear.

'Have you seen the medium again? Heard anything more about your boy?' he asked, wanting to say something intimate. Wanting to make her look at him.

'Yes. I've talked to him on the phone since I

saw you last. It freaked me out this time actually. Charlie's messages were different. He seemed to be trying to tell me something . . . '

'You must make sure seeing him isn't going to upset you,' said Oliver.

'I can't stop now. I can't leave him alone again,' said Carrie.

'You don't blame yourself for what happened do you?' asked Oliver.

'I fell asleep. It *was* my fault, I wasn't watching him.'

'You can't watch children every single minute of the day.'

'It was my job,' said Carrie stubbornly.

Oliver looked at her and he saw that she would never give in to what was easiest for her. Her mouth was set tight, her hand brushing her forehead in that endearing way she had as if her thoughts were a nuisance to her, not worth having.

'I lost someone too,' said Oliver. 'It was a long time ago.'

'Who was it?' asked Carrie.

'My brother,' said Oliver, wondering why he was telling this woman he barely knew something he had not spoken about for years.

'What happened?' asked Carrie, unconsciously moving closer towards him.

'We were racing our bikes. There was this hill near where we used to live when we were kids. It was really steep. We would stand at the top and then launch ourselves down. We did it all the time. He was younger than me, but a real daredevil. He wasn't ever scared of anything and he really wanted to beat me, even though his bike wheels were smaller. I was egging him on, I suppose.' Oliver broke off and looked out across the water. Carrie could see that he was finding it difficult to tell her his story.

'There was this bend at the end of the road, you could almost see round it but not quite, so we always used to veer off at the last minute into the side of the road onto a grassy bank before we got to the end. It gave you just enough time to brake. For some reason George didn't that one time. He was beating me. He said he had put some oil on his chain or something . . . he just kept going. There was a car coming the other way. There was no way the driver could stop. George just went hurtling into him.'

'Oh how terrible,' said Carrie, thinking that she would never have imagined that he could look as sad as he did, his fists clenched, his voice just barely under control.

'My parents never blamed me, but I was the older brother. The one meant to be in charge. Afterwards there was always a George-shaped gap, however many holidays we took, however many parties my parents threw to avoid it. Leaving home was a relief because I thought I could leave the gap behind, although you never do, of course . . . '

Oliver stood up as if his words had provoked a desire for flight. Carrie got up too and put out a hand to him, wanting to console him. He looked intently at her and then slowly bent his face, his mouth meeting hers, gently at first, and then harder. Carrie felt a jolt of shock go through her and pulled back, but then felt herself responding to the sensation of his lips, silky and warm against hers. He put his fingers through her hair and held the back of her head steady. Her hands wandered down his back. She could feel herself beating against him. The clamour outside receded. There was only the two of them in the wide, open world. Outside, the muntjack deer skittered off, startled by a sudden noise.

★   ★   ★

Carrie couldn't remember the last time she had so thoroughly lost herself in someone. Possibly not since the far-off days when a half bottle of cider and a slippery-floored church hall had made her wanton with Saturday night lust. It certainly felt like adolescent behaviour. On the way back to the car, Oliver suddenly stopped and pointed at two bitterns flying together, large winged and ungainly against what was left of the pale light.

46

When Carrie arrived at the shop at nine o'clock on Monday morning a large cast had already assembled. It seemed that *Trove* was developing into something of a drop-in centre, and glancing through the window as she locked up her bike, Carrie thought that it looked more like someone's living room than a business. Enif was breakfasting in style from a bone china bowl in the centre of the floor, wearing what looked like some sort of tartan waistcoat. Paul was reclining in the lilac velvet armchair that Carrie had bought despite its scary price tag because she thought it would look great in the corner under the window and would provide somewhere to sit for people while their companions were trying things on. She saw with alarm that he had balanced his takeaway coffee cup on one of its sleek arms. Most worryingly of all she could see Pam wearing a pair of extremely high heels standing on the top of the stepladder, making jabs at the ceiling with a giant pink feather duster. Closing the door firmly against Little Bo Creep who had crept up behind her and was using his crook to get access to the basket of silk, beribboned knickers that had been placed rather unwisely by the entrance, Carrie looked around and spotted Jen who was sitting on the floor by the till in the midst of a sea of pink and cream tissue paper.

310

'Good morning, Carrie,' said Jen, ignoring Carrie's somewhat aggressive stare. 'I'm working on a new window display. It's going to have a wedding theme.'

'You might have consulted me. It's hardly the time of year for . . .' started Carrie crossly, but then seeing her friend's stricken face, she relented. 'Well, since it's fast becoming your specialist subject . . . What are *you* doing here, Mum?'

Pam turned a bright face to her daughter and shook her feather duster, which moulted a cloud of feathers. 'A spot of spring cleaning, darling,' she said, 'this place is going to wrack and ruin.'

★　★　★

After Enif and Paul had been despatched to hunt rabbits and stars and Carrie had sent her reluctant mother upstairs to do a stock check, Carrie and Jen spent the morning making the shop window look like wedding heaven. Jen had found a vintage dress on eBay in a soft, champagne-coloured brocade with a boat neckline and sparkling rhinestones round a full skirt and although it was too small to wear herself, she had decided it would make the perfect focus for a display and a cheery antidote to midwinter blues. The gown was pulled onto Dolly, the long-suffering shop dummy, who had resigned herself to a life of being mistreated by Jen. Dolly's feet were encased in a pair of satin ballet pumps and she was dragged from the ground to stand in splendour on the raised platform. The

311

floor around the dummy's feet was littered with the cream and pink paper roses that Jen had made and Carrie cut outsized confetti shapes from paper doilies and stuck them all over the window. While they worked Carrie told Jen a little of what had happened between her and Oliver.

'You really like him. Don't you?' said Jen.

'I think he's attractive. I'm just not sure he's relationship material. Maybe I don't really want a relationship. I don't know.'

'I'd be careful if I were you,' said Jen. 'You really need to look after yourself just now. After Damian and all this business with the medium and stuff, I'm just not sure you should be starting something with someone who lures people into sheds then seduces them.'

'It was a hide, not a shed.'

'Same difference,' said Jen, 'sounds furtive to me.' And she stood on tiptoe to fix a little headpiece trimmed with a short net veil onto Dolly's improbably blonde hair.

The two women went outside to look at the finished product through the window.

'Very pretty,' said Carrie. 'The dress could do with straightening out a bit.'

Jen looked at her friend who was standing on one side of the window and then the other and squinting critically through the glass, and felt a warm rush of affection and admiration for her. Carrie was so beautiful and so stoical and Jen hoped that something good would happen for her soon. She herself felt so full of happiness and gratitude that she wanted her friend to be equally blessed.

'What do you feel about what the medium said?' asked Jen. She still believed that Simon Foster had somehow found out the information he needed to make his story convincing and had used a potent mix of theatrics, intuition and a sophisticated understanding of behaviour to find the words that Carrie wanted to hear. It wouldn't have taken much, surely, for someone skilled in the mechanics of sadness to use the dropped clues, the small unconscious admissions to their own advantage. Nothing would convince her that Charlie could talk from beyond the grave, but she had supported Carrie throughout and would support her in this, even though she couldn't understand it.

'Hearing that he had drowned tore me up, but there was a part of me that felt something had been released in me, like the cork from a bottle. These later messages are much worse to listen to. I can't bear to think of him suffering.'

'But he's not suffering now,' said Jen. 'He can't be. I don't think you should listen to Simon Foster any more.'

'I can't just leave it though. I can't,' said Carrie. 'I can't turn my back on him. This is truly the last of him. I feel him slipping away.'

As they went back into the shop, Carrie's phone started ringing. Carrie listened for a minute and then rang off, her face white.

'What's happened?' asked Jen.

'Simon wants to see me,' said Carrie. 'Charlie has been sending some more messages.'

* * *

Pam, who had given up stocktaking and was sitting on an unopened box having a cup of tea, insisted that she go with her daughter. The taxi arrived almost immediately and fifteen minutes later, they were standing outside Simon's flat.

'The windows could do with a clean,' muttered Pam, eyeing them disapprovingly, and Carrie rang on the bell.

Simon opened the door looking as if he hadn't slept for a week. His pale eyes were shot through with veins, his shoulders were stooped, the lines on his face deeper than ever. Carrie noticed with alarm that even his usually immaculate clothes bore signs of neglect. His collar was dirty, his trousers stained. In the living room too there were signs of disturbance. The books had been turned over and there was just the faintest odour of food, some vegetable matter that had been left out too long that was now on the turn.

'I'm sorry about the mess,' said Simon, pushing some papers off the sofa to make room for them. 'I haven't been very well.'

'Are you well enough to see us?' asked Carrie. Something about the slightly-too-careful way that he was moving made Carrie think that he might have been drinking.

'I needed to see you,' he said. 'I think he won't ever leave me alone unless I can get you to understand what it is he is saying. The trouble is I don't really understand it myself.'

Simon passed an unsteady hand back and

forth across the top of his head as if to comfort himself.

'His messages have become more and more frantic. He often shouts, and yesterday I actually think I saw him flash across the corner of my vision. It was quick, as if he was trying to jump.'

Carrie felt saliva gather in her mouth as if she might be sick.

'What is he saying?' asked Pam.

'He talked about darkness and danger from a man. He started on again about not being able to breathe. A mother being hurt. The smell of water rising. Then he kept repeating *tell her, tell her, tell her she has to save Max.*'

Simon got up, bent over Carrie and touched her on the hand. She could smell alcohol on his breath and she looked up into his washed-out eyes.

'He told me to tell you he loves you every single day,' said Simon, and Carrie felt her heart contract as if it had been punched.

'Why is he talking about Max?' asked Carrie.

'I don't know,' said Simon sitting back down. The reporting of the messages seemed to offer him some relief. He rested his head against the back of his chair and shut his eyes.

★ ★ ★

'You look terrible. You need a stiff drink,' Pam said, bossily taking Carrie's arm and almost pushing her through the door of the first pub they came to. They drank several glasses of red wine, and were both quite drunk by the time they resumed their walk home. Pam got the heel of one of her teetering shoes stuck in a drain and broke it.

'Oh bloody hell,' she said, trying without success to reattach it.

'Marilyn Monroe did it on purpose,' said Pam as she almost turned her ankle trying to negotiate the edge of the pavement. 'She chopped a bit off the heel of one of her shoes. It's what gave her that famous sexy wiggle.'

'Why don't you just pull the other one off and even yourself out?' said Carrie.

'I'm getting this heel repaired and I'm not paying to have both of them fixed when I only broke one,' said Pam indignantly.

Carrie needed all her concentration to work out where the lampposts were positioned. The message from Charlie had hit her hard. She remembered all too clearly what her last words to her son had been. They were words that they had often said to each other, a kind of incantation to ward off evil. She felt absolutely exhausted, as if she no longer had the strength to feel anything at all. She imagined her body finally giving up under the pressure and crumpling like those pictures of cars that have driven into lorries, when you can't believe anyone has got out alive because there isn't anything recognisable left in the concertinaed metal.

★ ★ ★

When she got home Pam made her a cup of coffee and Carrie went to the drawer in her room where she had put the last photos of Charlie from her old camera. She lay down on her bed and curled her body around a pillow. She felt she needed to be careful with herself if she was to avoid further harm. The images tore at her all over again. She hated above all the fact that already they had begun to seem out of date. It wouldn't be long before someone would look at Charlie's hair, the style of his shorts, even the quality of the colour in the images and think of them as old, just as she did when she flipped through pictures in antique shops; piers that had long ago melted into the sea, family groups lined up outside shuttered shop frontages, children wearing strange-shaped collars and stilted smiles.

The last photograph in the pack was the one with Max in it. She had a sudden image of running up to him that day in the midst of her terror and asking him if he had seen Charlie. Was there some particular significance in this moment that she had failed to register because she had been in such mortal terror? In the photograph he was sitting on a towel looking straight at the camera with Charlie in the foreground. Because he wasn't at the centre of the picture, his face was a little out of focus, but it was still clear enough. Right at the edge of the photograph was Molly, her hair held back by a scarf tied into a bow, her face in profile. She was opening a picnic basket or a beach bag. Max had very distinctive, almond-shaped eyes and ears that stood enough away from the side of his head for other children to have surely drawn attention to them. Children had an unerring ability to seek

317

out the soft, unprotected spots of others. That was how children survived; their mothers opened up their softest spots and let them settle in there, recklessly heedless of the pain they knew would follow as a result of making themselves so vulnerable. He looked anxious. He certainly didn't have the face of a carefree child. She thought of the way he had stood so still in the shop, allowing her to hold him, as if he knew that it was comforting her. She felt a great, unexpected surge of anger against Charlie. She was shocked by the strength of the feeling that engulfed her. He had broken her heart and devastated her life and now he was tormenting her with messages she didn't understand. The dead were supposed to send messages of comfort to the living weren't they? Not cryptic warnings about children she hardly knew. Her anger gave her some respite from hearing the sound of his voice, and with the photographs still littered around her and with tears drying on her face, Carrie fell asleep. Pam, tiptoeing in a short while later, covered her with the duvet and drew the bedroom curtains.

★ ★ ★

Carrie dreamed she was back on the beach. She was making the walk out towards the horizon but this time she was alone. Everything else was as it had been. The sun containing within its tentative warmth a warning of incoming clouds, the sand giving slightly as she walked, emptying itself of moisture under the weight so that each footstep left a ghost of itself. When she came to the edge of the sea where the water sucked in and out, she rolled up her trousers and went in. Just ahead of her a child in yellow shorts was floating face down, moving slowly, rocked by the gentle rise and fall of the waves. Carrie ran towards him, but although she was soon up to her waist, she wasn't any closer. He drifted just out of her reach. She could feel the tug of the water, could sense its dangerous lure and she allowed herself to be taken, until she too was as light as flotsam on the waves. She floated out until she reached him and to her immense joy she could feel that he was alive. The pulse was leaping in his narrow neck and when she held him close she could feel his heart pumping. She used all her strength to pull him back to the shore, holding him around his neck and swimming beneath him and eventually arrived, gasping on the sand. When she turned towards him she saw Max lying looking at her.

47

Carrie woke in the late afternoon with a raging thirst and a throbbing headache. She went downstairs, poured herself a large glass of orange juice and drank it standing up, looking out of the patio doors. She watched a neighbour's cat walk across the lawn and then start to dig with delicate paws in a patch of earth. Carrie knocked half-heartedly on the glass door and the cat gave her a startled yellow-eyed stare and then made off back through the hole in the fence. A bit of cat crap would really make very little difference she reflected, since the garden was such a mess. The work she had done on it only seemed to have made it look worse and there were still plant pots full of rotting geraniums and the matted clumps of dead lobelia that she had yet to tackle. The flowerbeds too were in dire need of clearing and digging over. The whole place had an air of sodden neglect despite the silver light and the delicate strands of pink in the sky. She could see the place by the rhododendron bush where they had all stood one rainy afternoon and had a funeral for Bun the hamster. Charlie had wept great fat tears and wrung his hands while Damian had buried the creature in a rice box, but she had felt a great sense of release. The animal had been nothing but a source of guilt to Carrie. Whilst they sat around reading the papers and eating bacon sandwiches or watching TV, Bun had spent his miserable days and nights going round and round on his wheel, his horrible tiny claws clutching at the plastic.

Carrie felt suddenly lonely, unable to spend even another minute by herself, brooding about dead hamsters and Charlie and the messages. The house seemed to be closing in on her. She went upstairs, changed into clean jeans and a pale blue loose shirt tied around the neck in a big bow and ballet pumps in almost the same colour. She pulled on her coat, grabbed a bottle of wine from the rack in the kitchen and before she could change her mind, crossed over the street to Oliver's house and knocked on the front door. He came to the door barefooted, his shirt untucked.

'I'm not disturbing you am I?' asked Carrie waving the bottle of wine at him.

'Not at all, come in. I was just pretending to do some work,' said Oliver, smiling broadly and ushering her into his front room. He closed the laptop on his desk and turned on a lamp on a side table.

'You were working,' Carrie said. 'Please tell me if you would rather I came another time.'

'I'm honestly glad for the distraction,' said Oliver, taking her coat and sitting her down on a comfortable, cushion-littered sofa.

'I'll just open this and get us some glasses,' said Oliver leaving her to look around the room. Carrie hadn't seen the place in its usual state, only as it had been when cleared for the infamous Christmas party. An event that was still talked about on Almond Street in hushed tones. It seemed that an uneasy rapprochement had occurred between the Roses and the Foxtons. In fact, rumours were rife that there had been a spot of seventies-style wife swapping, but Carrie had trouble imagining any of them having sex at all, least of all putting their differences aside for long enough to muster up the necessary energy. She suspected the rumour had been started by Mrs Evans, who not only liked to indulge in gloomy, end of the world predictions mostly involving natural disasters and mass contagions, but she also had a somewhat prurient mind. Carrie determinedly put all thoughts of her neighbours' sex lives out of her mind and looked around her. The room was surprisingly cosy, with pictures and photographs on all the walls and bright rugs spread out on the wooden floor. There was a group of sculptures of birds on the windowsill, a vase of yellow roses on the coffee table and a great bowl of stones of all shapes and sizes on the desk. She had been expecting the rather more neglected home of the typical single man, with a focus on gadgets and ease of access to the fridge rather than this place, that looked as if a lot of thought had gone into the arrangement of it. Carrie wondered whether the room had been decorated by one of Oliver's ex-girlfriends, although it seemed unlikely that he had allowed one to remain in post long enough for her to pick out the soft furnishings. Oliver came back into the room and handed her a glass of wine.

'This is a beautiful room,' said Carrie.

'Thanks,' said Oliver, sitting down next to her

on the sofa. 'It was a bit of a mess when I moved in, but I enjoyed decorating it and making it nice. This is my first proper home and it was great to be able to get all my things out of storage and put them out.'

'Where were you living before?' asked Carrie.

'All over the place. I lived in America for quite a long time and then in London and then Italy and Spain. Wherever the work or my whim took me really,' said Oliver. 'Are you OK, Carrie?' he asked, looking at the bluish shadows under her eyes.

Instead of answering she looked at him and then put her mouth against his. She kissed him hard, opening his lips with her tongue, and then moved her hands under his loosened shirt feeling his smooth chest, his heart beating fast under her hands. She unbuttoned her shirt, pulled her bra aside and put his hand on her breast. He ran his flattened palm against her and she felt the pulse between her legs throb in response. She moved her hands down his thighs and then lower, and felt him straining against the fabric of his trousers. She heard his swift intake of breath when she unzipped his fly and put her hand inside. He ran the tip of his tongue down her neck, lapping gently at the little hollow in her throat. She released him from his trousers and stroked him, feeling him jerk under her hand. She was in a hurry now and pushed him back on the sofa, pulling his trousers down and straddling him. She bent and allowed her mouth to just graze, then lightly lick the end of his penis and she felt his body bucking beneath her as he positioned himself closer to her mouth. She wanted the forgetting that came with pure sensation. She wanted to stop feeling anything other than this obliterating passion. Almost at the point of no return, Oliver took hold of her hands and stilled her.

'Is this what you want, Carrie?' he asked gently, his eyes wide with desire, his breathing ragged. Although the last of his control was ebbing away he was nevertheless troubled by her sudden urgency and the speed with which they had got here. Her reply was to crush her mouth against his again and this time there was no stopping either of them. There was the inevitable negotiating of clothes, the awkwardness of being on a sofa that was too small to hold both of them, the not knowing which way their bodies fitted best, the giggling struggle out of jeans and fastenings, but above all that was the strength of the desire that ran through them, carrying them along as they moved together.

★ ★ ★

Afterwards, Oliver held Carrie as she cried and told him about Charlie's last words. He stroked her hair and then took her upstairs and wrapped her in his bed where they both slept a little and then woke to each other again, going slower this time and trying to find those places that made them melt, or cry out, or forget again what it was they had been thinking. Much later, Oliver put on a comedy underwear apron and she was relieved to see there was at least something in his

324

house that was as naff as she had expected it to be. He cooked her bacon and baked beans and fried bread and brought it to her on a large tray.

'You really are the most beautiful woman I have ever seen,' said Oliver leaning back in the bed and watching her eat the food as if she had never eaten before. He loved the fact she was sitting unselfconsciously bare breasted, the light from the bedside lamp shining on her skin and the curve of her neck.

'And you are as handsome as you think you are,' said Carrie tartly. She wasn't going to tell him that no man had the right to look as good as he did whilst wearing nothing but his slippers and an unsavoury apron. After scraping her plate clean, she took his apron off and he pretended to explore her body for crumbs and they fell asleep again with their legs twisted together under the sheet.

★   ★   ★

Carrie woke the second time with the same unease that she had felt the day before when she had first heard Simon's most recent message from Charlie. A memory of Max's face came to her with his sweet, grave eyes. 'Charlie is my friend,' he'd said. Oliver was still asleep, so she slipped quietly out of the bed without waking him and went back across the road to her own house. She tried not to visualise the other women she had seen treading this same path from his house. It was her turn to get to the shop early so she only had time to splash water on her face and brush her teeth before getting on her bike. Despite repeated attempts to get it fixed, the wretched thing was permanently stuck in third gear and so by the time she arrived she was panting with the effort of getting over the railway bridge.

She unlocked the door and turned off the alarm and then set about giving the place a vigorous sweep and polish. She wanted to keep as busy as possible so that she didn't have a chance to think too much about what she was feeling. Half an hour later the shop was gleaming, she had been out to buy milk and get change for the till but she still felt no respite from her thoughts. Charlie had liked Max, had felt a sense of kinship. What was it the other boy had disliked? Bats? Charlie had fluctuated between repugnance and fascination for the creatures, once even making her take his book with pictures of a bat colony outside the house and hide it where he couldn't find it. On impulse, Carrie went behind the till counter and pulled out a pile of paper that she had stowed there. She found the card that Molly had left at the shop with her contact details, and rang the number. The phone rang for ten rings and then went to voicemail. Feeling slightly foolish, Carrie left a message.

'It's Carrie Hudson here. From the shop . . . I'm ringing about your paintings. Wanted a quick chat. Could you ring me back as soon as you can? Thanks.'

Just then the door banged open, startling Carrie, and Jen burst in over the threshold in her usual noisy way. She slung her coat over the counter and started to unwrap what might possibly have been part of a hessian sack from around her neck. She fixed Carrie with one of her beady looks.

'You've slept with him. Haven't you?' said Jen. She had a disconcerting sixth sense for sex, although Carrie probably thought the evidence of lack of sleep around her eyes and a certain dishevelment in her attire were probably pretty big clues.

'I may have done,' said Carrie and went into the back to put the kettle on and to get away from Jen's scrutiny. Jen followed her out.

'I hope you know what you're doing,' she said sounding genuinely worried. 'I don't think you are particularly strong at the moment and I'm not sure Oliver is what you need.'

'I don't know what I need,' said Carrie. 'I just want to stop feeling this way all the time.'

She told Jen about her last visit to Simon's flat while her friend made them both tea.

'What do you think I should do about it?' asked Carrie. 'If I believe it is Charlie speaking to me, which I do, then I have to believe that what he is trying to tell me is the truth. He wants me to help.'

'What about going to the police?' said Jen.

'And tell them what? That my dead son has told me that someone he once saw on a beach is in danger?'

'Hmm . . . yes. It's not exactly going to make them leap into action.'

'I've got their address, the people on the

beach. Remember they came in here with her paintings?' said Carrie.

'Oh, yes,' said Jen, 'I was actually going to get in touch with her today because I sold one of them. The one of the man in the field.'

'Parson's Bridge, near Ely . . . don't think I know it, but I could Google it.'

'You are not thinking of going to the house are you?' said Jen.

'I might go this afternoon,' said Carrie.

'Don't go on your own,' said Jen.

'It'll be fine. They'll probably be there at the house, safe and sound. I'll feel stupid and have to make up a story about wanting to see more of her paintings or something, which if they are selling might be a good idea anyway.'

'Promise me you won't go haring off across the Fens by yourself,' said Jen. 'At least get that Oliver to go with you.'

48

After Rupert left, Max became hysterical about the eel. Cowering away, he demanded that Molly get rid of it. She tried to explain that there was nowhere to put it, no window she could get open to throw it out of, but then driven mad by his terrified entreaties, she hid it away as best she could under a loose stone, although she took the precaution of wrapping it up in a torn-off bit of plastic sheeting that she found under one of the drums. She thought that if they had to suffer another day of this, they might have to eat it. She knew Max was very hungry although he had stopped asking for food since last night.

Molly had wrapped the rest of the sheeting around Max and held him across her body all night, sharing as much of her warmth with him as she could, although she was chilled to the bone herself. At around dawn his cough became much worse and he started shivering and then claiming to be burning hot. He tried at one point to get out of the sheeting, but she held him fast, giving him the occasional drink from the bottle top, trickling it carefully through his dry lips. Pressing into her side was the rusty scythe that she had found under the sheeting and which she had attached around her waist under her shirt with a torn-off length of the plastic. There were a few other bits of old farming equipment, but nothing else that would serve as a weapon.

Her body ached. She had barely slept at all since the beginning of their imprisonment two days ago, and hadn't drunk any of the water in order to conserve as much as possible of it for Max. She strained her ears for any sound, but all she could hear was the sound of rain on a metal or plastic roof somewhere nearby. The noise reminded her of being in the caravan as a child. Her and her sister, endlessly playing cards while they holed up on some lay-by waiting for the rain to stop while her father fiddled with the radio trying to get a weather forecast and her mother made the best of things. She felt a sweep of longing so hard and childish that she cried out, causing Max to shift restlessly in his sleep. She would have given anything in that moment just to have her mother with her. She thought of the way she used to comb out her hair, teasing gently at the knots, endlessly patient with her wriggling complaints, and then brushing and brushing it until it shone.

'It's not your crowning glory, Molly,' she said once. 'You always say that about girls with nothing else special about them. But you have so many special things about you.'

She had been a bold girl, afraid of very little, keen to prove herself and to take on challenges. Once she had walked the whole length of a narrow log over a fast moving river just because her sister had told her sneeringly that she couldn't do it. She could still feel the sway of it under her feet and the dizzy rush of water and the taste of delight as she jumped clear onto the bank. She didn't know how she had become the person she was now. Couldn't remember any more when she had last felt that supple strength that used to come so naturally to her. She thought that maybe Rupert had seen that leaping self in her and had wanted to stop it in its tracks, to cut it off in case it jumped too high.

49

As she cycled back to her house, Carrie became more and more convinced that she was doing the right thing. The sense of unease and urgency that she had experienced earlier in the day had been replaced by resolve. She *had* to act on Charlie's words. He was frightened about something that was happening and she had to do all she could to take that fear away.

Through the clouded window of the swimming pool she could see strings of bunting and children lined up at the edge waiting to start a race. Fingers plucked the bottoms of their swimsuits, pale legs swung across the tiled floor. On Mill Road a crocodile of small children still unselfconscious enough to walk hand in hand meandered down the pavement, led by a stressed-looking young woman with a rucksack. She could still see his absence everywhere.

As she passed his house, Carrie saw Oliver moving around in his front room and so she stopped, rested her bike against his wall and knocked on the door. He came to the door quickly and she was obscurely pleased to see that he didn't look his usual groomed self. It was clear that their night together had made enough of an impact on him to stop him dwelling too much on his ravishing good looks.

'Where did you get to this morning?' he asked.

'I was all prepared to get you fried breakfast number two.'

'I'm sorry to have crept off like that,' said Carrie. 'I had to get to the shop early and I didn't want to disturb you.'

'You can disturb me any time you want,' said Oliver pulling her inside and kissing her. She felt herself responding to him straight away, feeling a flare of desire as soon as he touched her. He put his hand inside the neck of her shirt and rubbed her shoulder with his thumb, but Carrie pulled away.

'I can't stay,' said Carrie. 'There's something I've got to do, and I was wondering if you would help.' Carrie stopped because she noticed a pale-coloured silk slip hanging over the arm of the sofa, an item that definitely hadn't been there that morning. Looking around the room, she also saw a pair of black court shoes under one of the chairs.

'Although, on second thoughts, it doesn't look as if it's terribly convenient,' snapped Carrie and turned and walked to the front door.

'What was it you wanted me to do?' asked Oliver, surprised at the sudden sharpness of her tone.

'It doesn't matter,' said Carrie. 'I'm fine on my own,' and she opened the door and went out, shutting it firmly behind her. She knew that she shouldn't have allowed him to get as close as he had to her. The man was clearly incapable of keeping his dick in his trousers for longer than ten minutes. She was angry with herself for not trusting her first instincts about him. She didn't know what was wrong with him, but she didn't want to hang around to find out.

★ ★ ★

A quick search on her computer established the exact location of the house and she only tarried for as long as it took to swap her pumps for some boots and to put her anorak, the map and a torch in the boot of her car. Carrie got out of town as quickly as possible, and it was only when she was on the road to Ely that she allowed herself to think at all about what she was doing. She wasn't sure what it was she expected to find at Max and Molly's house, but it was the only lead she had and therefore the only thing she could do to try and work out what it was that Charlie was telling her. The sky was overcast and threatening rain and there was a strong wind picking up. Crows swirled over the fields or settled briefly in trees that had been shaped by their exposure to the elements into mean, hunched things. Her phone rang in her handbag, startling her, causing her to veer slightly into the side of the road and setting off an involuntary tingle up her arms. She passed the cathedral in the distance, its stately bulk anchored firmly to the horizon, and then turned right along a narrow road edged with hedging to one side and a channel of water on the other. She passed the odd house and some farm buildings and then, about four miles up the road, came to a cluster of houses. The area code for Molly and Max's house had indicated that it was just beyond this little hamlet, and so Carrie passed through Parson's Bridge and continued up a bumpy road for a further half a mile or so. She disliked driving this close to the ditch of water, and noted that since the light was already fading and with no lights other than her headlamps, she would need to be careful on her return journey.

She pulled up outside the house. It had to be this one, since there were no others near it. It was the time of day when lights would be on if there was anyone in. The house sat low in the landscape, its dark windows small, an overgrown yew tree partly blocking the front path. The place seemed deserted and Carrie felt a sudden jolt of dread. For the first time she wondered about the wisdom of coming here alone. Maybe she was too late. Maybe whatever dreadful thing Charlie said was going to happen, had already happened. She tried to remember exactly what it was he had said, but the words had been confused. She got out of the car, opened the boot and put on her anorak and took hold of her torch, which felt reassuringly heavy in her hand. She shivered as the wind cut through her, its strength allowed full rein in this unsheltered spot. She knew it was probably pointless, but she knocked on the door anyway and then pushed against it in case it had been left open. She peered in the front window, and by cupping her hands against the glass could see the living room with a fireplace that looked as if it had been used fairly recently, and some toys and books on the carpet. There didn't seem to be anything out of the ordinary. She went round to the back garden where there was some mouldy garden furniture and a balding Christmas tree leaning up against the wall. Carrie noticed that one of the windows had been left slightly ajar and, putting her hand inside to release the catch, Carrie opened it wide. She scrambled over the windowsill and the sink that was immediately below and landed hard on the floor. She shone the torch around the room, located the light switch and clicked it on to reveal a kitchen that had clearly been abandoned hastily. There were unwashed dishes on the side and some food in a pan on the cooker. The house felt cold and smelt musty, but it didn't feel as if it had been empty for any length of time. She went out into the hallway and, despite feeling foolish, felt compelled to call out.

'Molly? Max?'

Her words echoed round the empty house, and again she had that sense of prickling dread. There was a sudden noise from above and she switched her torch on, the beam picking out a pair of cat's eyes staring at her from the top of the stairs. Carrie started up the stairs and the cat disappeared with a low whimpering mew. She felt around the wall of the first room and switched on the light to reveal what was clearly a boy's room. A half-finished Lego model stood on the desk and there was a line of small cars crossing the carpet. The bed with its *SpongeBob* duvet had been made, but then disturbed, the corner of the duvet pulled back. It was instinct that made Carrie reach under the pillow and feel around. This was where Charlie used to leave messages for her. Unable yet to write anything but his name and very basic sentences, he often used to draw pictures as a way of explaining to her how he was feeling. She had kept many of his drawings of smiling Charlie and snarling Charlie and Charlie with teardrops as big as pears sliding down his face. Carrie found a small piece of folded paper under the pillow. She opened it up and read the hastily scrawled words.

My Dad is taking us. He hurt my Mum. Please help us. Max

Carrie let herself out of the house through the front door and got into her car. She rang the police straight away, worried that ringing 999 might not be appropriate, and yet not knowing what else to do. She spent some time explaining what had happened and then was passed to another person and had to explain the same information all over again.

'I really think something needs to be done now. I think it's urgent,' said Carrie, trying to communicate her unease to the police officer, who seemed to be more concerned with establishing her exact relationship with the people who lived at the address she had given him than providing her with the reassurance she was looking for. It was not surprising that the copper was confused; she would be too if someone rang up and told her they were following a hunch that had come via a message from a medium.

'We are aware of a potential situation at that address already, Mrs Hudson,' said the third police person she was put through to. 'We have already received a report of two missing persons from a neighbour of Mrs Reardon's. The matter's in hand.'

Carrie agreed to come into the station on her return to Cambridge. Still feeling anxious, but unable to think what she could usefully do, she set off back. The night had fallen suddenly and she had to use all her concentration to navigate the narrow road, the rain having made the surface of the road even muddier than it had been on the way there. Her tyres were sliding perilously near the edge of the water. Some movement on the periphery of her vision made her look in her rear view mirror. She caught a glimpse of a man standing quite still in the middle of the road, staring ahead, and then her car moved forward and the road went dark and she could no longer see anything at all.

50

It was around midday when Molly heard him arrive. He looked more unkempt than he had done before. The bottoms of his trousers were muddy and he had taken off his hat to reveal long dirty hair. He smelt of wet fur and damp earth. She wouldn't have recognised him now as her husband, as anyone she had ever known. He had become utterly alien to her now, another species. Max stared wide-eyed at his father. His breathing was laboured and he was too weak to do anything other than stay lying across her.

'Rupert, we are losing him. Do what you like to me, but please, let him go.' Molly gently pushed Max aside and got up. It took all of her strength not to reveal her fear to him.

'Please. Just open the door.' She approached Rupert as she would a wild creature. She moved slowly and then took hold of his arm in entreaty, but he shrugged her off and went towards Max. The boy looked at him, unmoving.

'We threw the eel away,' said Max, 'but I can still smell it.'

Rupert bent down and picked the boy up. He walked over to one of the large tanks in the centre of the room and opened the hinged door. Molly lunged at him, attaching herself to his back, digging her hands into his neck and biting him as hard as she could. Rupert barely acknowledged the pain. Batting her off, he slid an unresisting Max inside the drum and shut the door.

'No. Rupert no! He won't be able to breathe.' Molly screamed in panic, feeling what was left of her control slipping away.

Molly clutched him around the bottoms of his legs, trying to get the scythe from under her shirt, wrestling with the fastening. She couldn't get it free. He grabbed a handful of her hair and pulled her towards the other drum. Molly fought hard, feeling a great clump of her hair rip itself from her scalp as he dragged her along. He opened the second drum and began to push her into it. Molly held on to the metal rim resisting his attempts to put her inside. She kicked out towards him, making enough contact with his stomach to cause him to move back, winded, but it was as if he was oblivious to all obstacles. His eyes were blank. He felt as immovable as the flank of a large mammal. It was as if the man had gone and been replaced by this implacable being. All of him had become terrifyingly focused in this fierce, blind strength. He pushed her inside and then everything went black as the heavy metal door shut and she heard the metal slot slip into place. For a moment she panicked, feeling the space tight around her, her legs bent slightly against the end of the barrel. Time moved slowly and she could feel her breath ragged in the back of her throat. This is the last thing I'm going to feel, before I die, she thought, and then Max, oh Max. She turned her head and saw a series of holes the size of small coins at the side of the metal drum, through which came the faint traces of light. She put her mouth to the holes, breathing as if she had just surfaced from water.

'Max!' shouted Molly through the holes. 'Max, breathe through the holes. Breathe, Max.'

She stopped moving to listen, but there was no response and so she shouted again. She wriggled round onto her other side and managed this time to tear at the plastic ribbon holding the scythe in place. She knocked the wooden handle of the tool as hard as she could against the top of the drum. She stopped and listened, but there was still no response so she knocked again. Her body was icy cold and she was weeping uncontrollably, but she kept banging on the ceiling of her circular prison. She stopped again and listened. With a great leap of joy, she could just make out a gentle tapping noise coming from Max's direction.

51

At the police station Carrie got the impression they didn't quite know what to make of her story. They asked her again and again how it was that she had ended up in that place if it was true that she really didn't know Molly and Max, other than the brief sighting she had had of them on a beach three years ago, and one recent conversation with them in her shop. Every time she repeated her story it felt more ludicrous. The policeman who had been there the day she and Damian had looked at those terrible photographs was kind, going out to get her a cup of tea, hot and sweet and in a proper mug. She wondered where he was now, that child in the photographs, and whether he had found his way home. The world seemed to be full of lost children and Carrie felt a sudden sharp grief for all of them. For her Charlie, and this boy Max, and that other boy with his tight little fists.

★ ★ ★

When Carrie finally got back to her house, she found the place cold and cheerless and she shivered as she put on the heating and closed the curtains. Although she knew that there was nothing else she could do she still felt restless. She thought about ringing Simon to find out if Charlie had come through to him again, but changed her mind. The police had been given all the information available to her and it was up to them now to find out what had happened to Molly and Max. She had done her bit. Her stomach growled. She tried to remember the last time she had eaten and realised that it was probably the midnight breakfast that Oliver had made for her. Despite what had happened this morning, she felt a wave of longing for him. He might be a bastard, but he knew how to make the world go away and she could certainly do with a bit of that at the moment. She put some slices of cheese on toast under the grill and more for form's sake than any real desire, chopped up a green pepper with some cucumber and a splash of olive oil. She ate her hastily prepared meal in front of *EastEnders* and then went upstairs to run herself a bath.

* * *

She was lying in a bath of fast-cooling water, too tired to get herself out, when she heard the doorbell. She got out hastily, pulling her dressing gown on without drying herself, and dripped all the way down the stairs. Oliver was standing on the doorstep.

'Hello Carrie, can I come in?' he asked.

Carrie hesitated. 'I'm really tired, Oliver,' she said. 'I've had a bit of a day . . . '

'Please. I want to know why you left my house so suddenly,' he said.

'Are you telling me you really don't know?'

said Carrie, reluctantly, opening the door wider to let him in.

'I have an idea,' said Oliver. 'But that's what I want to talk about.'

Carrie led him into the front room and rather ungraciously offered him a drink.

'A glass of wine would be great,' he said, sitting down on the revamped sofa.

Carrie poured two glasses and then went to sit away from him on the armchair by the fireplace. She didn't bother to light the fire. She didn't want him to think that she was in any way interested in having him stay longer than absolutely necessary. She would hear what the lying scumbag had to say and then he could go.

'I expect you saw the clothes around the house and jumped to a conclusion,' said Oliver.

'Yes. The conclusion that four hours after I had left your bed this morning, another woman came round and took her very expensive slip off in your front room,' said Carrie, wishing she hadn't mentioned that she thought the slip looked expensive. It suggested too close a scrutiny of the offending object. 'And then followed that by discarding her fairly sluttish heels on your floor,' she went on.

'I can see how it must have looked,' said Olive. 'But I didn't sleep with her.'

'Right. So what *did* you do with her?' asked Carrie. 'A spot of wrestling? Some gardening perhaps?'

'Jasmine is an ex-girlfriend. She has a rather . . . chaotic life, sometimes she ends up at my house, sleeping it off; in this case not in her

344

underwear but in some pyjamas I lent her.'

'What's the longest relationship you've had with anyone?' asked Carrie.

Oliver took a sip of his wine and looked away from Carrie.

'My life hasn't exactly been conducive to long-term relationships,' he said. 'I've travelled a lot. Not really met anyone I wanted to stick with or who wanted to stick with me.'

'What would make you want to stick with someone?' asked Carrie.

'I don't know. I think I'll know it when I see it. Maybe,' said Oliver.

Carrie went over to sit beside him.

'I just can't afford to start something that's going to hurt me, Oliver. I haven't got the strength. I want something right and good. Something sustaining,' she said, feeling the pull of him despite herself and the careful way she was sitting apart from him.

'I don't think I fit the job description,' said Oliver. 'In my parents' house George's room is still exactly as it was the day he left it. I mean every detail, down to the clothes on the bed, his scuffed shoes on the carpet. He is still the bit of them that they thought the most precious. I did that to them. I don't mean to, but I cause harm.'

'I don't know your parents,' said Carrie. 'But I would lay money that they don't think the way you are describing.'

'I don't know,' said Oliver. 'I just know I can never make it better for them.'

'It's not your job to make it better for them. They have to find a way of doing that for themselves,' said Carrie.

'I like you, Carrie,' said Oliver. '*Really* like you. I'd like us to be together, but I can't tell you it will work out. My track record isn't exactly impressive.'

Carrie looked at him for a moment. She wanted to throw herself into his arms and allow herself to be carried upstairs to bed, but she knew that being with Oliver would open her up to the possibility of more pain and she didn't think she was equipped to deal with it.

'I can't,' said Carrie. 'I can't take the chance.' Carrie put her glass on the floor and stood up.

'I'm sorry, Oliver,' she said, and was surprised by the regret she saw in his face.

As he left, Oliver stroked her cheek with one finger. Afterwards as she lay in bed, she thought she could still feel where he had touched her.

52

Carrie woke the next morning to see Pam standing at the end of her bed, surveying her. Her mother pulled open the curtains to reveal a bright blue sky and roofs iced with frost, then settled herself on the end of the bed.

'You sleep on your side with your arms stretched out,' Pam said. 'That means you are what sleep specialists call a yearner, someone with an open nature but who is prone to suspicion.'

'I yearn to be left alone by my mother,' said Carrie, rolling over and burying her face in her pillow.

'Listen Carrie, Simon's downstairs. He's had another message. I think you should come down,' said Pam, stroking her daughter's head and getting to her feet. Carrie felt a sinking sense of dread. This thing wasn't going to leave her alone after all. Still half asleep, she got up and followed her mother downstairs.

Simon was sitting at the kitchen table with a cup of tea. Carrie noted that Pam can hardly have been in a hurry to come upstairs to wake her if she had taken the time to make him a drink. Her suspicions about her mother's intentions were confirmed when she saw Pam put an almost proprietorial hand on the back of the chair Simon was sitting on. He looked up as she came into the room.

'I hope you don't mind me coming here,' he said.

He looked less unkempt than he had when they had last seen him, as if he had made a special effort to look respectable before leaving the house. He was freshly shaved and had a small bloodied nick on his chin. She wondered how he had found out where she lived, but Pam answered her unspoken question.

'I answered your mobile this morning when you were still asleep. I saw it was from Simon and I thought it might be important,' said Pam. 'He said he had something more from Charlie.'

Carrie sat down at the table and Pam put a cup of tea down in front of her.

'Is it about Max again?' asked Carrie. 'Because I went to his house yesterday and he isn't there and the police are involved.'

'You went where yesterday?' asked Pam, looking shocked.

'He was describing a strange kind of building,' said Simon. 'Over and over, he kept talking about a very tall chimney. If you get me some paper, I'll try and draw you what I think he was describing.'

Pam bustled off to get the required paper and pen and gave them to Simon who began to sketch the outline of a building, or rather a series of buildings connected to each other. In the centre was a tall thin chimney. The buildings looked Victorian with their sloped roofs and brick facades and high, small windows.

'He said that Max was inside somewhere very dark and he was finding it hard to breathe,' said

Simon. 'He also said that Max was coming to join him soon.'

Carrie looked at the sketch that Simon had made and it didn't look like anywhere she had been to or seen in a photograph.

'I think you should take this straight to the police,' said Pam. 'You can't deal with this by yourself.'

'I'm not sure the police don't think we are all a bunch of nutters,' said Carrie. 'I got the distinct impression last night that they thought that grief had addled my brain. Which it very well may have done.'

She thought for one wild moment that perhaps she had dreamed the whole thing and that her sorrow and guilt about the death of her child had caused her to have elaborate hallucinations. In many ways the idea that this might be the case was more comforting than the reality. If she could be sitting in her own kitchen, believing that her dead son was communicating with her through an alcoholic medium who was currently drawing strange pictures on the back of her telephone pad with a pen, then anyone could believe anything at all.

Carrie went through to her front room and got her laptop and brought it through to the kitchen. She did a Google search for chimneys in East Anglia and got page after page of chimney sweeps and chimney renovators. She refined her search to tall chimneys in East Anglia and almost straight away got a picture that looked very similar to the one that Simon had drawn. It was of a steam pumping station situated in a village

349

near Ely. Now a museum, the building used to pump water from the Fens and into the drainage ditches that marked out the edges of fields and roads. The configuration of the buildings was just too similar to Simon's drawing to be a coincidence. The group of buildings consisted of a scoop wheel, an engine room and a boiler room to which the chimney was attached. Carrie didn't understand how a museum could possibly be the place where Molly and Max were being kept, but it was a lead and she intended to follow it.

Carrie had a quick breakfast and shower and got herself dressed. Bowing to pressure from Pam that she wouldn't go anywhere by herself, she rang Paul and asked him if he would come with her. She drove around to his and Jen's house and he was standing, anoraked and ready outside the door. Enif picked his way disdainfully into Carrie's car, as if he couldn't believe he had sunk so low as to travel in such a shabby vehicle.

'I'm sorry to have to involve you with this,' said Carrie as she navigated the congested streets around the centre of town. 'Mum's convinced I am going to get myself into trouble.'

'It's no problem at all,' said Paul. 'Glad to get away from the computer. The dots do start to swim before the eyes after a while.'

'Did you go into the shop yesterday?' asked Carrie. 'I feel really guilty about the amount of time I'm having to be away.'

'I like being in the shop, besides, I need the

extra cash if I'm to get through the next bit of the research project. Enif is getting to be a faddy eater.'

They found their way to the museum without any trouble and parked the car on a narrow strip of grass by the canal. The building was solid and imposing, the square chimney being the highest landmark for miles around. The arched wooden door was locked and it was clear that the museum wasn't open to the public. An elderly man who was passing with his dog shouted out to them.

'It's closed. Only open on certain days of the week, I'm afraid,' he said, his small, low-bellied dog eyeing Enif fearfully as if he knew he was in the presence of the devil. Carrie and Paul wandered over to the man, who had stopped to let his dog do a trembling crap. That was the Enif effect for you.

'It's worth a look though, if you are round this way again,' he continued. 'If it wasn't for these old steam pumping stations the whole place would have stayed a bog longer than it did. Imagine how cut off this area was when most of it was underwater.'

'Were there many stations like this one?' asked Carrie.

'I think there were about a hundred at one time, but this is the last preserved example in this area of the country. It wouldn't surprise me if there were the remains of a few still dotted around, probably mostly ruined, maybe some of them used as farm buildings.'

Carrie suddenly thought about the painting

351

that Molly had brought into *Trove* to be sold — the picture of the strangely configured ruin. She was almost certain that the building had had some sort of broken-off chimney with vines half covering it. Where had she said it was? Near her house, Molly had said. They had stumbled upon it when they were walking.

Enif made a sudden lunge at the other dog's hindquarters, so Paul hastily pulled him away and into the car. The man made a point of waving Carrie and Paul off, before continuing up the road. Carrie thought that he probably liked to pass the time of day with the odd stranger who strayed into his path, but he also liked to know that they weren't hanging around for too long on his patch.

53

Molly wasn't sure exactly at what point in the night Max stopped his regular bouts of tapping. For a while, she consoled herself with the thought that he had drifted off to sleep and she tried to do the same, despite the fact that she had severe cramp in her legs from lying with them bent up against the end of the barrel. On a number of occasions in the night, she thought she heard the door of the building open, and each time it happened she held herself ready in case Rupert opened the door of the barrel, but he never did. She also thought that she could hear objects being dragged across the stone floor. She tried banging against the top of the drum to attract his attention, but Rupert seemed to be ignoring her. She had stopped feeling hungry now, but an overwhelming weakness had taken hold of her and she was desperately thirsty. She thought longingly of the half-full bottle of water they had left at the corner of the room. She thought of the colour of the sky through a green canopy of leaves. Of her father pacing the blue carpet. Of the way Rupert had held her wrists on the first anniversary of their marriage and of the strange undulations that Max had set off across her swollen belly as he moved inside her. She tried calling out to him and then banging louder with the handle of the scythe, but this time there was no answering tap.

Max lay curled up like a baby in the tunnel. He thought he heard his mum tapping nearby, but he didn't have the strength to answer her. His head felt big and hot and his body had swollen up too and was floating over water. He thought of the way his mother had of cupping his chin when she had something to tell him and of the soft feeling of her hair after she had washed it. He thought of the way that Craig at school had pushed him hard in his stomach so that all his breath went. He thought of the way he used to line his animals down the hallway. He could feel the sway of the water, could see Charlie a little way ahead, holding out his hand to him. It wasn't far now to the edge of the sea where Charlie was.

Molly came to with a start. The door of the barrel was being opened. She held herself ready. She knew she only had one chance. As the door opened Molly swung her arm as hard as she could at Rupert's face. The scythe sliced through his jaw and lodged in his cheek and he fell backwards in shock. She quickly pulled herself out of the drum, wincing as her legs took the weight of her body and almost buckled underneath her. He tried to bat the scythe away as if it was a fly, but it was stuck too far in. Rupert flailed around the room, trying to dislodge the implement from his flesh and at last, with a snarl of pain, he freed it. His hands went up to his face and blood dripped through his fingers and down his front. He seemed blinded by the blood. Molly ran to pick up the fallen scythe, taking advantage of his temporary confusion to strike him again, a great swipe at his side that caused him to double up in pain and hold himself. Again she slammed the scythe into him and the force of the blow sent the rusty blade into the side of his neck. This time he fell to the floor. He lay with his hands up to his throat, great streams of blood pouring from the wound. Although she could hardly bear to touch him, Molly quickly felt in his pocket and pulled out the key. She was vaguely aware of the fact that there was now a great pile of hay bales in one corner of the room, and she could smell the sweet, dry odour. She ran over to the barrel that had Max in it and opened the door and pulled her son free. He was unconscious but still breathing. She held him in her arms and ran to the door, balancing the bulk of his body across her bent knee as she put the key in the lock and tried to turn it, crying out in frustration as she jiggled the key in the lock, trying to find the right position. She felt the key turn and at the same time a hand clamped itself around her ankle, bringing both her and Max to the ground.

54

Paul and Carrie decided that it was worth at least having a look for the other pumping station. It was a long shot but it was just possible that this was where Molly and Max were being kept. Carrie could feel Charlie urging her on. The sky was full of huge shifting clouds that were being chased across the sun by a keen wind and so the light changed constantly, by turns bright and then almost dark. A tractor full of manure held them up for a while as it lumbered down the road ahead of them, dropping great steaming lumps in its wake.

Carrie had no problem finding her way back to Parson's Bridge and retraced the route she had made the day before along the road that had become even muddier overnight. Enif had begun to get restless and was making a warning noise at the back of his throat.

'I think he might be thirsty,' said Paul. 'I'll give him some water when we stop.'

Beyond Molly and Max's house the road became even rougher and Carrie worried for her car suspension as they bounced alarmingly over the stony surface. It began to seem unlikely that there was anything other than the sodden fields stretching out as far as the eye could see and the whirl and sweep of the crows. Occasionally they went past a copse of trees and Carrie slowed, thinking that the branches might be obscuring a building, but there wasn't anything. Finally the track petered out into what was nothing but boggy grassland and Carrie no longer felt confident about driving. It would be all too easy to go the wrong way and end up nose down in a ditch. She parked the car and they got out. Enif had a quick slurp from the water bottle that Paul squeezed into his mouth and then he was off, nose down, tail up.

'What's he doing?' asked Carrie, alarmed to see the dog disappear so quickly.

'He usually knows where he is going,' said Paul and set off after his dog. Carrie had no choice but to follow. They walked for a while past reed beds and the occasional patch of water and then came to a small wood of beech and willow trees. Enif still romped ahead, sniffing deeply. This was the most animated Carrie had ever seen the creature. Gone was the fatigued and sardonic air he usually adopted and in its place were bright eyes and an eager gait. He looked like a dog on the trail of a whole heap of trouble.

Beyond the trees the ruined pumping station came into view. Most of the building other than the tall central section had crumbled and was open to the elements. The top of the chimney had also deteriorated and was now half the height of the one at the museum, which would explain why you couldn't see it from any of the roads. There was evidence that someone had been making improvements to the ruin; a water butt had been placed up against the wall and the one wooden door had been reinforced with a new frame studded with nails. It looked as if someone had been sleeping there too; a makeshift tent had been set up with some plastic sheeting and some string. There were also various tools, some containers, a rope and a length of piping that had clearly been put there recently. Otherwise the place was steeped in neglect. Ivy had twisted its way along the branches of the nearby trees and then attached itself to what was left of the walls, growing violently through the brickwork, heedless of the damage its relentless progress was making to the fabric of the building. Moss and mould clung to the bottoms of the walls where water had once breached and would do so again.

Enif had stopped, ears pricked, his head alert and Paul got hold of his collar and slipped his lead on. For just a moment they all stopped to listen, at first hearing nothing but the slide of the wind in the trees and the oddly human cry of lapwings some distance away. Then faintly, but distinctly, they heard the sound of a scream coming from inside the building. Carrie ran over to the door and tried opening it, but it was locked. She looked at her phone and saw that there was no reception and she turned to Paul.

'Has your phone got coverage here?' she asked.

Paul took a quick look at his phone and shook his head.

'I want you to go and take Enif with you so that you are sure to find your way back to the nearest place to phone the police from,' said Carrie.

'I'm not sure I should leave you,' he replied.

'One of us has to go and phone for help. If we wait any longer it may be too late. Enif won't come with me. Go on. Don't waste time. You may have to go as far as Parson's Bridge, I'm not sure. I know I phoned the police from Molly and Max's house so you should be alright when you get there.'

Reluctantly, Paul turned to go. Enif too seemed unwilling to leave the spot to which he was rooted; Paul had to tug at his lead several times before he could be persuaded.

'You'd better take the car keys too,' said Carrie, passing them to Paul.

'Come on Enif, back to the car,' he said, and the two of them set off at a run.

Carrie went up to the door again and banged on it but there was no reply, so she walked around the building to see if there might be another way in. There were no other doors and the only window she could see was set high up, almost at the roof. She went round to the front again and this time picked up a stone and banged repeatedly on the door. She waited a couple of moments and then to her surprise she heard the key turn in the lock. The door opened and she looked in, blinking to adjust her eyes to the dark interior. At first she could see nothing, so she stepped inside. A shape loomed up in front of her and she felt a blow on the side of the head. She fell to the floor, banging her head on the stone, and felt herself slip into unconsciousness.

She could only have been out a few moments and when she came to, she lay still, aware that she shouldn't alert whoever had hit her to the fact that she had regained consciousness. She turned her head sideways so that she could see more of the room. She could smell blood and something else that smelt of animal fat and also nearer, something dank and alien. As she moved her head again she dislodged a stone and froze, thinking that the noise would cause whoever was there to look in her direction. She found that she was staring straight into the face of what looked like a dark snake. She stifled the scream that came to her lips and edged herself away from the creature, which emanated a brackish, ancient odour. She heard the same scream that she had heard from outside and turning her head again to the other side of the room, this time saw its source. Molly was tied around the neck by a rope, which was connected to a chain hanging from the ceiling beam. The chain was attached to a hook in the wall in a pulley system which was presumably how she had been raised up into position. Her feet were just resting on a pile of hay bales that had been heaped up in one corner of the room, but any sudden movement might knock over the precarious tower. As Carrie's eyes adjusted further to the lack of light, she could see that Molly was staring in fixed terror at a man standing at the foot of the hay pile. Carrie's best view was of his feet in boots caked in the mud that rose halfway up his trousers. He was the source of the smell of animal fat that rose up from him in sickening waves so strong that Carrie felt herself gag. She tried to lie as still as possible. She knew that if he turned and saw that she was awake, she would be in real trouble. The air was thick with fear. She could hear Molly breathing in and out, the sound ragged and desperate.

The man turned and Carrie saw his face, which was covered in blood and had an enormous gash across one cheek that stretched in a half circle from his ear to his nose. She also could see that his jacket was stiff with dried blood and that he clearly found moving difficult. Despite his obvious injuries, his face was expressionless. He moved away from Molly to the centre of the room where there were two metal barrels with circular doors. The man moved to the end of one of the drums and raised a length of piping with a funnel attached to it.

Molly moaned. Her feet were desperately trying to keep purchase on the tower. 'Please Rupert. Please. Don't,' she said. Her voice sounded scratchy and rough, as if she had been screaming for days. It was clear that the rope around her throat had been tied tightly. Her hands repeatedly went up to her neck, trying to loosen the pressure on her windpipe. The man ignored her, and holding the funnel steady with one hand, began to pour what looked like water from a plastic container into the funnel. Carrie assumed that the pipe was attached in some way to the back of the drum and that for some reason best known to himself the man was filling the drum with water.

'Please. Tell me what you want. Please. Don't do this to Max,' said Molly who was weeping. As Molly spoke, Carrie realised with a sickening lurch of her stomach that Max must be in the drum and that if this man was filling it with water he was attempting to drown him by slow degrees. She didn't know how long it was since he had embarked on the exercise and hoped for Max's sake that he had just begun. She thought of the little boy curled up inside, bewildered by what was happening to him, cold and terrified, and she felt more angry than she had ever done in her life.

Carrie looked around her for anything that she could use to give herself an advantage over the man and then froze as she was aware that he had stopped what he was doing and had started to walk towards her. Had he seen her moving? She lay as still as possible, her eyes closed and her breathing as regular as she could manage it. He stood above her for a while, presumably checking that she was still unconscious, and then, seeming to decide she posed no threat, moved away again. She tried to calculate how long it would take before Paul managed to alert the police. Would they take his call seriously? Would he be able to explain exactly where they were and would they even be able to get police vehicles to such a remote location? She opened her eyes again and saw that she didn't have time to wait and hope that they would be rescued. The man was pouring what smelt unmistakably like petrol onto the bottom of the pile of straw bales. He reached in his pocket and brought out a box of matches and lit the bottom of the pile. The hay caught fire, but slowly and so he crouched down and blew out great gusts of breath, to encourage the hay to catch more quickly. He shook the petrol can and seemed angry that it was empty. Casting a quick look in Carrie's direction, he crossed the room and opened the door and went outside. This was the only chance she was likely to get. She got to her feet and taking hold of the loose stone, ran across the room and positioned herself behind one of the drums.

'Be careful. He'll kill you,' said Molly, who seemed to be at the end of her endurance. Her voice was all but gone and her head kept hanging down and then jerking up as she felt the noose tighten around her neck. The fire had taken hold and the room had begun to fill with smoke. Carrie, who had her head down as she crouched in her hiding place, heard the door open and she steadied herself. The man noticed immediately that she was no longer lying on the floor, and made a snarling exclamation of rage. He looked wildly around the room and then walked around looking for her. He checked behind the pile of hay bales and then moved around so that he was standing with his back to her.

She moved as quickly and as quietly as she could, raising the stone high over her head and bringing it down with all her strength on the back of his head. He slumped instantly to the ground. Carrie ran over to the wall and unhooked the chain and released Molly who fell onto the pile of hay bales and sent them toppling. Not looking at Molly, Carrie ran over to the drum and opened the door and as she did so, released a stream of water that fell on her arms and legs. She looked inside at Max, who was lying completely still. As the water dripped from the drum she reached inside and pulled him out with her hands under his arms. He slid forward without resistance and she caught him before he fell to the floor. The room was now full of smoke and it was hard to see where she was going. The flames were creeping across the hay. She held Max close and fought her way to the door through the smoke and was relieved to find it open. Gasping and coughing, Carrie ran outside and laid him on the grass.

His face was bluish grey and his eyes were closed and when she put her face close to his mouth she couldn't detect any breath. She unbuttoned his shirt, which was stuck to his narrow chest. She tried to remember where exactly on his body she was supposed to press. He looked so pale and small and she was terrified of hurting him. She tilted up his head, closed his nostrils with one hand and then put her mouth around his and blew gently. She looked along his chest and watched it rise with her breath. She waited a short while and then repeated the process a number of times, hoping that she was doing what she was supposed to be doing. She had a dim and panicked memory of some lurid diagrams she had once seen in a doctor's surgery. She felt for his pulse, but could detect nothing, so she found what she hoped was the right point above his rib cage and pressed down five times with the heel of her hand. Still nothing. She tried to stop herself from losing focus, could hear herself whimpering, pleading with God, with anyone. She took a deep breath and started the whole process again, alternating the breaths with the compressions, and then, just when she had given up hope and was weeping with the effort, Max stirred, turned his head and vomited into the grass. She lifted him up and held him to her, feeling the slow beat of his pulse gain traction. She covered him in her coat, left him on the grass and ran back inside. The room was now so full of smoke she had to feel her way around the wall, but she could see the blaze in the centre of the room. As she moved towards it, she saw Molly's body lying just beyond the fire as if she had used the last of her strength to crawl out from the burning debris. Carrie could feel her lungs filling up with the smoke and felt her vision going. She grabbed hold of Molly's arms and pulled her across the floor to the door. Twice she fell down, overcome with the smoke, but she managed to get Molly outside. Taking great gulps of air, she leaned against the doorframe but then felt herself being dragged backwards into the room. As she turned, she could see the man's eyes still blank in his bloodied face. He pulled her by her hair towards the burning hay, and threw her onto the centre of the fire; she felt the heat and the smoulder as her clothes caught alight.

His arms were pressing her down, keeping her pinned to the heat, his strength fearsome and unstoppable. His arms caught fire and yet still he continued to hold her. She pushed against him with all her strength, but he was like a wall. She felt his hands around her throat, pressing down on her neck, cutting off her breath and she felt herself slipping away. In the last moment before she lost herself, she felt a great blast of cool wind and the man toppled sideways, releasing her. She opened her eyes and looked into Charlie's face. She saw the dear shape of his head, the perfect arched eyebrows above the dark brown eyes, the radiant smile. It was all of him. The essence of him. It was as it had always been and as she felt his arms around her, she finally let herself go and the world went dark.

55

Carrie sat by the river on a blanket watching the two swans that had sailed into view, their necks making a wedding accessory heart. After weeks of strong, punishing wind this day had turned miraculously still, so that barely a ripple moved on the surface of the water. The air felt luxuriantly balmy. Carrie and Jen had spent the night before together at Carrie's house drinking margaritas, making favour bags stuffed with goodies from the shop and talking about all the things they had done and all the things they still wanted to do. Jen had identified a potentially ideal site for *Trove 2* and they had talked about how the new shop might look. At around the fourth margarita mark Jen had started to get a little overexcited about the concept of a grown-up toy shop with a particular emphasis on sleek sex aids and old school sweets and had to be talked down by Carrie. In the morning Carrie had had to administer paracetamol and coffee and a bath full of reviving foam. There had been a minor crisis when Jen had turned breathless and sweaty at the thought of waking up with the same person EVERY DAY, but the moment passed when Carrie talked her through the considerable assets of her husband to be.

'Remember his way with pebbles, Jen,' she said. 'And think of all the lovely circular walks you will be able to do together.'

Despite all Carrie's earlier misgivings, the dress was a triumph. It turned out to be the very first one that Jen tried on; a fifties-inspired design made of cream lace threaded through with strands of silver. The full skirt finished just below the knee giving Jen the perfect excuse to buy the oyster satin Miu Miu peep-toes she had set her heart on. The dress's tightly fitted bodice and low scooped neckline gave Jen a creamy, buxom air, a look that made Tom stagger visibly when he turned to her as she came to stand by his side in the church.

The rest of the day had run according to plan. The church smelt of the old-fashioned pale pink roses that were tied to the end of every pew and which Jen carried a small posy of. The guests threw clouds of lilac and blue delphinium petals in the churchyard outside. Jen's father made a surprise appearance with yet another rather-too-young woman with delicate skin and a regretful look in her eye. Both Jen and Carrie cried a little when Carrie made her speech. Tom kept telling everyone how lucky he was. Someone's teenager was sick in a handbag. Paul and Enif, whose fur had been slicked back with some sort of shiny gel, were first on the dance floor and of course, the bride was the most beautiful bride anyone had ever seen.

Now the party had decamped for the evening to a marquee in a friend's riverside garden from where the guests were taking dangerous and noisy punt trips. There had already been an incident when someone had got his punting pole stuck in the mud at the bottom of the river, refused to let it go, and had been left clutching it for a teetering mid-river moment before making a spectacular descent into the water. After lighting the small candles in their clouded glass holders that were placed strategically around the garden, Carrie had taken some time out from the hurly burly to sit by herself and have a glass of white wine. There were still moments when she needed to walk away from people to think and gather herself. Although it had been four months since the day at the pumping station, she hadn't yet quite regained her former strength. She looked down at her hands and lower arms, which were very badly scarred by the effects of the fire and were still tender to the touch.

★　★　★

When she had woken in the hospital without him the grief had felt as sharp as it had done when he had first gone. To have seen him so close, to have felt his breath on her and his arms around her and then to have lost him again felt too painful to bear. For the first couple of days, she had done nothing but weep great scalding, bitter tears that seemed to have no end to them. There was nothing else to her but this terrible feeling of loss and abandonment. She knew that he had gone finally and forever. When she stopped crying for long enough, people ventured into the room and filled in the parts she had missed. Pam stayed with her night and day, holding her bandaged hands and giving the passing doctors the glad eye.

One afternoon Carrie woke up to find Oliver sitting in the chair by her bed looking at her. She told him to go away and he did, but he kept coming back. He brought ridiculously large bunches of flowers and extravagant chocolates and talked to her about a bird with a broken wing he had found just outside the hide and about how Mrs Evans had an alarm fitted to her house which went off when anyone approached her front door. A policeman, who had been first on the scene at the pumping station, described the miracle that had saved her.

'It was as if something had extinguished the fire around you. It was still burning elsewhere, but just where you were lying it had gone out completely,' he said. 'It was just the strangest thing.'

Rupert had died in the station due to the combination of the effects of the fire and the severity of his wounds. Molly and Max had survived, although both of them had been in hospital for some time. About three weeks after Carrie was discharged Molly and Max came to visit her. Both of them were still bruised and fragile and moved with the characteristic tentativeness of people who have been recently hurt. Molly wept and held Carrie's sore hands and told her that she couldn't find the words as no one can when they feel something with all their heart. It was easier for Max. Unlike most adults, he had not yet unlearned the power of speaking what he meant. He came and sat very near to her and put his hand on her knee.

'Thank you for Mum and my lives,' he said. 'I

370

can't be your boy like Charlie was, but I would like to be your friend if you want me to be.'

He also told her in a whisper, as if it was a secret for them to share, that Charlie had stayed with him all the way through, talking to him, telling him to hang on, singing him songs to comfort him.

* * *

Carrie shivered slightly. The air was turning cool. She looked up to see Oliver walking towards her, and just behind him, doing that infuriatingly gleeful dance, was Jen grinning widely and pointing in a childish way at Oliver's back. He sat down beside her on the blanket.

'Hello Carrie,' he said, looking at her face, which was held resolutely away from him.

'I didn't know you were invited,' said Carrie.

'Jen rang me up a couple of days ago. I think I was a last-minute addition,' said Oliver. They sat in silence for a moment.

'Would you like to go for a punt?' asked Oliver.

'Not really,' said Carrie shortly, thinking, despite herself, how good he looked in his dark suit and white shirt. 'You don't really look dressed for the job.'

'I was thinking that you might do the punting,' he replied. 'Come on, Carrie. You might even enjoy it.' She reluctantly got to her feet and waited while he brought the boat alongside and lit the lantern.

'All aboard,' he said, holding the chain tight so

that the boat rested against the edge of the bank. Carrie took off the gold vintage heels she was wearing and threw them onto the floor of the punt and then stepped on, feeling the boat rock to one side and then right itself as she sat on the cushioned seat. Oliver took off his jacket, stowed it under the front of the boat and took hold of the pole. Just as they were pushing away from the bank, Jen came running up with a bottle of wine, two glasses and Carrie's pink cashmere wrap that she had left in the marquee.

'Thought you might need these,' she said, giving Carrie a conspiratorial look and earning a scowl in return. 'Bon Voyage!' shouted Jen, oblivious to Carrie's furious stare and in any case, too drunk on happiness and wine to care.

They pulled away and started up the river. Most of the others had called it a day, so they had the quiet water to themselves. Oliver punted with concentration, the water dripping down his arm in silver drops as he placed the pole and then pulled it out with each push forward.

'Shall we try?' asked Oliver, stopping for a moment to look at Carrie in her red dress, the light from the lantern on her face.

'Try what?' said Carrie.

'Try to love each other,' he replied.

She knew there was a chance she could love him. Maybe she already did. It wasn't loving him that was the problem; it was the thought of exposing her bruised and battered heart to further damage. It was risking more loss and more pain. The odds were not good but they were, after all, the only odds on offer. He laid the pole down and moved from the deck of the punt towards her. She felt the sway of the river beneath them as he kissed her.

Epilogue

Carrie arrived at the beach half an hour before the others. The car park was almost empty, but the kiosk had opened for business. The buckets were swinging from the awning, the fishing nets and sea shoes were laid out for sale and the smell of hot fat already hung in the air. People on their way to the beach would hope that equipping themselves with the requisite seaside paraphernalia would mean that they were making the most of the day, despite the weather, despite the lack of crabs to fish for. Families came to the sea drawn by a fantasy too entrenched to change, and which bore little resemblance to the reality.

Today they had been lucky. The sun was warm and the air had a kind milkiness. Carrie thought that the beach looked exactly as it had on that day, the same colours, the same smells, the same geography, and yet, of course, it was quite different. New sand had covered the old, each grain as distinct and different from the other as snowflakes were. Patterns had blown away and reformed and would continue to endlessly shape and reshape themselves. She stood looking out at the sea and the horizon. It was there, on that steadfast line, always visible yet always out of reach, that she fixed her thoughts of Charlie. She knew that she would always look for him there, at the point where the earth met the sky. It didn't need to be this beach. He was anywhere where edges blurred, where mystery and beauty caught you up.

The rest of them came in twos and Carrie was reminded of the ark that Max had given her when he had come to visit after she had come out of the hospital. He had lined the animals up in pairs on her mantelpiece and set the little wooden Noah up on the gangplank. First to arrive was Damian, who had brought a grey-eyed woman called Sarah with him. Sarah held Damian's arm and smiled carefully at Carrie. Next was Pam in unsuitable shoes and Simon, with whom she had cadged a lift. Carrie saw with a sigh that her mother took every opportunity to clutch on to his arm and laugh in a girlish fashion. Then Kate and Dave Jefferies, with their two girls already dressed in matching pink swimsuits. Paul came with Enif who immediately escaped from his velvet lead and led his owner a merry dance across the dunes. Molly, with Max running ahead, arrived just before Tom and Jen and a small bump under the worst smock dress Carrie had ever seen. Last of all was Oliver, who had brought the food and a seaside bucket full of flowers.

It was a simple ceremony. They set up in a sheltered part of the dunes and established their territory as is the form and the instinct, with blankets and bags and umbrellas and then went to the sea, the children running shouting across the sand, unable to simply walk in this space that was made for moving fast in. There was no body to bury, no ashes to scatter. The only marker was love. Damian read a poem and Max sang 'Cheek to Cheek' in a clear, sweet voice, and everyone cried. Carrie watched Sarah wipe Damian's face tenderly with a tissue and was reassured. Afterwards they walked back together to eat sandwiches and crisps and to toast Charlie's memory from plastic picnic cups.

After the food had been allowed to digest, the children, accompanied by Carrie, went to splash in the sea. They made a sandcastle for Charlie decorated with mussel shells and surrounded by a maze of tunnels and when they had finished Max inserted a damp, gritty hand into Carrie's and stood beside her in the shallows.

'Max,' said Carrie, looking down at him. 'Have you had a nice day?'

'Yes,' said Max, scooping his feet through the wet sand at the edge of the water. She noticed that he no longer had the fleshy marks on his ankles that she associated with small children. He had grown even in the short time she had known him, and before too long would inhabit that awkward, bony stage when boys and their bodies were at war. Just now he had an easy stillness that was unusual for a child of his age.

'The sea took him, didn't it, Carrie?' asked Max.

'Yes. It did,' said Carrie. 'It took him while we weren't watching.'

'I think it wanted him for its own,' said Max.

'Maybe,' said Carrie, feeling the tears start.

'He's alright, Carrie,' said Max.

'Do you still see him or does he talk to you any more?' Carrie couldn't help asking. She needed to know if she would hear from him again.

Max looked up at her with his beautiful, serious eyes.

'He's gone now. I don't see him any more and he doesn't speak to me. But he's inside me,' said Max, bending to scoop up a shell with one hooked, pruned finger.

★ ★ ★

They all stayed on the beach until the air turned chilly and then wrapped wet swimsuits in wet towels, gathered up the sandy remnants of the picnic and made for home. Carrie and Oliver stayed on for a while after the others had driven off. They sat with a blanket over their knees and watched the tide slip further out.

'Do you think it's time to go?' asked Oliver after a while, putting his arm around her, knowing she would find it hard to let this day end.

'Yes,' said Carrie. 'It's been as good as I hoped it would be. Better.'

Just as they were reaching the car park, Carrie turned back one last time. It was a hard habit to break, having this feeling that she was leaving Charlie behind. But then she rubbed her forehead with a sandy hand, wrapped her arms around herself and walked on, taking him with her.

Q & A
with
Madeleine Reiss

Q **What inspired you to write** *Someone to Watch Over Me?*

A It was that moment of terror that I think any parent can understand when they look around them and realise that they can't see their child anymore. I just had this image in my head of a woman standing on a beach, knowing that the thing she fears the most has happened.

Q **Carrie's experience is intensely painful. How difficult was it for you to write about what happened?**

A I did get quite emotional at times because although what happens to Carrie has not happened to me, I think the losses I have experienced in my life informed what I wrote. I found that writing about grief made me re-live my own. People say that writing can be therapeutic, but I am not sure I want to sit weeping at my desk. I think I'll write something just a little jollier next time around. Although it will probably still be sad — I think I am drawn to sad things.

Q **Landscape is an important part of the novel. What is it that you love about the area?**

A I am obsessed with the sea. Whenever I am even the slightest bit low, I make for a beach, sit for a while and it restores me. I particularly love the Norfolk coast because of the bleached-out quality of the light. I am also very fond of the Fens, which feature in the book. Although people sometimes find them flat and dull, I think the big sky and the black earth create a very dramatic landscape. I like places where you have to work a bit to find the beauty.

Q **There is a strong supernatural element to the story. Is this something you have encountered yourself?**

A I have never seen a ghost and would probably be terrified if I did. I do believe that spirits linger and that they can be very real influences on our lives if we allow ourselves to listen to them.

Q **Rupert is a monstrous presence in the novel. Which literary baddies have inspired you?**

A Baddies are so much more interesting than goodies. Snow White's stepmother was an early source of terror. I couldn't even *look* at the cover of my book of fairy tales I was so scared of her. After that it was the terrible tapping of Long John Silver's wooden leg in *Treasure Island* that chilled me. Then Mrs Danvers creeping around in *Rebecca*, Bill

Sikes's remorseless thuggery in *Oliver Twist*, Tom Ripley's madness in Patricia Highsmith's *The Talented Mr Ripley*, the manipulations of Alec d'Urbeville in *Tess of the d'Urbervilles* and Pinkie Brown's violence in *Brighton Rock*. I could go on . . .

Q Describe your typical writing day.

A I know that if I am not at my desk by nine, I am doomed. Any later and I feel the day is slipping away from me and that feeling distracts me from focusing properly. The plan is to write until I am hungry and have lunch watching Bargain Hunt and then write some more until 3.30ish when I am supposed to go to the gym. However, I mostly skip the gym and eat biscuits instead.

Q What would you like to write about next?

A I want to write a love story. Something romantic and lush.

Q If you were stranded on a desert island, what books would you like to have with you?

A It would be absolute torture to have to choose! If forced, I would pick *Vanity Fair* by Thackeray because I always find new things in it; *The Mill on The Floss* by George Eliot because it is so familiar to me, it would act like a comforting refrain; *Celestial Navigation* by Anne Tyler because it is about loneliness and I would be lonely on the island; *Cold Comfort Farm* by Stella Gibbons for its ability to make me laugh; and *Heat* magazine (as long as I was sent a new one every week) so that I could keep in touch with bonkers celebrities.

We do hope that you have enjoyed reading this large print book.

Did you know that all of our titles are available for purchase?

We publish a wide range of high quality large print books including:
Romances, Mysteries, Classics
General Fiction
Non Fiction and Westerns

Special interest titles available in large print are:
The Little Oxford Dictionary
Music Book
Song Book
Hymn Book
Service Book

Also available from us courtesy of Oxford University Press:
Young Readers' Dictionary
(large print edition)
Young Readers' Thesaurus
(large print edition)

For further information or a free brochure, please contact us at:
Ulverscroft Large Print Books Ltd.,
The Green, Bradgate Road, Anstey,
Leicester, LE7 7FU, England.
Tel: (00 44) 0116 236 4325
Fax: (00 44) 0116 234 0205

THE DRESSMAKER

Kate Alcott

Tess, an aspiring seamstress, is stunned at her luck when the famous designer Lady Lucile Duff Gordon hires her to be a personal maid on the Titanic's maiden voyage. When disaster strikes, Tess is one of the last people allowed on a lifeboat — her employer also survives. On dry land, savage rumours begin to circulate: did Lady Duff Gordon save herself at the expense of others? Tess's dream of becoming a skilled dressmaker is within her grasp but now she is faced with a terrible choice. Suddenly she finds herself torn between loyalty to the fiery woman who could help her realise her ambitions and the devastating truth that her mentor may not be all she seems . . .

INDISCRETION

Charles Dubow

Harry and Madeleine Winslow are a devoted couple, blessed with talent, money and charm. Bonded by deep devotion, their marriage is both envied and admired by friends who spend summers at their East Hampton idyll. When a holiday fling goes disastrously wrong, 26-year-old Claire falls into the Winslows' welcome orbit. They are enchanted by her youth, intelligence and disarming naivety. But over the course of the summer, reverence transforms into dangerous desire. By the end, it is no longer enough to just be one of their hangers-on ... Seen through the eyes of Maddy's childhood friend Walter, *Indiscretion* is a story about the complexities of love, and how obsession can tear apart even the most perfect of worlds.

THE GRAVITY OF BIRDS

Tracy Guzeman

Sisters Alice and Natalie were once close, but adolescence is wrenching them apart. Alice is a dreamer who loves books and birds; Natalie is headstrong, manipulative — and beautiful. On their lakeside family holiday, Alice falls under the thrall of a struggling young painter, Thomas Bayber. But Natalie seems unmoved, tolerating sittings for a family portrait with surprising indifference. By the end of the summer, three lives are shattered. Decades later, Thomas, now a world-renowned artist, reveals the existence of a portrait of himself with Alice and Natalie from that fateful summer. The sisters themselves have disappeared. And Thomas is torn between taking their secrets to the grave, or using the painting to resurrect the past before it closes up on all of them for good . . .

THE LOWLAND

Jhumpa Lahiri

In the suburban streets of Calcutta where they wandered before dusk, and in the hyacinth-strewn ponds where they played for hours on end, Udayan was always in his older brother Subhash's sight. So close in age, they were inseparable in childhood — and yet, as the years pass, their brotherly bond can do nothing to forestall the tragedy that will upend their lives. Udayan — charismatic and impulsive — finds himself drawn to the Naxalite movement, a rebellion waged to eradicate inequity and poverty. He will give everything — risk all — for what he believes, and in so doing will transform the futures of those dearest to him. For all of them, the repercussions of his actions will reverberate and seep through the generations that follow.

LIFESAVING FOR BEGINNERS

Ciara Geraghty

She has lots of friends, an ordinary job, and she never ever thinks about her past. This is Kat's story. None of it is true. Milo McIntyre loves his mam, the peanut-butter-and-banana muffins at the Funky Banana *café*, and the lifesaving class he does after school. He never thinks about his future, until the day it changes forever. This is Milo's story. All of it is true. And then there is the other story. The one with a twist of fate which somehow brings together a boy from Brighton and a woman in Dublin, and uncovers the truth once and for all. This is the story that's just about to begin . . .